Sleazy Rider

As I showered, I tried to make sense of what had just happened. It wasn't the first time Kit had got off by sharing me with another man, but it was the first time the other man had taken control of the situation so completely. My mind ran round in circles, but I was too tired and drained to get a handle on anything, so I focused on my body instead, slathering on a richly scented lotion I had found in the bathroom, rubbing at my tired limbs. My skin smarted where Max's belt had caught me.

I craned my neck to see the sore parts in the mirror. The pink weals clearly showed where the leather strap had hit me, their criss-cross pattern marking my rump. I ran a fascinated finger along the skin, feeling the heat where the blood still pumped harder. Since we met on the ferry, I had worn Max's badge on my leathers; now, for an hour or so, I would wear his marks on my skin.

By the same author:

Up to No Good

Sleazy Rider
Karen S. Smith

BLACK LACE

Black Lace books contain sexual fantasies.
In real life, always practise safe sex.

First published in 2005 by
Black Lace
Thames Wharf Studios
Rainville Road
London W6 9HA

Design by Smith & Gilmour, London
Printed and bound by Mackays of Chatham PLC

ISBN 0 352 33964 0

1

I was pressed against the handrail, palms flat on cold metal, gazing across a calm, turquoise sea as the south coast of England receded into the distance. Against my back I felt the heat of Kit's body, his muscular arms slipped under mine, holding me tightly in place. He rubbed himself slowly against me, to cause a friction of leather on leather, and the bulge of his excitement nudged against my back. To the other passengers there was nothing to see – just another biker couple enjoying the last view of home. They strolled past, oblivious, discussing their choice of autoroute or their duty-free shopping.

Except one. From the deck below, a pair of pale-blue eyes held mine with an expression of interest so frank that I felt my face burn in a blush. I recognised this blond man, who was now seated among his friends, as the dude who had tethered his motorbike next to mine in the hold below. Or rather, had let one of his group tether it for him, while he had watched me yanking on a strap to secure my own bike across its saddle. Even then I had noticed him – the neatly trimmed goatee, the well-worn black leathers – but, more than anything, I'd registered the air of quiet power about him. Now he sat like a king among his courtiers, watching me as Kit's subtle caresses roused me, turning my limbs to fire and water.

And over my shoulder Kit was watching him.

'It seems we have an audience,' he whispered, his lips brushing my ear. 'Shall we give him something to watch?'

Dropping his head to trace a line of sparks down my neck with the tenderest of kisses, he slid his hands over my body. While his left hand squeezed my breasts through the tight leather suit, his right hand slipped between me and the handrail. His long fingers slipped between my legs and stayed there, the gesture unmistakable to anyone watching.

Still the blond guy sat, legs apart, hands folded calmly in his lap, our one-man audience. Embarrassed, but also aroused by the way I was being turned into a public show, I tried to turn my head to meet Kit in a kiss, and to break the gaze holding mine. Firmly, Kit turned my face back towards the watcher, his grip strong on my cheeks.

'If you're going to start eyeing up other men on our honeymoon,' he whispered with a touch of steel, 'the least you can do is give them something to remember us by.'

His cunning fingers were strumming me like a guitar, making my legs tremble with helpless excitement. If I wasn't held so tight between Kit's hand and the erection I could feel pressing into my back, I felt I would fall.

At last our impassive observer stirred in his chair. In spite of myself I strained to see any trace of excitement in him, but his leathers, unlike Kit's sleek racing suit, were bulky and creased by long usage. At his first movement, though, each of his companions looked to him, instantly ready to respond. Still he looked only at me, at my body trembling on the brink of orgasm but held tight by my husband. Though I was covered from neck to toe, my face half veiled by the red hair falling over it, I felt completely naked in those cobalt eyes.

Following their leader's look, the group of bikers also turned to see us above them. If I could have run away then I would have done so, but I was trapped. I could only bite my lip to keep from crying out as I came, pushing myself against Kit's fingers, my hands gripping the steel balustrade like a shipwrecked sailor clinging to a spar. As the last aftershocks quivered through me, Kit planted a kiss on the nape of my neck.

'That's my girl,' he said. But the ripple of satisfaction that ran through me was for the smile that shone, at last, beneath the ice-blue eyes below us.

Only a few hours into our honeymoon and I was already thrilled by the interest of a complete stranger. But then, our relationship had never been exactly conventional, and Kit had seemed to enjoy sharing me with the voyeur almost as much as I had enjoyed being turned into a sex show. As he half-steered me towards the front of the ship, I could tell he was as disappointed as I was to see the coast of France already approaching. There was no time to get a cabin and finish what we had started so publicly.

Kit looked around the deck, desperately hoping for some private corner, and I laughed, remembering the second time we'd met, stranded with a full hand of hormones and no hotel room for hours and hours. He gave me a rueful look, his caramel-brown eyes reminding me exactly what I saw in him. That mixture of bravado and boyish openness had disarmed me even more than his slender good looks. And now he was my husband. A rush of affection rose through me, and I tilted my face up to kiss him.

'Don't start what you haven't got time to finish,' he said as he kissed me back. But I was looking past him at the edge of the white tarpaulin above. It was one of the ship's lifeboats, hanging ready above the handrail, but the cover was unhooked, leaving a gap big enough to wriggle through.

Motorcycle leathers are not designed for discreet wriggling, however, and, by the time we had creaked our way in, safely stowed in the empty lifeboat, it was swinging conspicuously and we were breathless with effort and laughter. The wooden boat smelled damp and salty, and the odd shafts of brilliant sun picked out small puddles of water on the bottom of the small craft. More by feel than sight I found the zip of Kit's suit and opened it. I pulled up his T-shirt, damp with sweat, and found his smooth, warm penis nosing into my hand.

My mouth locked on his, I squeezed gently, and felt his deep groan vibrate through me. As I moved my hand up and down, each stroke slightly quicker than the last, I could hear the voices of other passengers outside, already making their way back to the vehicle decks in preparation for arrival. The urgency of what we were doing made this seem more exciting, more furtive, and I rubbed my body against Kit's as I pumped him, squeezing his thigh between mine. I could feel him tense as he neared his climax, and quickened my rhythm, running my thumb over his most sensitive ridge.

Then I froze. Inches from my head I heard a voice: 'See that?' it said.

'What, the lifeboat?'

Had we drawn attention to ourselves, rocking the little boat on our own waves of excitement?

'The tarp's loose,' the first voice went on. 'Better sort that before Skip sees it.'

I held my breath, unsure which was worse – the threat of discovery, or the threat of being secured into the lifeboat by a zealous crew member. Beneath me Kit trembled, frustratingly held on the verge of orgasm but not daring to move. He could hardly relish his ultimate moment of pleasure with a couple of geezers so close by, engaged in work chat.

A scraping sound outside told us that one of the crewmen was attempting to reach the loose tarpaulin. As I opened my mouth, trying desperately to think of some plausible excuse for our being here, a loudspeaker crackled into action. Car drivers were being called back to their vehicles.

'Leave it,' said the voice so close to our hiding place. 'It'll do till later.' Two sets of departing footsteps told us that we were safe for now.

With renewed eagerness I caressed Kit, determined to bring him to climax before we could be interrupted again. With a few more strokes he shook, groaned softly, and flung his head back in pleasure. His hot tribute poured over my hand and a powerful scent, clean and salty, filled the confined space. Smiling shyly, he kissed me once more.

Then we rushed to restore ourselves to presentability. I stuck my head carefully out of the gap in the tarpaulin, only to see a steady flow of passengers hurrying past. This one would have to be brazened out. Stealing a last kiss, I swung myself down on to the deck. A family of Dutch holidaymakers looked surprised to see me emerge, but were too preoccupied with regaining their car to give me a second glance. Or maybe they guessed what we were doing and didn't care – being Dutch, after all. As Kit landed beside me we exchanged a 'got-away-with-it-again' look and giggled as we prepared to disembark.

We joined the crowd gathered around the top of the staircase, waiting to get back to the hold. Although we'd be unloaded last, it would take a couple of minutes to unstrap the bikes and don helmets and gloves. To my surprise, when I let my eyes wander upwards, I saw the blue-eyed watcher standing on the viewing deck, looking down at me. This time Kit, who was in front of me, hadn't seen him.

I held his gaze, hoping for another flash of that smile, but instead he gave the merest flick of his head, a peremptory summons. Then he walked along the deck out of sight. Before I could think about what I was doing, I said, 'I'm just going to the toilet,' and ran up the stairs to the viewing deck, my heart thumping, looking for that blond head and dark, powerful silhouette.

He was standing at the apex of the deck, his back to me, looking down on the narrowing strip of water between ship and quayside. I stopped beside him, suddenly confused. What was I expecting? Why had I so readily obeyed that arrogant gesture? Following his eyes down, I felt a moment of disorientation.

'Afraid of falling?'

His voice was quiet, but not nervous. He sounded as if fear was something he only observed in others. The thought flashed across my mind that he intended to throw me in, see me crushed between concrete and steel or drowned beneath the foul, dark water. Then he smiled once more, and I felt foolish.

'So,' he said, turning now to face me, 'is that your husband?'

I nodded, wondering what I was doing talking to this man.

'I saw the wedding rings,' he went on.

'It's our honeymoon,' I said, and blushed again, remembering my surrender to sensual pleasure in front of this man and his friends. He shook his head in mock despair.

'And already you act like a slut.' His accent was slightly odd, a mid-Atlantic drawl with something more musical mixed in.

'I'm Max,' he said, and held out his hand. Though the gesture was oddly formal under the circumstances, I shook it. His palm was dry and hard, the grip light but masterful.

'Emma,' I replied.

He unpinned a metal badge from his jacket, took hold of my collar and pinned it to my leathers pulling me close into his body. As I craned to see what the design was, he took a business card from his pocket and slid it into my hand. Then he dismissed me with another toss of the head. Feeling slightly humiliated, I turned and walked back to the staircase, stuffing the card into my pocket.

Kit was already in the hold and chatting to Max's followers as he unstrapped my bike.

'Straight back to Amsterdam, then?' he was asking.

Seeing me, they gave polite nods of greeting, ignoring the fact that they'd all seen me lose control under Kit's skilled touch. Then one of them caught sight of Max's badge on my leathers. Before he could repress it, a look of surprise, almost fear, flashed into his eyes. Now he met my gaze differently, a new respect mingled with something else.

It shook me. I looked down and saw the emblem pinned to me, an eagle's claw gripping a snake that writhed in agony, exquisitely modelled in silver. It meant nothing to me. Who was this Max? And how come he had such an effect over a group of hardened bikers?

The strangeness stayed with me as we rode on to the quayside and through the town, but once we hit the open road I had more immediate things to consider. First, I thanked my lucky stars that Kit's mother, a petrolhead like her son, had chosen a pair of matching Ducatis as a wedding present. Then, I concentrated on riding mine at least as well as Kit who, as a bike journalist, had an unfair advantage.

Every curve in the road was a joy, as we swung the bikes in and out of the corners. Light and perfectly balanced, but with enormous power lurking beneath the throaty gurgle of the engine, this motorbike could handle everything the road threw at it. All I had to do was handle the bike itself. Coming too fast into a tight bend, I frightened myself by locking up the back wheel for a moment, feeling the rear tyre catch and skip sideways on the road. After that I took it more gently, giving myself time to get used to the bike. There was no hurry, after all. We had a month to spend and every road in Europe was ours for the taking.

For mile after delicious mile we rode through the countryside, meeting hardly any traffic apart from a herd of placid cows, their sleek brown flanks almost brushing us as they passed. Ancient stone houses and hideous modern outbuildings were scattered among the trees and hedges, apparently without any regard for aesthetics. Their very randomness brought a smile to my face. I spent my working life trying to make buildings look exactly right. My architect's eye couldn't help looking critically at every farm we passed. This month off was long overdue. Perhaps eventually I'd stop trying to fix everything and learn to relax.

Though I was aching and sore, my back and wrists crying out from the hours in the saddle, I still felt a pang of regret to see the first signpost for our destination. 'Château Victoire, 5 kilomètres'. Though I was longing for a hot shower, a cold beer and a good dinner, I was still buzzing with the excitement of the ride. I relished each twist of the tiny country roads that took us away from the open country and into shady forest, the air honeyed with the scent of blossom and pine. Then we came round a long curve and saw, at the end of a long avenue of cypresses, the Château Victoire.

In England it would have been one of the finest stately homes in the country. Here, it was a masterpiece in a state of dissolute neglect: nothing wrong with it that some superficial restoration wouldn't solve (there I go again) but looking as if it simply couldn't be bothered to worry about its appearance any more. It was like finding one of the great screen beauties of the 1950s sitting in a village café somewhere, slumming it in an old sweater with no make-up. Kit flicked open his visor and glanced across at me, eyebrows raised, seeking confirmation.

'It's perfect,' I breathed, and he glowed with satisfaction.

The tyres crunched on the gravel drive as we rolled slowly up to the entrance. The stone glowed golden in the evening sun, and the columns of the portico cast long violet shadows down the steps. Enormous dark wood doors, polished to a sheen that reflected the sun on to the marble floor beyond, stood open. Before them, a man stood waiting. His rather dressy jacket was cut tight at the waist, which gave it the appearance of a frock coat. Our shiny red machines looked completely out of place in this baroque setting of faded elegance.

With quiet efficiency, the concierge showed us the stable block where our mounts would be locked for the night, conjured a couple of smartly dressed young men to carry our luggage, and led us up the sweep of the stone staircase. Life-sized oil portraits stared haughtily from the walls, and the high dome of the ceiling was painted with a riot of cherubs and thinly draped nymphs. Our boots echoed on the parquet floor as we followed our frock-coated guide along the corridor. While he unlocked a panelled door I looked through a high window across the parkland. Rolling meadows receded to the horizon, with neither a road nor an electricity pylon in sight. A small herd of deer grazed near a lake in which a miniature Greek temple was reflected. We seemed to have left the twentieth century far behind us.

Then I stepped into our room, and felt as if I'd truly travelled back in time. Mirrored panels lined the walls and an ornate marble fireplace was surmounted by an extravagant oil painting depicting an orgy, thinly disguised as a scene from classical mythology. But the room was dominated by a vast, canopied bed, draped in deepred brocade. Our porters tucked the all-too-modern luggage into the dressing room and withdrew discreetly. Kit tipped the concierge, who nodded his thanks.

'Feel free to dress for dinner,' he said as he pulled the door shut behind him.

At last we were alone together, but the moment for flinging ourselves on each other had passed. We were both too intrigued by the room. I pushed on one of the mirrored panels to reveal the bathroom. White tiles, crazed with age, reflected the light from the sash window, in front of which an enamel bath stood on lion's feet. Wisps of steam rose from it, and I stepped forwards to see it already full, a faint scent of lavender rising off the water. As well as the usual furnishings of a well-equipped French bathroom, a brass showerhead as big as a sunflower hung from the ceiling, relying on nothing more than a sloping floor and plenty of space to keep the water from flooding the room. Thick, rough white towels were piled on a wooden clothes stand.

My weary limbs couldn't resist the warm water.

'I'm going to have a bath,' I called to Kit, and I instantly abandoned my leathers and underwear in a pile by the door, and stepped into the tub. I slipped down into the scented water, my joints relaxing in the silky heat, and watched through the curtainless window as woodpigeons cooed and circled against the blue. The only other sound was Kit moving around next door. It was almost too quiet for my London ears.

This is what it would have been like, I thought, to be a grand lady of a bygone age. I would lie in this bath while in the next room my servants would lay out my clothes, ready for me to dress for dinner. I indulged myself with such fanciful notions, imagining how wonderful it would be to have servants fulfil my every need. The hot water I was lying in would have been carried up the stairs in buckets and poured into the tub. In fact, a maidservant would probably be helping me even to wash myself. I stretched a wet arm in the cool air, and imagined a uniformed maid pouring a pitcher of water down it and over my breasts, ready to lather me with fragrant soap. To be serviced in such an intimate way was an arousing thought.

I closed my eyes and slipped a soapy hand between my thighs, imagining it was that of a country housemaid whose innocent face was gazing down at her mistress's body. She too might be aroused as she rubbed me between the legs, feeling her own body echoing the sensations. Or would relieving the mistress's frustrations merely be part of her job? Perhaps the master of the house was even now finding satisfaction elsewhere, bending the groom over the watertrough round the back of the stables, leaving his wife to seek her pleasures where she could.

But my husband was here now and I wasn't going to waste any more time alone in the bath with Kit so close. I wrapped myself in a towel and stood dripping in the doorway of the bedroom. Kit had thrown open all the mirrored panels to reveal a wardrobe already full of clothes, and was holding a corset made of green satin. Turning to smile at me, he held it up.

'Would Milady care to dress for dinner?' he asked.

It was spooky for a moment, as if he'd been reading my mind. There were dozens of garments there, of all designs and sizes. For the gentleman, dress trousers, silk breeches and oriental robes filled a third of the rails. But the ladies' clothes were infinitely varied. From severe black riding habits to extravagant crinolines in pink satin, every possible dressing-up-box wish had been fulfilled. And for every dress there was the underwear to match: corsets, bustles, stockings and stays; layered petticoats and lacy bloomers. Letting my towel drop in a damp heap on the Persian rug, I joined Kit.

For him I chose a white tailored shirt with a high starched collar, a long jacket in hunting red, and black trousers that showed off his muscular thighs and bottom. He even found a pair of riding boots to fit. Then it was his turn to dress me. Soon the bed was covered in a riot of silk petticoats, white stockings and a green dress with a full skirt.

'That's tiny,' I protested, as he held it up against me, its waist smaller than mine even without underclothes. 'I'll never fit into that!'

'Wait and see,' he replied, laying aside the dress and holding up the green corset.

With the laces loose, it was easy enough to wrap the corset around me and clasp the front panels together. Already it pushed my full breasts together and up, giving me the most magnificent cleavage of my life. Then Kit began to tighten the laces. At first the pressure was gentle, almost reassuring, like being tucked snugly into bed. As he worked the laces harder, the pressure on my ribs grew stronger, a bear hug against which each breath was an effort. I abandoned the struggle to push my diaphragm against the constraint, and let my breathing work up and down instead, a true heaving bosom.

By the time Kit tied the laces off, I was squeezed from hip to shoulder blades, aware only of that part of my body which was now held almost rigid. He turned me to look into the mirror, and I caught my breath to see the shape I had become. Usually curvy, I was now a classic hourglass. With my waist cinched unnaturally tight, my hips looked fuller and my bust was as high and proud as a ship's figurehead. No wonder Kit's eyes shone with lust.

No longer able to bend at the waist, I found it awkward to pull on the white stockings and tie the ribbon garters above my knees. Kit had to hold each petticoat open for me to step into, and knelt down himself to button me into white leather boots with neat heels. Finally, he pulled over my head the green dress which fitted, as he predicted, perfectly. In the mirrored panels a pair of French aristocrats stared back at us.

As if on cue, a discreet knock at the door announced the return of the concierge to tell us that pre-dinner drinks were being served in the drawing room. He made no comment, or indeed any sign of surprise, at the way we were dressed. I guessed that we weren't the only guests to join in the spirit of things. Picking up my skirts as if born to it, I swept through the bedroom door and accepted Kit's arm to walk down the grand staircase.

We were the only residents that evening and, as the candlelight glistened in the crystal glasses, I felt as spoilt as a fairytale princess. We sipped our aperitifs on the terrace overlooking the grounds, the constriction around my middle a constant reminder of my role as a Lady. Kit, too, was living up to his costume, striding in his boots as if he'd just swung himself down from a horse after a day's hunting. I found myself simpering bashfully, my eyes lowered as a respectable girl of yesteryear should.

Dinner itself was magnificent, the big dining room bright with candelabra, the long table dazzling with silverware. Seated at each end of the long table, we dined in near silence, rather than raise our voices in the stillness. Instead, each look and gesture became intensely focused. The smell and taste of the food absorbed us, every subtle flavour appreciated and lingered over.

By the time the dessert plates were removed, with the merest smudges of chocolate clinging to them, we were in a truly sensitised state, attuned to sensual pleasure in all its forms. Kit put a hand on my narrow waist as we walked back to the terrace for a final glass of brandy, rubbing a thumbnail down my ribs between the boning. I felt like a package, tied up tight with ribbon.

The night air was cooling, but the chorus of cicadas reminded us how far south we'd come already. The dark garden gave off the heavy perfume of flowers, adding sweeter top notes to the sharper scent of the brandy. We rolled the dark amber liquid round our glasses, letting our hands warm it and release the volatile spirit. As I bent my head for the first sip, it prickled my nostril before my tongue tasted the smooth fire.

We kissed, the brandy awakening my mouth to each touch of Kit's questing tongue. He took another sip before taking my lower lip between his, sucking gently, then letting the cold night air awaken the stinging of the alcohol. As he did so, he burrowed a hand under my many petticoats. I was wearing no knickers, so his curious fingers traced their soft path up my thigh and into my cleft, which was already moist to his touch. Quick and light, his fingers flicked over my bud and teased the entrance to my sex. As my breathing quickened with excitement, I felt the constriction of the corset even more.

Kit put his hands around my waist, and his fingers almost met at my back. Without ceasing his kisses, he lifted me on to the stone balustrade and pushed my skirts up above the tops of my white stockings. Then he took another mouthful of brandy and knelt between my legs. As I felt his soft tongue press gently between my folds, a burning heat spread through me, right down the crack of my sex. As the alcohol trickled over my tenderest skin, I cried out in shock, but the warmth was already turning to the most intense pleasure.

The rough stone bit into my hands as I steadied myself against the strokes of Kit's tongue. The burning faded to a glow of arousal, then to coolness as the spirits met the night air. Then another tongueful of brandy cascaded over me. Waves of sensation kept me reeling, Kit's lapping bringing me inexorably towards my climax. But just as I felt the big wave gathering – the one that would break over me and have me crying out in sweet release – he stopped. A grunt of annoyance escaped me, but Kit was already lifting me from my perch and shoving me gently towards the doors. 'Bedtime,' he said.

Our room had been transformed; a small fire was burning in the grate and a generous blaze of candles multiplied in the mirrors. I would have started pulling my clothes off as soon as the door was shut but, since I had been laced and buttoned in from behind, only Kit could undress me. I offered my back to him, one hand on the back of a chair for balance, but instead of undoing the dress, he put an arm around me and caressed my breasts, squeezing out of the top of the bodice. His other hand was stroking my buttocks through the silk under-skirt. I sighed in pleasure.

Following Kit's nod, I saw us reflected in the mirrored panels, a lady dressed so primly, yet writhing under the lascivious hands of her man. Our eyes met in the mirror, and I bent forwards over the chair, brazenly offering my rear to him in a gesture of lewd abandon. He pulled my skirts up, the flash of my naked buttocks pink among the crumpled white underwear. With the impossibly svelte silhouette of my corseted waist, I looked like a 'What the Butler Saw' film show, or a naughty Victorian photograph.

Seemingly hypnotised by the picture we made, Kit ran his hand over my flanks, watching them shiver in response. I could clearly see his erection straining against the tight black trousers, and I was longing to feel it inside me, but he seemed intent on making me wait. His hands strayed over my cheeks, down my inner thighs and back up the crease of my bottom, without ever touching the most sensitive spots. The very lightness of his touch increased my suspense, contrasted as it was with the firm pressure on my waist and breasts.

At last, slowly and deliberately, he unbuttoned his flies and let his prick stand out, a graceful curve crowned with a big head. Never taking his eyes off the reflected scene, he placed it at my soft, warm entrance. Only when I whimpered with frustration did he begin to slide it in, rubbing past every tiny ridge inside me, each small movement adding to my desperation to feel his whole length penetrate me.

Suddenly he pulled back, nearly coming right out of me, and then slid himself all the way in. With fierce urgency, he rocked against me as if riding a horse, one hand pressed against my clit. After so much waiting, it took only a few moments for me to come, his cock filling me from behind, his hand rubbing me in front, and the vision of myself in corset, petticoat and button boots filling my mind. From the animal passion of Kit's thrusts I expected him to come just as fast, but he continued to rock until my climax was subsiding.

Before I'd regained my breath, I was thrown backwards on to the bed, skirts in disarray. This time, it was only in Kit's expression that I could see what an erotic picture I made. He gripped my ankles as he entered me again, my stockinged legs over his shoulders. The pounding of his cock set another climax going deep inside me, and his body banged against my clit with each thrust. Seeing my excitement, he gripped my confined waist and pulled me against him harder, reaching his own climax just as I called out his name in mine.

We lay, sweating, in a crumpled heap of satin and silk across the bed.

'Would Milady care for anything else?' Kit asked. I laughed.

'Thank you, Parker, that will be all,' I answered back.

2

By the third day, the tightening twists in the road and the cooling air told us we were approaching the Alps. Spending hour after hour hunched over the handlebars felt natural to me. My eyes and brain were fixed only on what the road would throw up next: a tractor pulling out of a farm gate; a stray dog, or a patch of gravel that could send the tyres stuttering across the tarmac. Now the contours of the road were a challenge, as every corner was different – one opening out into a gently curving climb, the next masking a hairpin bend behind a rocky outcrop.

Kit and I took it in turns to lead as we climbed higher into the mountains. The clean scent of pine replaced the heavier blossom smells of the lowlands, and in the shadow of the trees the air was cold on my face. Kit was a superb rider, taking the tightest corners so fast that his back tyre slid out behind him, and the gentler ones with the bike leaned over far enough to touch his knee along the road. I followed him as close as I dared, watching his technique.

I was learning fast, and I could feel my riding improving with every hour. When I overtook Kit and rode ahead, I tried to put every lesson into practice, and was gratified to flick my way through a windy uphill stretch so fast that the red muzzle of Kit's bike disappeared from my mirrors for a minute or two. The adrenaline coursed through me, and I let myself think for half a second that I was a better rider than he was. It wasn't true – all I am is nearly as good and twice as reckless. When he caught up with me on the next straight he overtook me and deliberately slowed the pace, making the point that I was getting too throttle-happy.

In fact, when we stopped for petrol I got a bit of a telling-off.

'Don't push yourself too far,' he said as I stretched my legs. 'You're good enough to know your limits. You were riding right to the edge of your ability back there, with nothing in reserve for the unexpected. What if you'd come around a corner to find a cow in the road? You wouldn't have stood a chance.'

I knew he was right, but his sensible words had the opposite effect to what he intended. Instead of accepting that I'd got carried away, I got sulky and resentful.

'What's the matter?' I asked. 'Worried that a woman might become a better rider than you?'

He walked away without replying, taking off his gloves, and I felt childish and stupid. He had never tried to prove his superiority in riding, or ever made a cheap crack about women drivers. It was only caring about my safety that had provoked his little speech.

My clumsy apology didn't really dispel the bad atmosphere, and I meekly rode behind him for the next couple of hours, trying to show by actions instead of words that I'd taken his point on board. It was frustrating, but I wanted to let Kit know I was sorry for my unreasonable outburst. I promised myself to behave responsibly for the rest of the day.

Though we didn't ride through snow, we saw plenty as the road wound up through the passes into the high Alps. Warm in the summer sun, I shivered whenever the road plunged into a dark, chilly tunnel. Each time I emerged, blinking in the brightness, another fantastic mountain vista towered above us. Then the terrain started to fall away before us, and we were actually looking down on white peaks. Shining through broken cloud against an improbably blue sky, the snowy Dolomites looked like some artist's vision of heaven. It was like flying down towards a lost world, and a feeling of intense happiness burned through me. This was exactly what a honeymoon should feel like; this joy in life, with the anticipation of unknown delights shining before us.

Indeed, the following morning's breakfast brought an unexpected pleasure. As I walked into the restaurant overlooking pine-wooded slopes, I saw a familiar figure sitting at a table by the window. The shaved head and powerful body, the tattoos on the arms wielding a knife and fork with relish, were unmistakable. But what was Geoff, of all people, doing in our honeymoon hotel? I turned to Kit, asking with a look if this was another of his surprises, but he only shrugged. As I wondered how to handle the situation, Geoff turned to look for a waiter and saw me instead. A broad smile broke across his face, and he waved us both over to his table.

It seemed that, for once, Geoff's appearance was pure coincidence. Given his central role in my hen night, it was strange to share a honeymoon breakfast with him, but both he and Kit were relaxed, so I could see no reason to worry. There were no secrets between the three of us, after all, and Kit had no cause to feel threatened.

Between mouthfuls of cooked breakfast, Geoff explained his presence in Italy. He was stunt co-ordinator for an action film being shot in the mountains – a huge job that would keep him there for several weeks. Today was a day off, so he planned to go climbing with some of his fellow stunt performers.

'Not enough danger in your working life?' I teased him.

'I don't do it for the danger,' he answered seriously. 'Excitement, yes, but I don't set out to get hurt.'

Kit shot me a meaningful look, and I felt myself blush.

'Kit thinks I'm a reckless fool,' I told Geoff.

'Not a fool,' said Kit, 'but slightly too much taste for taking risks.'

Geoff nodded in agreement. 'He's got the measure of you, then.'

Sensing that I was beginning to feel put upon, Kit smiled sympathetically.

'More coffee?' he asked and, as I nodded, he took my cup for a refill.

Geoff put his big hand on top of mine.

'Emma,' he said quietly, 'if I know you well, it's because you're a lot like me. Don't get hooked on danger. Taking risks is fine, but don't let the risks run the show. Stay in charge, or you're heading for something bad.'

Before I could reply, Kit returned with more coffee.

'Going to take her climbing, then?' he asked Geoff cheerfully.

'If you like,' said Geoff. 'How about you?'

Kit shook his head as he lifted the cup to his lips. 'I don't do heights,' he answered, 'but I wouldn't want that to hold you two back.'

I was tempted. Before I met Kit, Geoff had taken me climbing several times, and the thrill was different to biking, but just as strong. However, this was our honeymoon, and I wasn't about to abandon Kit for the day.

Later, after we'd fully digested our breakfast, Geoff threw his climbing equipment into the back of a pick-up truck, and me and Kit mounted our bikes, ready to hit the road south. We were heading for a planned rendezvous this time; one with my best friend, Jane.

We descended so fast that my ears popped, and only hours after leaving the hotel, we were riding along the shores of Lake Garda. I was astonished at the scale: sailing boats were tiny white flakes on the blue water below, and the far shore disappeared in the haze. The road alternated between dazzling sunshine and the pitch black of tunnels, gradually dropping down the rocky cliff to water level.

It was funny to see sunbathing tourists when we'd woken that morning to a view of snowy peaks. Riding in leathers was also too warm for comfort. I understood why the locals rode about in shorts and T-shirts, but the habit of wearing protective layers was too ingrained in me to copy them. Instead, I tried to keep enough speed for the air to cool me, and looked forward to a swim in the lake.

As the gurgling roar of the bikes' engines died away, we exchanged a smile at the sudden silence. Only the quiet lapping of the lake on a small, sandy beach could be heard. Jane was staying in a rented villa right by the lake, and its whitewashed walls reflected enough heat for us to feel it through our leathers, but the deep shade of the terrace promised inviting coolness. We walked towards it, peeling off as many layers as we could. Before we could sit down, Jane emerged from the dark doorway and wrapped me in a soft, blonde, Chanel-perfumed embrace.

It didn't surprise me at all to learn the nature of the work that brought her here – a photo shoot for a men's magazine, ostensibly about Italian fashion, but in reality an excuse to show off beautiful women in stunning locations, wearing as little as possible. Since we'd arrived in the heat of the day, the models and stylists were lying around indoors with cool drinks, waiting for the temperature to fall before resuming work.

Jane laughed as we draped our sweaty leather suits over two sunloungers to air; they did contrast comically with the skimpy swimsuits everybody else was wearing. I wasted no time in changing into my own swimsuit and slipping into the silky waters of the lake. After long, hot hours in one position, it was bliss to float freely, my limbs stretching out in relief. My skin felt as if it was drinking in the cool liquid through every pore, and each nerve ending was awake to the soft motion of the ripples over my body.

Kit swam alongside me, brushing his slender, muscular body against mine. I shivered as the hairs on his chest dragged against my shoulder, and rolled over in the water so our faces were close together. His mouth found mine, and we kissed, warm tongues and cold lake water flowing together into each other's mouths. His arm, warmer than the element surrounding us, slipped around me and pulled me closer.

We were floating, feet finding the sandy bed and losing it again as we bobbed up and down. Through the thin fabric of my bikini and his trunks I felt Kit's penis stir and begin to swell. A small crowd were sitting or lying near the beach, but nobody appeared to be paying us much attention, so I ran a hungry hand over the bulge and gave it a squeeze of encouragement. In response, Kit cupped his hands under my buttocks and pulled, pressing my clit against his hip bone.

I wriggled against him, wrapping my thighs around him so my leg pressed on his erection, and began to rock myself against him. A steady rhythm pulsed sharp and sweet inside me. He released the halterneck of my bikini top, letting the triangles of cloth fall away as my breasts floated in the water. My nipples were lapped by each tiny ripple in the surface as I bounced, warm air and cold water alternating to make them stand alert, tingling with sensation.

Kit dropped his head to take a nipple in his mouth, his teeth gripping it till pleasure blurred with pain and I gasped. I was getting very excited, wanting something more than this mutual rubbing, but uncertain how much we could do without attracting attention from the shore. Kit must have felt the same way because, with a glance at the lazy forms on the terrace, he turned us around so I was concealed from the shore by his body. One hand continued to caress my breasts, sliding over the wet skin, while the other found my bikini bottoms and pulled them down.

I wrapped my legs around his waist and Kit pulled me on to him, his long fingers rubbing me while his long cock slipped inside me. Now it was he who set the pace, bouncing me in the water so each wave added to the movement of his thrusts. He was deep inside me, the water adding to the delicious friction, and his hand keeping time. Though I was trying to steady myself by holding on to him, I was rapidly losing control of my limbs.

The sensation of hanging weightless on his cock was intoxicating. From the way he was squeezing my breasts and kissing my neck and shoulders, I could tell that Kit was just as excited as I was. Faster and faster his fingers flicked at my clit, harder and harder he pounded into me, till he gave a final lunge, groaning in his orgasm. Only then did the tension in my sex and the fluidity all around me join together in one electrifying circuit, and I quivered with release, Kit holding me tight in his arms.

It took a few minutes for me to regain my swimsuit and my composure, as we bobbed breathless in the water. With fantastic timing we walked ashore just as Jane brought a jug of cool orange juice on to the terrace, the freshly squeezed fruit far sweeter than anything that could come out of a carton.

I was planning a lazy afternoon lying in the sun, possibly venturing back into the lake for more swimming, but Jane had other plans.

'Those motorbikes are Italian, aren't they?' she asked, eyeing up the sleek lines of the Ducatis. 'Do you fancy being in a fashion shoot?'

That was Jane all over, always looking for something

new to throw into her plans. I suspected that it was the bike, not me, that she was really after, but it did sound like fun.

'All right,' I said, 'but I'm not getting back into those sweaty leathers.'

Jane looked mischievous. 'I had something cooler in mind,' was all she said.

Barely dry from our swim, it was deliciously cool to ride along the lakeside road in shorts and a skimpy top. One of the stylists had rustled up an open-face helmet and some stunning shades, and Jane had found a pair of black patent-leather boots with high heels, in which it was just about possible to ride a motorbike. Sitting behind Kit, Jane snapped away as he rode alongside, shouting instructions at both of us, most of which were carried away by the wind. I was showing off shamelessly, pouting for the camera and leaning forwards to simultaneously show off my riding style and my cleavage.

But Jane wasn't satisfied yet. When we got back to the villa she beckoned to one of the models, a Frenchwoman called Colette, darkly feline, with straight, bobbed hair. While Colette changed, Jane pulled my skimpy T-shirt off. I felt self-conscious, standing in my cut-off jeans, but everybody else was oblivious. To them, nudity was part of the job. Jane threw me a denim halterneck top, and I gratefully put it on.

This time I rode with Colette behind me in matching helmet and shades, white cowboy boots and the tiniest white bikini. She had been sunbathing till Jane called her, and her sun-kissed skin burned against my naked back. Even her thighs were hot where they brushed mine, a sensual contrast to the cool air blowing over my front.

Colette was utterly relaxed on a motorbike, as languid

on the little pillion seat as she had been on her sunloun-
ger. Occasionally I caught her scent, slightly musky but
with some floral perfume coming through, but usually
the wind swept everything away. She was enjoying this,
her husky laughter a counterpoint to Jane's shouts. I
couldn't see Colette's face, but I could see Kit's as he rode
beside us, and I recognised the spark of lustful interest
in his eyes as he watched the two of us.

Partly for Jane, and partly for Kit, I ran my hand over
Colette's thigh, warm and smooth. Jane was certainly
delighted, and shouted at me to do it again. Colette
gripped me with her legs, and gave my arm an encouraging stroke. I repeated the caress, playing it up a little
for the camera, a girl-on-girl parody of the classic bike
mag shots in which the guy gets both the bike and the
girl of his dreams. Inside, I was starting to enjoy it for
real, and the shiver that ran up the lithe brown leg told
me that Colette was too.

She hooked her legs over mine and lay back, so I could
run a lazy hand right down to her boot. In my mind's
eye I saw her, arched back, small pointy breasts thrown
up towards the sun. I wanted to feel more of her, but
Jane was directing this shoot, and I would have to hope
that her mind was running in the same direction as
mine. For now, I leaned forwards over the tank, so my
own breasts lay against her legs, and my face almost
touched the leather of her boots. The powerful vibrations
of the engine went right through me, pressed as I was
against the metal between her legs.

Then she was sitting up again, rubbing herself catlike
against my bare back, skin and fabric teasing every
nerve with the alternation of rough and smooth, cool
and vividly warm. I felt her breath at the nape of my
neck and a shiver of excitement answered between my
legs. I was longing for Jane to order her to kiss me, so I
could mask my own pleasure behind the photo shoot.

Instead I felt Colette's small, slender hands stroking my thighs, sending currents of energy ricocheting from toe to clitoris and back again.

It was getting hard to concentrate on riding the bike, as the throbbing of the twin pistons began to blend with my own rhythm of arousal. A couple of drivers coming the other way tooted their horns, but any embarrassment was overwhelmed by the urgency of my desire. Besides, if Kit was enjoying the spectacle of two half-naked women riding together, why shouldn't other men like what they saw?

Colette's hands, light but decisive, worked their way up and her nails scratched at the rough denim at the curve of my hips. In spite of myself I pushed backwards against her, and felt her grind herself against my rear. I hoped guiltily that her hands would find their way down inside my shorts, that she would run those clever fingers along the cleft, already moist, that was begging to be touched.

From the look in Kit's eyes, he would have enjoyed that almost as much as me, but Jane was bellowing her orders. 'Belly!' she shouted, still photographing furiously, and Colette's obedient caresses ran over the bare skin of my midriff, warm on the air-cooled skin. All I could do was try to focus on keeping control of the motorbike, while Jane demanded more and more provocative touches and my body responded helplessly to them.

One hand squeezed and pinched my nipples through the cloth, then from the corner of my eye I saw a scrap of white go flying on to the verge. Before my brain could work out what it was, two bare, soft breasts were pushed into my shoulder blades. I was dying to take them into my mouth, to hear Colette moan as I sucked on them, but still I was forced to passively endure the teasing contact, the agonisingly incomplete pleasure.

Now at last I felt the wetness of her tongue at the

back of my neck, the pressure of Colette's lips and tender little nips from her teeth. Desperate for some release, I slid forwards on the seat and pressed my mound against the petrol tank, revving the engine harder to increase the vibrations rising through the metal. Two quick hands burrowed into the tightness of my top, expertly caressing my breasts and, at the same time, pulling her own tighter against my back.

Jane's photographs, Kit's rapt face, the astonished drivers going past, all were forgotten as I pursued my climax. The bike was the only thing over which I still had control, and I was riding it like a lover, gripping it between my legs and building the momentum towards my own orgasm. Our speed was rising too and, as the needle swung past vertical, Colette hung on to me more tightly, her breath coming quicker at my ear.

Faster and faster we went, but still I hung on the edge of the precipice, so close to coming but unable to reach it. I could see the end of the straight hurtling towards us, and a traffic light turning from green to red. Shaking with frustration, I slammed down through the gears and braked hard, ramming us both forwards against the tank. Even the violence of our stopping was not enough to bring me off, and I stood trembling at the lights, Colette damp and heated against me.

Kit rolled up alongside us and Jane gestured to us to turn right. Resigned to ending the shoot in a state of unredeemed arousal, I obeyed, to find us riding down a shady lane towards the water. At Jane's direction, I rode on to a wooden deck alongside a boathouse, and parked overlooking the lake. Colette dismounted but, when I went to do the same, Jane motioned me to stay on.

Kit and Jane worked together as one, as if they'd discussed it in advance: in no time my bike was secure on its stand, and Colette was back on it, this time lying on her back in front of me, her slim body an elegant curve that echoed the line of the tank, and her arms thrown back over the handlebars. Jane picked up her camera again, and Kit leaned against the boathouse, watching.

I put my hands to Colette's throat and released the strap of her helmet, leaving a faint red mark on her brown skin. Her glossy black hair fell over the red of the tank, and she lay back, eyes half closed, smiling at me. Removing my own helmet, I let my hair fall forwards, copper in the sunlight. As it lightly brushed her breasts, the nipples rose, nut-brown, to meet it.

My tongue ran over them, flicking swiftly, and as she groaned in pleasure I felt an echoing stab of response in my own nipples. I pulled off my top and lay on top of her, breast now pressed against breast, her wet nipples against my dry ones. Hands on the handlebars, I rubbed my body up and down hers, and she wrapped her supple legs around me. I was aware that Jane was still capturing all this on film, but no longer had any illusion that this was for the benefit of an audience.

Now that I was freed from the constraint of piloting the bike, I no longer felt the urge to hurry towards the end. I lingered over the softness of Colette's body beneath mine, enjoying the whimper of pleasure that escaped her shining lips. I kissed her on the mouth, my lips enfolding hers, and my tongue pushing in to meet hers. Her hands wrapped themselves into my hair, holding my head over hers, nails touching my scalp.

I thrust my hips into her clit, the metal buttons of my shorts grinding into my own as I did so. My questing hand traced a path along the edge of her g-string, setting off a ripple of excitement that I could almost feel in my own body. Finding its way underneath her arching back, my finger followed the deepening crease down and felt the puckered muscle of her buttocks clench in response.

Half lifting her, my hand delved further and slid into the dampness that mirrored my own.

As I rubbed, Colette writhed against me, saying something that was muffled by our kisses. I was too aroused to stop, excited by the effect I was having on her, and by the way her bucking body jerked against my hot spot. Her hands now dug into my shoulders, half resisting me, half holding me tightly to her. I could tell she was near to coming, but I didn't want her to climax yet, so I was holding back on the rhythm of my hand in her cleft.

'Stop there.'

Shocked by the commanding tone of Jane's voice I did what I was told, looking up in astonishment.

'Take off your shorts,' said Jane, 'and you, Colette, turn around.'

It felt weird to interrupt our lovemaking so near the peak of passion, but also perversely sexy to be denied the release, as if we were shooting a porno film and I had to drag out the action. Even as I bent over to slide the denim over my boots, I was aware that Jane had chosen a low angle to capture the curve of my flanks above the cloth.

Following Jane's pointing hand, I remounted the bike, where Colette was stretched again, this time with her legs slung over the handlebars. The white triangle of the thong, an arrow pointing forwards to the speedo, only drew attention to the way her sex was offered up. As I bent my head and pulled aside the scrap of cloth, I felt her arms around my waist, pulling me down towards her flicking tongue.

Now Colette was the bike I rode, my fingers gripping her ankles through the boots and my mouth between her legs, controlling the power and rhythm of her vibrations. Instead of the motor roaring through the bike, it was the vibrations of her tongue, lips and eager fingers that set me shaking. Every time I changed pace or tried a new angle of attack, I felt her response in the way she worked on me, as sensitive as any finely tuned performance bike.

As the woman beneath me quivered, fast approaching her climax, I felt like a racer nearing the finish line. Wild though my own abandon was, part of me still kept control, determined to bring Colette roaring to victory with me. Feeling my own orgasm begin to break through me, I put her clitoris between my lips and sucked, pushing my fingers into the wetness beyond. I came then, groaning into the soft musky hair of Colette's sex, and hearing her cries muffled between my legs.

3

Kit was even more keen than usual to get me into bed that night, but I enjoyed putting off the moment. For hours his hungry eyes followed me around the villa, as I partied with Jane and her models and helpers. They were a very mixed crowd, all nationalities and sexual persuasions. When somebody put on some Cuban music, and I danced a raunchy tango with Colette, kissing her tequila-soaked lips, I saw a slender Moroccan lad pull Kit on to the dance floor. Normally Kit would have run a lecherous hand over his partner's firm buttocks, if only to tease me, but for once he seemed indifferent to his muscular grace, not taking his eyes off us. As the song ended, I relented at last, and we slipped upstairs to our room while the party continued.

'That was quite a photo finish,' he said as he pulled the cotton dress over my head. 'Do all Jane's fashion shoots end with both models naked?'

'Not quite naked,' I reminded him. 'We both had our boots on. Besides, a Ducati is an Italian fashion icon.'

'Nobody will be looking at the Ducati,' he said between kisses.

Through his shorts I could feel how excited he was, and that aroused me still more. Having teased him for so long, I wanted this one to be just for Kit. Rolling over to lay him on his back, I slid down to peel off his clothes. He sighed and closed his eyes as I ran a lascivious tongue over the head of his cock, tasting the first salty drop of moisture that already hung there. Watching his face, I took him in my mouth and sucked gently, working my lips over the tender ridge.

Then I straddled him, lowering my hips with taunting slowness to take his shaft into me. I worked myself up and down on him, touching myself as I did so. He ran his hands up my flanks and over my bouncing tits, but let me set the pace. I enjoyed being on top, being able to set the rhythm I needed, and to rub myself off as I rocked. Kit enjoyed it too, lying lazily where he could see my whole body and share my pleasure.

I could tell he was already close to coming, so I paced him carefully. I enjoyed the feeling of power it gave me, watching him tremble with suspense as I brought him to the edge and then kept him hanging. His full lips moved and I heard one whispered word, 'please...' Then, at last, I had mercy and gave him release, feeling him flood into me, hot and wet, and then lie limp and sated beneath me as I bucked in my own orgasm.

Sometimes we liked to lie long in bed in the morning, enjoying slow, sleepy lovemaking, and get up late and ravenous. That morning we woke full of other appetites; we were both itching to get back on the bikes and find some more demanding mountain roads. I tiptoed in to say goodbye to Jane, a tousled mess of smudged mascara in the arms of some model.

'Good to see you,' she mumbled. 'Come back whenever you want.'

I'm sure she was asleep again before I left the room.

By lunchtime we'd left the lake behind and were switchbacking along a mountain road, one side edged by a cliff face and the other a sheer drop to a river far below. There was no room for mistakes, but I was full of confidence and felt I could do no wrong. I'd reached the moment when the bike felt like a part of me; when I had only to look where I wanted to go, to feel the weight shift, and the wheels found the perfect line around each bend.

I was speeding ahead when we caught up with a group of Italian riders, three men on fast sports bikes, having as much fun as we were. We rode behind them for half a mile, then the road opened up to a longer straight before the next bend, and I felt an irresistible urge to turn a few heads. Though they were already accelerating I knew I could beat them, so I pulled the throttle open and felt the surge of power almost lift the front wheel as the bike flew forwards. In two, three seconds, I was past them all and braking hard to go into the corner ahead of them.

I was still moving way too fast, and got round on pure instinct and adrenaline, my eyes fixed on the road ahead as it disappeared behind the rock face. As I positioned myself for the next corner, I got a glimpse of the first of the Italian boys in my mirror, and was wickedly pleased by how much distance I'd already put between them and myself. Speed on the straight is one thing, but how fast you can take a corner is the real test of a rider, and I knew that in a matter of seconds there'd be three Italian men behind me with something to prove. As soon as they realised they'd been passed by a woman, the competition would really be on.

Sure enough, the rider behind me did a double take as he lined up and then overtook me with a move so risky his tyre tracks touched the edge of the tarmac. The race was on. For the next mile or two, the two of us passed each other every chance we got, his two friends mere dots in our mirrors. On these narrow roads, there was barely room for two bikes to race, let alone four.

Or five. Because, of course, Kit was still riding behind us all, no doubt thoroughly disapproving of my recklessness. I couldn't help myself, though. One glimpse of my rival's face as I passed him was enough to instil in me the thrill of fierce competition and sexual challenge all at once, and I forgot all my vows to be more sensible. Kit might tell me off when we finally pulled up, but for now I had eyes only for the road and the stranger on the bike that was clearly a match for mine.

Then, to my amazement, I was passed not by the Italian, but by Kit's red Ducati. Perhaps he didn't want to spend another afternoon as a spectator, watching me playing with somebody else, or perhaps he'd just remembered how much fun it could be to push things to the edge. Certainly, as he nipped in front of me with inches to spare, I was half a second away from clipping his back wheel and sending him over the cliff.

Now there were three of us in the race and, with Kit's years of experience in the mix, the riding went up another level. It was time for Kit and the other man to overtake each other halfway round a blind bend, to corner so fast that the back wheel slid sideways into the gravel, and I was fighting just to stay in the game. If I'd ever forgotten how much better a rider Kit was, I was being given a reminder.

But the Italian wasn't about to concede victory. Three engines screamed as we tore up the empty mountain road, Kit or the Italian in the lead and me doing well to take second place from time to time. We'd come down this road two days before, and I remembered the worst bends, trying to use my mental map to give me some advantage over the Italian. As we approached one blind bend with Kit in the lead, I moved towards the centre of the road, preparing to overtake when it opened up into the straight that I knew was coming next.

The Italian must have known it too, because he boldly went for the inside of the bend as Kit started to turn, planning to steal the lead before we even hit the straight. Just as he pulled level with Kit, I saw with horror that he had nowhere to go. A bus was coming the other way, filling more than half the road, and the Italian was about to ride straight into it.

In slow motion, the bus braked, wheels screeching on the tarmac. At the same time, moving in perfect synchronicity, both the Italian and Kit made an abrupt change of direction. The Italian missed the corner of the bus so tightly that his boot touched the bumper, and Kit missed the Italian, taking the corner so wide that his wheels found the edge of the tarmac. As I found my own line between him and the bus, I saw the bike lean further and further over and then slide along the tarmac. Kit slid behind it for a few yards and came to rest against a tree as the bike disappeared off the edge of the road.

Without even being aware of it, I was off my bike and running back to him. It felt unreal, like a nightmare. Like all motorcyclists I had heard many terrible accident stories, but I had never imagined being in one of these scenes myself. Could our honeymoon really be over like this, in a couple of seconds? I couldn't accept the worse thought – that I might have become a widow in the blink of an eye.

The other Italians, riding behind us, were on the scene in a moment and racing to where Kit lay. At the sight of his chest rising and falling, I felt the biggest rush of relief I have ever known. Then he raised a hand to his visor and, as I knelt beside him, pushed it up and said, 'That'll teach me to take it to the limit.' Tears filled my eyes, but I could only think about what needed doing for Kit.

As we checked Kit for serious injury the fastest Italian appeared, looking stricken. It was, after all, his fault that Kit had come off. One of his friends called for an ambulance. By the time it came, Kit had reassured us that he still had feeling and movement in all his limbs.

'At the moment, all I'm feeling is quite excruciating pain,' he said dryly, 'but at least I don't seem to have lost the use of anything.'

None of the Italians spoke much English, but they managed to reassure us that one of them would bring my bike to the hospital so I could ride in the ambulance with Kit. It was only then that I gave a thought to his bike, lying smashed somewhere below. Now I began to cry, knowing that the dream was over so quickly. Though Kit would recover and life would go on, we would never again have that perfect feeling that everything was ours.

I sat in the ambulance, holding his hand, as it retraced the bends that we'd just ridden up. He lay quiet, catching his breath when a sharp corner jarred him. The paramedic smiled encouragingly at me, and said a few words of comfort in Italian, but I sat and wept. I knew that this accident wasn't really the Italian's fault. I was the one who started the competition, and without me Kit would have enjoyed the ride in his usual calm style. By now we could have been sitting in a restaurant having lunch and enjoying the view. Kit's warm brown hand would have brushed affectionately over mine, and I would have smiled back at him, knowing we had all the time in the world. Instead, his hand was cold with shock, and he had given up trying to smile bravely and lay, eyes closed, waiting for the pain to stop.

At the hospital I felt lost and useless as he was whisked away behind green curtains by nurses talking urgently in Italian. I didn't know what was happening or what I should do, so I stood waiting. I thought I heard Kit's voice, but I couldn't make out what he was saying. At last, a doctor came out of the cubicle and spoke to me in English.

'You are the English rider's wife?'

'Yes,' I said, 'how is he?'

The doctor managed to look serious without making my heart sink too far.

'He will mend,' he said, 'but it will take time. He's broken several bones – arm, leg, pelvis – and inside he is bruised and sore. A few days in hospital, then he will need some weeks for the bones to set. Now they are putting the plaster on, then you can see him.'

Contradictory emotions washed through me, relief that the injuries were nothing worse, worry about how I could look after Kit while he healed, and irrational anger that our honeymoon had been spoiled. Kit was so sweet about the whole business that I felt even worse. He never once said anything to blame me, in fact he apologised for frightening me. When I started saying, 'I'm so sorry, it's all my fault,' he hushed me.

'Nobody forced me to ride that hard,' was all he said. Then the sedation started to take effect and his eyes closed. Soon his steady breathing showed that he was asleep.

Outside, the Italian riders stood around awkwardly. They had brought my motorbike, but to my miserable eyes it looked forlorn without its companion. Desperate to do everything I could to make things right again, I asked them to take me back so we could search for Kit's bike and see what state it was in. From the glances they exchanged, I guessed they had already looked, and that the news was bad, but I was determined to take everything in hand at once. I did accept the offer of a ride on the back of one of their bikes, though, accepting that my state of mind was not ideal for riding at the moment.

Normally, I enjoy riding pillion behind someone. Even if I don't know them well, there's a physical closeness and a level of trust that forms a human bond between you. This afternoon, though, it was a lonely experience to hold on to a stranger and return to the place where everything had turned so abruptly from joy to unhappiness. Naturally, they all rode as slowly and carefully as was possible for three Italian men on fast bikes.

Seeing the marks on the road – the black rubber from the bus's tyres, the scrapes left by Kit's bike, and the gash in the verge where it had slid off the tarmac – I felt sick. It could, after all, have been so much worse. With no engine sound it was so quiet, with scarcely a bird to break the silence. Steeling myself, I walked to the corner and looked down. Hundreds of feet below, a flash of red among the grey stones showed where the Ducati had come to rest. Imagining what would have happened if Kit had gone with it, I was plunged back into the nightmare feeling. I had to do something, to avoid dwelling on how much worse things could have been, but what could I do? Retrieving that bike from its stony bed was going to be a hell of a job for anyone, let alone mending it.

The Italians watched me nervously. I'm sure they expected me to call a recovery service and leave the bike to the professionals, but I couldn't be without something to do for that long. Again I felt useless, marooned without speaking the language. Could I get these lads to help me rescue the bike, maybe borrow a local tractor to pull it clear?

I turned to the leader, trying to frame my opening sentence. His eyes were fixed on my leathers, just below the collar. Hoping that I wasn't going to see a smear of Kit's blood, I followed his gaze down to the eagle-and-snake badge that Max had pinned to me on the ferry. The Italians were regarding it with the same mixture of respect and wariness that Max's own companions had shown.

I still didn't know who Max was, or why all these people seemed to recognise his mark, but I did know three things. First, Max spoke perfect English. Second, he would know how to get a bike back from anywhere it could possibly land, and how to get it made as good as new, and, third, somehow, I felt certain of this without knowing why, he would come if I needed him. My fingers found his card in my pocket. There was a mobile phone number on it.

My hands shook with nervousness as I opened my phone and punched in the number. It rang three times, then that voice answered with a curt 'Yes?'

'Max,' I said, trying to keep my voice steady, 'it's Emma.'

If I had thought about it with a clear head, I would have realised that he might be anywhere in Europe at that moment. In the time it had taken Kit and myself to reach Italy, Max and his companions could have been in Sweden, Poland or southern Spain. I don't believe in fate, so I'm forced to call it luck that he answered my call from somewhere in Austria and was with me in a few hours.

Rather than go back to the hospital, where Kit lay between anonymous, clinical sheets in a drug-lined sleep, I sat waiting in a roadside café. The three Italians waited with me, keeping me supplied with a steady flow of coffee, hot chocolate and water. They tried to get me to eat something, but my mouth was dry and my stomach a tight ball. At their urging, and knowing that it had been hours since our early breakfast, I accepted a bowl of polenta, but the first mouthful made me feel sick.

Since my call to Max, the Italian rider's visible sense of guilt had turned to something more like fear. Helpful and attentive before, now he couldn't do enough for me. His two friends exchanged worried glances when they thought I wasn't looking. I didn't care. Swamped with my own guilt and misery, I had no room left for sympathy.

I was sitting with my back to the window; the breathtaking view of the mountains was spoiled for me now. Before Max pulled up outside, though, I heard the throaty gurgle of his bike and my spirits rose, knowing he would be able to take charge of the situation. When the engine sound stopped I was surprised to find that my heart was pounding. The Italian had turned white, his eyes fixed on the doorway. I gathered my nerve to stand and greet Max.

He stood in the doorway, silhouetted against the sunlit road. Again, his presence embodied the promise of enormous power, held within a near-perfect stillness. I wanted to go to him, but I couldn't move until he did, his eyes perhaps adjusted to the dark café and now fixed on me. I was suddenly aware that all conversation had ceased, and that the sound of his boots on the floor was all I could hear. I walked towards him and we met in the middle of the floor.

In my mind he was taller – in fact, he looked down at me from only a couple of inches above me. I had also forgotten how intensely blue his eyes were, and the effect they had on me. I was trembling, all the emotions of the day suddenly washing through me, and to my deep humiliation tears were rolling down my face and dripping off my cheeks. I couldn't speak.

Max looked at me, not at all embarrassed by this display of weakness. Simply, as if comforting a child that has fallen over in the playground, he got a handkerchief out, handed it to me and, as I mopped pathetically at my face, put a hand on my head and drew it to his shoulder. Abandoning any pretence at dignity, I leaned against him and bawled. He just stood there till I had stopped, saying nothing. Only when I had regained control of my breathing, stepped back and dabbed at the wet patch on his leather jacket, did he say with a slight smile, 'So – this motorbike.'

Now I was aware that he had been joined by three of his friends, who were greeting the Italians with nods and handshakes, one of them speaking Italian, apparently asking where the accident had happened. After a short exchange with the three Italians, he turned to Max and said something in Dutch. Of course – that explained the slight lilt in Max's impeccable English. Max answered in Dutch, and the other men all set off at once for their motorbikes.

'Peter will arrange it,' Max said over a chorus of engines starting up and receding along the road. 'Now, I think a drink and then I take you back to the hospital. And for you, some food.'

So relieved that everything was being taken care of, I feared I might cry all over again. I sat back at the table while Max spoke to the barman. Gratefully, I accepted an espresso, but the first mouthful burst on to my tastebuds like a flamethrower.

'Grappa,' said Max, 'Eau de Vie. You look as if you need a little injection of life in your coffee.' I smiled at him, and for the first time he gave me back a full smile.

When a bowl of soup appeared in front of me, I actually felt hungry. Ravenously hungry, in fact. I burnt my tongue on the hot, spicy liquid, rich with meat and pasta, and emptied the breadbasket to wipe the bowl clean. Food, grappa and emotional comfort fuelled a warm glow inside me. Max spoke little as I ate, watching me attentively as he sipped a beer. When I sat back, he nodded for the bill.

'Now we visit Kit,' he said.

I climbed behind him on to the massive cruiser. After the tiny perch on the sports bike, the pillion seat felt strangely low and pleasantly padded. There was even a little back-rest, against which I rested wearily. Max's black leather-clad back rose in front of me, though I could see little over his shoulder of the road ahead. As much for comfort as for stability, I put my arms around him and felt the solid strength of his body.

Max looked totally out of place in the clean, white hospital, his heavy boots echoing in the hushed corridor. Expressions of disapproval flitted across the nurses' faces as we passed them, but the doctor greeted us both warmly.

'Your husband is awake,' he told me. 'And we hope he will be ready to leave in a few days.'

Kit was more alert than when I'd last seen him, and reached his intact right arm across the bed to shake Max's hand.

'Thanks for coming to the rescue,' he said. 'I owe you one.'

'It's my pleasure,' Max replied. 'I'm sure you'll be able to do something for me one day.'

Though Max withdrew tactfully to the corridor, I felt awkward with Kit. He didn't seem to think it odd that I had called this guy, a man I had met once for a few moments, to help us through this crisis. In fact, I thought I had seen a look of complicity pass between them, as if they shared an understanding that excluded me. This unsettled me. I would have felt easier to meet a jealous or suspicious response. Still, it meant I could continue to rely on Max's help.

Kit eased my mind by chatting normally, reassuring me that his injuries were expected to heal fully, and smiling with real affection. He was still heavily dosed with painkillers and seemed drowsy.

'Don't get into any trouble while I'm not there to keep an eye on you,' he murmured, and then his eyes closed and he drifted back into sleep. I planted a kiss on his soft mouth before I quietly left him there.

Outside, I found Max already waiting by our bikes. When I arrived he pulled on the plain black helmet that left his face open to the oncoming wind and bestrode his bike without a word.

'Where are we going?' I asked, but he simply jerked his head in a command to follow him. Again, even as I obeyed, I felt a cold trickle of humiliation at my own willingness to be summoned like a dog.

Following him through the city on my own bike, I stuck as close as I could to avoid losing him in the hectic traffic. Cars, bikes and the ubiquitous scooters came from all directions, treating traffic rules with grudging compliance or, more often, ignoring them altogether. Miraculously, there were no collisions, and the cacophony of horns never seemed to escalate into real anger. Keeping my eyes fixed on the black figure ahead, I wove through the maze.

The broad main streets became side roads, then we were riding through lonely back streets between warehouses and empty buildings. The sky was darkening, blue turning to a coppery brown in the west, with a few golden clouds drifting across the snowy peaks that were now shining bronze.

Max turned down a narrow lane that sloped steeply between wooden fences, the end blocked by a high gate. As he neared it, the gate swung outwards and I followed him into a yard. The gate crashed shut behind me and a heavy-set, bearded man in jeans and leather waistcoat looked suspiciously at me as I pulled up beside Max. Max nodded to him, as if answering his unspoken question, and the man held open the door of an anonymous building with metal-shuttered windows.

Max walked into the lighted room, and I stepped in

behind him. A basic bar was serving alcohol, and several men were carrying beers away from a counter in the corner. Other men sat on benches at bare wooden tables, and two were playing pool. In fact, there were only men in the room, all dressed in denim and black leather. I had been in a gay bar in London once where all the men wore leather and denim that looked as if it was fresh from the manufacturers, and the overall effect was of play-acting, a parody of masculinity. This place was the diametric opposite of that. This was maleness in a raw, dangerous form, and I felt like an intruder. Even my colourful one-piece leather suit looked gaudy and inappropriate here.

I drew closer to Max's side, and the hostile eyes that were on me from all directions flicked from me to him and back again. Max placed a protective hand on my shoulder, his grip strong even through the leather. Seeing that he acknowledged me as his guest, they nodded a wary greeting to me and turned back to what they had been doing.

I wanted to ask what this place was, and why he'd brought me here, but the words stuck in my throat. Instead I sat meekly where he indicated, opposite him at a table in the corner. When a man dressed the same as everybody else approached the table, Max ordered two beers in perfect Italian. I opened my mouth to decline, mindful of having to ride back through that traffic later that night, but he simply said, 'You won't be riding anywhere.'

I didn't know what he meant; was his plan to leave my bike here and take me as his passenger again, or did this weird place have bedrooms? My mind shied away from the next question, but it lurked at the edges of my consciousness. Did he intend me to sleep with him? And if so, what would I do? Since our first encounter on the ferry a dark mixture of fear and attraction had drawn me to him; but I had never foreseen being with him in a situation such as this.

Many of the men seemed to know him, but they kept their distance. Exhausted by the day's events, I would have welcomed company so I could fade into the background and rest my numbed mind while Max talked to his friends. Not that he was badgering me with conversation. We were halfway down the glasses of beer before he spoke.

'Your first accident?'

I nodded glumly. 'First serious one,' I replied. 'I've had a few tumbles, and seen a few more, but nothing worse than bruises. This one was . . .' I couldn't finish, thinking about how bad it might have been. Those cool blue eyes watched me, waited for me to find the words.

'It shook me up –' was the best I could do '– to see Kit go down so fast.'

Max nodded gently. 'Sometimes it's good to be shown what the risks are,' he said. 'Riding motorcycles is a risky game. You can push it as far as you like, but there is a price.'

I felt awkward, being with Max in a completely alien place. I could tell that without him I would be an unwelcome visitor, and yet he himself was pretty much a stranger to me. In fact, I hadn't felt so alone and far from home for many years. I was also starting to be aware that I had been in the same sweaty T-shirt and leathers for many hours, and was feeling grubby and dishevelled.

We finished our beers and, with a peremptory nod, Max ordered two more. I was relieved to see two women come in, to be greeted with familiar smiles by the men. I felt less exposed, now I was no longer the only woman in the place. I hoped they might join us at the table, but they went through the bar, stopping to speak to a few of the men, and disappeared into another room. Seeing my face fall, Max laughed softly.

'You were hoping to join them? Maybe another time.'

The jukebox got louder as the evening went on; pounding rock beats with caterwauling guitar solos that made conversation near impossible if I had wanted to speak. The truth was, I didn't know what to say to him. The only questions I had were too frightening to ask: Who are you? Why are you helping me? What happens now?

As I finished my beer, Max looked at my weary face and said, 'You want to sleep?'

Too tired even to care what came next, or to resist, I nodded. He stood, and I followed him to the door through which the women had left. In a dimly lit corridor, a narrow staircase rose into darkness. Like a true gentleman, Max indicated for me to go up first.

As I turned the corner on to another murky passageway, I heard the voices of the women from downstairs, laughing together as they came out of some room. A burst of noise as the door opened told me they had gone back into the bar, and again I felt a pang of isolation. Max opened the door of a small room and I went in. Whatever happened now, I was too much in his debt to refuse, I told myself. The truth was, I didn't have it in me to resist his natural authority.

The room was plain, a single bed covered with a blanket, and a chair. Max turned on a lamp that was positioned on the windowledge, and I saw that everything was clean, if threadbare. He pointed to a door in the corner.

'Shower and toilet in there,' he said. 'Breakfast downstairs at eight.' Then he was gone, closing the door softly behind him.

The music in the bar below got suddenly louder and

a growl of approval went up from the men. Of course, the women I had seen earlier were the cabaret. How could I have been so naïve? Below me they were teasing that roomful of testosterone with some kind of striptease act. And I had been hoping for girlie company!

I sat on the bed, shaking with anticlimax. Though I was unutterably weary in body and mind, and knew I would be asleep as soon as I lay down, I was shocked to taste a bitter thread of disappointment. Max was, after all, the perfect Good Samaritan, asking nothing from me in return for all his help. He was not going to use me in degrading and perverse ways to service his dark desires. But I wanted him to, I recognised at last with a thrill of shame. I wanted him to use me.

4

Breakfast was at eight, as Max had promised – milky coffee and a sweet roll. The room was empty except for us, spartan with white walls and plain wooden furniture. Showered and fresh from a deep sleep, I felt far more able to handle whatever might happen. I was glad, I told myself, that Max had not tried anything on last night, as by now we would both be regretting it.

If I was honest with myself, what I was regretting was not having felt the touch of those strong, square hands. I watched the way he handled his cup, precise without being in any way prissy. I could imagine him working on his motorbike in the same measured way, the broad fingertips locating each tiny bolt and wire by touch alone. His broad shoulders and muscular arms, profiled by a solitary ray of sunshine piercing the metal shutters, would lift a heavy bike with ease. So what could he do to me, so strong and yet so painstaking in every detail?

He looked up from his cup and caught me staring at him. Though I looked away at once, I felt the colour rise to my cheeks and I thought I saw a ripple of amusement twitch at the corner of his eyes. It was hard to say how old he was. I guessed late thirties, but that was more from his gravitas than his physical condition. There was no trace of grey in his short blond hair, and hardly a wrinkle on his skin.

As we stepped out into the yard, Max laid his hand on my shoulder again, this time for my benefit rather than for any audience. On the back of a pick-up truck lay the remains of Kit's bike. The fairing was completely smashed, jagged pieces sticking out at gruesome angles like broken bones. Everything I could see, mirrors, handlebars, even the exhaust silencer, was twisted and bent out of line. I caught my breath for the ruined beauty of the machine, the perfect lines destroyed in a few seconds.

'It will be made good,' said Max. 'I will make sure of it. But you should remember this. When you ride in the sunshine, the road is dry and your heart takes flight. Let this remind you that you are not immortal.'

'I will,' I replied, and felt I would never forget the picture of waste and ugliness that lay before me.

'But, since we are not immortal,' he went on, 'let us get on with our lives at once and live them to the full.'

Somehow I had assumed that Max would be off again once the retrieval of the motorbike had been sorted, but he showed no signs of being in a hurry to leave. It was true, there were plenty of things to sort out, and I was very grateful of his language skills, to say nothing of the clout he seemed to have with the locals. In a few hours Kit's motorbike had been placed in a local workshop for repair, and we'd arranged for Jane to come and collect Kit so he could convalesce at her lakeside villa.

I checked myself into a hotel, rather than face another evening under the glowers of the bikers.

'What is that place?' I asked, trying to sound casual.

'A clubhouse,' was his enigmatic reply.

'And you're a member?' I pursued it.

He nodded, but 'In a way' was his only answer.

In the impersonal comfort of the hotel I lay sleepless, worrying. All this would cost money, lots of money. We had planned a cheap honeymoon so we could stretch the money over at least a month. Now it was looking anything but cheap, and yet Kit would be unable to go back to work for weeks, at best, and I was unwilling to leave him behind in Italy and go back to work myself. At heart, I still blamed myself for the accident and all its consequences.

Towards the end of the week I went back to the hospital, taking him some fruit and local cakes. He was mending well, already more lively and chafing at being confined to bed.

'Those nurses are teasing me something rotten,' he said to me as a young blonde in a crisp white uniform walked briskly past his room. 'This morning they gave me a bedbath and, by the time they'd finished working over my back with those wet sponges, I was in no state to turn over.'

I thought of him lying there helpless, his cock swelling between his belly and the warm sheet as the nurses stroked his skin with a clean cloth.

'Did they give you a hand with it, then?' I whispered in his ear, sliding my own hand over his chest as I spoke, feeling the coarse hairs spring back beneath my palm as I worked downwards.

'Ooh, don't start,' he groaned, as my finger traced the line of dark hairs below his navel. 'You know somebody's bound to come in just at the wrong moment.'

'You're right,' I said briskly, replacing the sheet over him and tucking it firmly under his chin. 'No sex till you're completely better.'

'No!' he said in protest, but the doctor was already halfway into the room.

'I'll leave you to it, doctor,' I said demurely, ignoring the fierce signals Kit's eyes were flashing at me. As I left the room, I managed a sly look at Kit, licking my lips suggestively.

When I turned my mobile phone back on outside the hospital, I had a message from Geoff: 'Hey, sexy redhead,' he said, 'I've got an offer you can't refuse. Call me as soon as. *Ciao, bella.*'

I laughed to think how little I was in the mood for a day of climbing, or paragliding, or whatever he was planning for his next day off. Still, Geoff wasn't to know what we'd been through in the last few days. I called him right back. If nothing else, he was the kind of friend I needed at a time like this.

But this time he wasn't trying to tempt me with a day of recreational danger. Not exactly, anyway.

'I know it's your honeymoon and all,' he said, 'but I've got some work for you.'

'What kind of work?' I asked, bemused. Who could Geoff possibly know who needed an architect in the Italian mountains?

'My kind of work,' he said. 'Stunt work.'

Normally I would have bitten his hand off, hearing that offer. The film he was working on needed a stunt motorcycle rider to double for the female lead. They'd been working with a stuntman but, small as he was, he was too obviously the wrong shape.

'I know you don't want to interrupt your holiday,' he said, 'but it's only a couple of days, and it's good money.'

Could I really make enough to pay for bike repairs and all the other expenses? The figures Geoff was quoting me were staggeringly high. In three days I could make enough to cover all our costs, and even have some left over to do something special for Kit. But did I still have the bottle for it? Two days ago I had been riding like a stunt rider, and look where that had got us.

I had to explain to Geoff why I was hesitating, and when he heard about the accident he whistled through his teeth.

'Nasty,' he said. 'I can see why you might be feeling a bit more careful. But remember, in a stunt shoot, *all* the drivers know exactly what they're doing. There's not going to be any unrehearsed bus coming round any corner on *my* gig.'

I still felt a cold fear at the prospect of riding fast and under pressure, but I wanted to do it. The idea of making back all the wasted money felt like somehow making reparation for the trouble I'd caused. There was also a part of me that refused to let fear rule me. I'd never before turned something down because I was scared, and I didn't want to start now.

When I visited Kit the next day he was more encouraging than I had expected.

'Do it,' he said, 'but not for the money. Do it because you need to get straight back in the saddle. It's like falling off a horse.'

'If you think so,' I replied. Already the idea was starting to appeal to me. After all, I would get to practise each dangerous stunt before I did it for real, unlike our capers on the public roads.

'But I do have one condition,' said Kit.

'Of course,' I answered eagerly. I was going to jump at any chance I had to make amends to him.

'I want you to suck my cock.'

'Now?'

I could see the house doctor doing his rounds, and there was every danger he would walk in to check on Kit, or that a nurse would stick her head around the door.

'Yep,' he answered. 'Now.'

He put his right hand behind his head, aiming for a pose of relaxation that was slightly spoiled by the left arm in plaster that lay heavily beside him on the bed.

He was having trouble keeping a straight face, but my practised eye could tell that he was also very turned on by the idea of getting a furtive blow job under the noses of the hospital staff. Perhaps he even hoped that one of the teasing nurses would catch us at it. Perhaps I quite liked that idea myself. Whatever it was, I feigned a sigh of exasperation at his unreasonable demands, and pulled back the sheet that covered him.

His penis was already stirring, growing under my appreciative gaze and lifting its head like a blind, hungry pup. My own desire rose in answer, and I bent to take him between my lips. As I let him stiffen in my mouth, I felt his warm hand stroke its way up my thigh and push between my legs.

I was so glad that for once, not expecting to ride anywhere that day, I was not impenetrably zipped into my leather suit. Kit's fingers made a meandering path up my bare skin, under the hem of my summer dress, and around the edge of my knickers. I sucked harder on his cock, sliding my lips along it so it filled my mouth completely. From the way Kit's fingers shook, I could tell I was having the right effect.

I ran my fingers through the hair on his chest, softly scratching the warm skin beneath, then down across his flat stomach. More urgently, his hand pushed under the elastic and into the hair that covered my sex. I took the hint and gripped the root of his cock, pumping in time with Kit as he flicked my clit with a lazy finger.

He always hit the spot, but more exciting still was the danger that one of the crisp, clean nurses might come in and find me bent over like this, servicing their patient. I had seen their lips purse when I walked along the corridor with Max, his dirty leathers representing all the filthy thoughts and deeds that they worked so hard to banish. Like little nuns, they tried to make everything pristine and simple. I hoped one of them would come in; I wanted to see her little pink mouth open in horror as Kit pumped his seed between my scarlet lips.

I pictured it as I came, Kit's fingers deep in my cleft, my groan muffled by his cock deep in my throat. He was also on the verge, I could tell, but unable even to thrust his hips, he lay shaking with excitement, waiting for me to give him release. For a few seconds I tortured him with suspense, running a slow tongue over the silky head, teasing the shaft with the subtlest of squeezes, then with a few strong strokes I brought him there and felt the hot liquid flood my mouth.

As I cleaned him up with the hospital tissues, Kit smiled a contented cat grin.

'Now, why can't they teach them that in nursing college?' he said softly.

'Don't worry,' I answered, kissing him. 'Jane'll take you back to her place tomorrow. I'm sure she'll be happy to give you personal care till I get back. Her or one of her models.'

Geoff was so sure I was going to say yes that he'd already booked me a hotel room for that night.

'That way we make an early start in the morning,' he told me.

When I heard just how early, I agreed that I'd arrive the night before, so I put the faithful leathers back on and went to say goodbye to Max.

This time the gate of the clubhouse stayed shut as I rode up to it. As I dismounted the alleyway seemed ominously quiet, and the reverberating rumble of the Ducati's idling engine only added to the feeling of menace. A small hatch slid open in the gate, and a bearded face scowled at me.

'*Voglio* Max?' I tried, kicking myself for the millionth time for my lack of language skills. The face looked surprised, then suspicious. Unable to continue verbally, I pointed to the metal badge on my leathers. This had an instant effect. The hatch slammed shut, and the gate immediately began to open. By the time I had ridden into the yard, two hefty men stood respectfully waiting, reminding me comically of the concierge at the French chateau.

One of them held out a hand for my helmet and gloves, and the other opened the door for me. This time I walked into the barroom alone, but my reception was very different. The eyes of the men who sat at the tables or stood by the bar were wary, not hostile. As I passed them, each gave a nod of acknowledgement, and I nodded back to each in turn. But I couldn't see Max anywhere.

Then the door to the back corridor opened and Max stepped into the room. All eyes were on him.

'Emma,' he said. 'Come this way.'

I felt the collective gaze of the room on my back as I walked behind him, and heard the door close behind me. The buzz of masculine conversation started again as Max led me into a side room.

I took a moment to work out that it was quite a small room, because three of the walls were mirrored. There was no furniture except a black leather armchair, unless you count the motorcycle that stood opposite the chair, chrome reflecting the million points of light scattered by the mirrors. Gesturing for me to sit on the armchair, Max perched casually on the saddle of the bike.

'I came to say thank you and goodbye,' I said, 'in case you ... I mean, I have to go away today, for a few days. I thought you'd probably be ...'

I didn't know quite how to put it. He'd come here to help me, and though I had no reason to expect him to stick around any longer, I couldn't quite face the thought of not seeing him again.

Instead of helping me out, Max sat and looked at me as I floundered. He hardly seemed to blink, his ice-blue eyes as steady on me as a laser.

'I mean, I'm sure you've got things to be doing,' I blundered on, 'places to go to, and people to see.'

Still he just looked at me, till I wanted to beg him to say something, anything.

'I can't thank you enough. All you've done for me, for us. If there's anything I can do for you, anything at all...'

Now he answered, but not with words. In his eyes I read the thoughts of what I could do for him as frankly as that first look on the ferry, when Kit had played me like an instrument for Max's entertainment. I looked down, embarrassed and confused. Between my legs I felt a shudder of lust. Max knew what I'd like to do for him, yet he showed no sign of wanting to take advantage of the opportunity.

'Anything at all?' he said, letting the words hang in the air. I screwed up my courage and looked up at him. His leather jacket hung open, showing a black T-shirt that clung to his powerful chest. Black leather jeans formed heavy folds that followed the contours of his legs, and disappeared into heavy black boots. The only adornment was the buckle of his belt, a massive silver eagle that held a writhing serpent in its talons.

I wanted to fall to my knees and crawl to him, to open that buckle, take out his cock and service him, to show him just how completely I was at his command. But he was so still, so contained. I could do nothing until he said the word. Inwardly, I begged him to order me to do it, but he just looked down at me. I could hear nothing but my own heart pounding.

Finally he spoke: 'That's good to know.'

Then he smiled a little, a mysterious smile that lit up his eyes but barely curled his lips. A smile that was the opposite of reassuring, a door on to the unknown held open for a moment. He stood and held out a hand to me, palm up. Uncertain, I also rose, and placed my hand in his. He lifted it to his lips and kissed it. The touch of his lips left tongues of fire dancing on my skin. But as he raised my hand his grip was tight, not on my palm as in a handshake, but around my wrist like a cuff.

While the gatekeepers handed me my helmet and gloves, Max simply said, 'Till the next time.'

All the way back to the hotel in the mountains my body and mind were in turmoil. I forgot to be nervous about the ride, or even to enjoy it as much as I should. Over and over again, I played the scene in my head, and the feelings ricocheted around my body. I had called Max, and he had come. Did I have to ask for more?

5

The sun was barely over the slope of the mountain when I got into Geoff's jeep the next morning and we left the hotel behind. There was no traffic on the twisty roads, and we were soon away from the town and into a small valley where there was no sign of civilisation. The fresh scent of the pines filled the cool morning air, and the birdsong was almost as loud as the engine noise. I was about to say how quiet and beautiful it all was, when we came around a corner and found the shoot setting up.

I was amazed to see so many people looking so busy, so many vans and so much equipment. There was a crane with an articulated arm that lifted camera and cameraman high above the road and then swooped in low. Two lights the size of small cars were being raised on scaffolding towers. I looked around, as wide-eyed as a child.

Geoff pointed to a white van at the end of the row.

'That's the most important truck,' he said. 'If ever you can't find me, I'll be there.'

'What is it? Stunt equipment?' I asked.

'Catering,' he answered with a twinkle. 'Come on, let's get you a bacon buttie and some coffee, then we'll see what's what.'

I stood, eating my breakfast and sipping scalding hot coffee from a polystyrene cup, trying to take everything in. It wasn't as random as I'd first thought; teams of people were working on different tasks, some running power cables along the ground, some rearranging the vegetation to make it look more natural, some running around with clipboards checking what everybody else was doing.

'Which one's the director?' I whispered to Geoff. He pointed to an unkempt man with his hands in his pockets, nodding in earnest discussion with the men gathered around the camera. Everyone was dressed the same – expensive outdoor jackets, jeans and trainers. There was an air of important bustle, but not much glamour.

Geoff beckoned me over to a car that was just pulling up.

'This is Diana,' he said, introducing a tall, beautiful woman who was getting out. 'Diana, this is Emma, who'll be doing your stunt riding.'

Diana smiled warmly and shook my hand.

'Well, thanks,' she said, with a hint of Texas drawl. 'You're a braver woman than I am.'

I smiled back, feeling braver already.

'Yes, but I've been riding since I was sixteen,' I answered.

Diana raised her eyebrows. 'In that case,' she said, 'I don't feel so bad. I only started a month ago.'

Before we could say any more, one of the clipboard people was plucking at Diana's sleeve.

'Make-up, I know,' she said cheerfully. 'See you guys later.'

I watched her walk off through the mayhem, a graceful figure with dark curly hair.

'I don't look anything like her,' I muttered to Geoff.

'You will,' he replied. 'They've put a wig on your helmet.'

They had also made a copy of Diana's costume to my measurements – at least, my measurements as remembered by Geoff. In the wardrobe truck I was pulled, taped and pinned into it by two very matter-of-fact women. I wasn't delighted to see that this skintight suit was designed for looks, not for protection. Black PVC wouldn't last long if I were to come off and slide along the tarmac, and the boots were clearly intended more for the catwalk than for changing gear. I wasn't sure how spiked heels were going to work on footpegs, but I was about to find out.

On the other hand, it did look good – very good indeed, if Geoff's appreciative face was anything to go by. I made a mental note to ask if I could take it home. Kit would love to see the way the shiny material stretched over my rump as I bent over, and to feel the long PVC gloves on his body. I tried a wiggling walk through the crowd, and felt a ripple of interest follow me.

For somebody who had learned to ride especially for the film, Diana sat a bike well. She only had to do the close-up shots, of course, when her face could be seen.

'Yes, I'm very good at arriving,' she joked, as I complimented her on the way she rode three yards, pulled up on the chalk mark, and looked into the waiting camera, as if scanning the road ahead. Then she handed the bike over to me for the long shot – the one that would show the whole scene from a distance.

I felt that I was under scrutiny as I started the bike for the first time. Not only my reputation, but Geoff's too, was at stake here. If I didn't look as if I knew what I was doing, he'd look stupid for having hired me. Still, riding a strange bike was something I'd done a million times, and this was a fairly standard Japanese sports bike – powerful and fast but easy to handle. I listened carefully as the director pointed out the key moments in the scene, then rode away to the first marker.

The riding was easy enough at this stage, but I was under a new kind of pressure. I'd showed off for an audience before, but riding for a camera was different.

My mouth was dry as I felt the bike throb beneath me, waiting for the signal to go. I could see Geoff's shaven head among the throng around the director. He had faith in me, so I had to believe I could do it. The crew member waiting beside me smiled and I smiled back beneath the curly hair of the helmet.

The walkie-talkie crackled, his hand fell in the signal, and I kicked the bike into gear. My first mark was that same chalk mark, to pull up and look into the camera just as Diana had done. It felt a bit silly, knowing that my face was the last thing they'd ever want to put on screen, but that was what they wanted to make the editing easy, so I pulled up and scowled into the lens. My own distorted face scowled back at me.

Then I continued down the road, pretending not to see the dozens of people hidden from the camera's view behind rocks and in ditches. My nerves had left me, and I felt very calm as I rode, stopped, avoided imaginary perils, and finally pulled up a mile away beside the last clipboard.

No time for euphoria yet, of course. I did that same shot again, taking on board the few simple points made by the director: 'Remember, in that first section, you're looking for them. After that, they're after you, and you're trying to get out as fast as you can. And make it look harder.'

It seemed I was expected to act with a motorbike as well as ride it fast. In fact, we did the shot five times, sometimes so I could improve my performance, and sometimes because one of the crew had reported technical problems. No wonder films took months to shoot, I thought, as I rode back yet again to my start point. I was starting to enjoy the play-acting, and to forget my worries.

I grabbed a sandwich while the stunt crew set up for Diana's close-up. She came to join me on a bench by the catering truck, and the stills photographer appeared from nowhere. He must have shot an entire roll of film of us eating our lunch. Diana was highly amused.

'Do you want us to pretend we're making out?' she called to him.

We posed playfully, draping an arm over each other's shoulders. She was right, of course; it was a classic male fantasy scene: two girls in PVC suits, one dark and one a redhead.

She had a lot of fun filming the scene I'd just done. The bike was now rigged on a trailer behind a truck, so the camera could film her from the front. She sat on the bike, pretending to ride, but even the lean of the bike as she took a corner was done for her. Each tilt was controlled from the truck by a man turning a handle. As the whole rig drove back to the start point for another take, she lay back lazily over the bike, resting a spike-heeled boot on each handlebar. The stills snapper ran alongside, nearly falling into a ditch in his distraction, and Diana pouted and arched shamelessly for him.

'You could shoot a great porn film on that rig,' Geoff muttered in my ear.

'You could,' I whispered back, the memory of my ride with Colette suddenly vivid. 'We should do it, make a bit of money on the side.'

'You slut,' he joked, his breath warm against my neck as he pressed close against my PVC-shiny body. 'I thought you were on your honeymoon?' Then somebody appeared with a clipboard and it was back to work.

I was really warming to the job now, loving the way the whole crew's attention was focused on me when I rode, and relishing the glamour of the sexy costume. I no longer cared that it offered slightly less protection than a pair of jeans. To the camera's eye, I embodied the daring, sexy, biker chick, and I felt every inch the part.

The first day flew by. Everything was so strange and

exciting, and the riding took so much concentration, that I couldn't believe we'd been at work for ten hours. As soon as I got into the jeep, though, exhaustion hit me. Geoff had to shake me awake when we arrived at the hotel, and I barely managed to eat dinner before falling into bed.

I did find the strength to call Kit at Jane's villa, but she answered the phone and said he was asleep.

'Don't let him call me later,' I told her. 'I'll be asleep myself. Just give him my love – and look after him for me.'

'It'll be a pleasure,' she purred suggestively.

I laughed – she really was too naughty.

'Don't look after him *too* well!' I joked. 'I want him back, you know.'

'Oh, don't worry.' She sighed in mock despair. 'Nobody's going to pry him away from *you*.'

Putting the costume on for the second day felt like a familiar routine. The stunts were a little harder than the previous day's, and a lot more technical, too. In the film, Diana's character is chased by a helicopter which swoops low over the motorbike, and one of her pursuers jumps out, lands on the bike behind her and, after a struggle, she knocks him off. Completely implausible, of course, but it was an action film. Geoff was going to jump out of the chopper, but the riding was down to me.

Even the basic shot, dodging the helicopter as I rode along the open road, was harder than I expected. The wind from the rotor blew me about, and every time the chopper changed direction I was buffeted by the air. It took all morning just to film that and Diana's close-ups. Watching her crouched low on the bike, as the camera on the truck captured the chase, I realised just how precise the helicopter's movements were, and how skilful the pilot.

With the bike strapped on to the trailer they went on to film the actor landing behind Diana, and their fight on the motorbike. I watched carefully; as much as safety would allow, I had to recreate the same movements with Geoff while actually riding the bike. I had always thought his job required skill and courage, and I was starting to realise just how much of both he must have. I was only here for one scene, and I was being pushed to the edge of my riding ability.

We rehearsed a dozen times before I felt ready to film, each time speeding up a little. Geoff's assistant was co-ordinating this stunt, giving the go for each action. His voice was calm in my ear, as he asked each of us if we were ready. I gave the thumbs up, and heard each member of the stunt team say: 'Standing by chopper.' 'Standing by winch.' 'Standing by.'

I rode along the straight, keeping one eye on the road and the other on the speedo, needle steady on 40. Not fast, by my usual standards, but quick enough for what was about to happen. My front tyre passed the first marker, and the voice inside my helmet told me to expect a passenger. I braced myself, ready to balance the bike.

Suddenly, a movement in the mirror and the bike sat back on its suspension under the extra weight. My uninvited guest had arrived, winched from the moving helicopter on a wire and on to my pillion seat. Instinctively I pulled the throttle open a little more, feeding in extra power to compensate for the weight. If I didn't keep pace exactly with the chopper, Geoff might be pulled off the bike before he had time to release the wire.

Even as he unclipped himself, we had to make it look as if Geoff was fighting me for control of the bike, and I was struggling to get rid of him. As rehearsed, he reached around me and put his hand at my throat. Using my right hand to keep the bike on its steady course, I grasped his wrist with my left, trying to give the effect of a fight.

'Wire clear,' came the voice, and we were free to move independently. Geoff's hand shot to the left handlebar, resting there lightly so I could use the right bar alone to swing the bike from side to side, as if we were pulling it to and fro between us. Then I grasped his wrist, so I could steer through his grip. The helicopter followed, high above us.

Geoff's powerful body felt familiar even in this strange situation. He and I went back years, and getting married to Kit had not ended the affection I felt for Geoff, or the glow of attraction to his tattooed, muscled frame. This play-fighting was new to us, and was too serious to be distracted from, but I was glad to have Geoff's friendly shape wrapped around mine on this moving bike, and not anybody else's.

I raked the heel of the spiked boot down his leg, and placed my hand back on the left handgrip as he withdrew his arm. We were nearing the top of the hill, and the finale of the action sequence. Placing the pointed boots carefully on the footpegs, I stood up, bracing my arms for balance. Geoff steadied himself against me, grabbing with his hands in gestures that must have looked rough, though in fact he was taking care not to disturb our equilibrium.

Bang on cue, the helicopter appeared ahead, hanging low over the road. Geoff's hands were on my forehead, lightly holding the helmet just above my eyes. In the close-ups the actor had covered Diana's eyes – but she wasn't actually steering the bike.

'Go!' came the voice in my ear.

I dropped low on the bike, and Geoff's weight was gone as his hands grabbed the skid of the helicopter. In the mirror I could just see a swinging leg, as he let me get clear, then he dropped on to the ground a couple of feet below.

In a final flourish that was my own idea, I waggled my fingers in a derisory wave before riding over the brow of the hill and out of shot. Actually, I had suggested a far ruder gesture, but apparently it wasn't that kind of film.

There was a lot of hanging about, but half an hour later the word came back – both cameras reported a good take, and we didn't have to do it all again. Tomorrow we would do the hardest bike stunt of all but for today it was, as they say, a wrap. Buzzing with excitement and achievement, I climbed in beside Geoff for the drive back to the hotel. Tonight I wouldn't be going straight to sleep; I was much too excited and full of myself for that.

As we pulled on to the main road, a silver motorcycle flashed past us.

'Flash bastard,' said Geoff, good-humouredly.

In reply to my enquiring look, he added, 'Michael. Helicopter pilot. They always have to go that bit further than anyone else.'

'Does he do bike stunts too?' I asked.

'Nah, not dangerous enough,' was Geoff's joking response.

I hadn't really spoken to Michael, except to plan the days stunt, but now I was curious to meet him. After dinner we found him in the hotel bar, a handsome man with short hair and a disarming smile. To my surprise, he was diffident to the point of shyness, bashfully dismissing his flying skills as being 'no harder than driving a van'.

This was clearly not true, as my questions revealed. Michael's attempts to explain the principles of helicopter flight with a few scribbles on the back of a beer mat only proved to me what a feat of mental and physical co-ordination it must be. I made a mental note to try it myself some time.

As usual in Geoff's company, the beers were flowing freely and I excused myself to call Kit from my room before I got too drunk to talk sensibly. I found him awake and lively, and the background noise told me that another party was in full swing in Jane's villa.

'I hope she's looking after you right?'

He moaned in reply. 'No! She's teasing me worse than those Italian nurses.'

'Oh dear.' I feigned sympathy. For all Jane's reassuring words, I wasn't crazy about the idea of my best friend providing too much consolation in my absence. If anyone was going to be my stunt double in Kit's bed, I'd much rather it was a stranger.

'She's even bought a nurse's uniform, just to torture me really thoroughly,' Kit went on. 'One of those rubber ones with the very short skirt.'

I couldn't help sniggering. The whole thing was so absolutely typical of Jane – out of loyalty she wouldn't actually sleep with my husband, I was sure, but she would get as much mileage as she could out of playing a perverse game of 'doctors and nurses'.

I lay on the big hotel bed and closed my eyes.

'Tell me more,' I coaxed, knowing that it would only add to Kit's arousal.

'She's giving me two sponge baths a day,' he wailed, 'and the only bit she won't wash is the bit that's standing to attention in her honour.'

'Shocking.' I giggled. 'I'll get her run out of the Royal College of Nursing. What else?'

'She doesn't wear any knickers when she comes in to see me.'

I could tell Kit was getting into this conversation.

'Then she drops something, and bends over to pick it up . . .'

'Just too far away for you to reach her?' I suggested.

'Exactly. If I wasn't a helpless invalid I'd grab her and give her the fucking she's after, but all I can do is lie there and look.'

'A rubber uniform, you say?' I was enjoying this long-distance stimulation too, and I ran a languid hand over my body as I spoke.

'That must cling very tightly indeed.'

Kit answered with a noise of pleasure. 'Especially at the top, where her tits stretch it almost to splitting.'

'And her bum,' I fed him.

'Every curve,' he agreed.

'So naughty of her to tease you,' I said, slipping my hand between my legs, 'when what you'd really like is to feel those shiny curves pressed against you.'

'I want to squeeze them till they squeak,' he growled. 'I want her to straddle me on the bed and push those tits right into my face.'

I could picture the scene: Jane filling the play uniform to bursting, and Kit's face lifting towards her cleavage, biting at her nipples till the rubber was slippery with his spit.

'And while you're doing that, she can slide herself on to your cock,' I said, playing with myself as I imagined sliding down his length and teasing him just as Jane had been.

'Ooh, yes,' he said, his voice thick with excitement.

'She'd be slipping up and down,' I went on, 'with that little rubber skirt flapping around your balls.'

I could tell from his breathing that he was wanking as he listened.

'You wouldn't have to do anything except watch her bouncing up and down on top of you. You could just lie there as she got faster and faster, using you as her helpless plaything.'

I heard Kit grunt, close to his climax.

'And then,' I whispered, 'she'd stick her slippery finger right into your arse, and you'd shoot your load inside her while she came like that, impaled on your cock.'

For a moment there was silence; then I heard Kit gasping for breath. I had timed it perfectly, and he had come just when I knew he would.

'Have you left your spunk all over Nurse Jane's clean sheets?' I asked, with mock severity.

'Yes, doctor,' he said.

'Tut tut,' I scolded him. 'She will be cross, won't she?'

'I daresay she will,' he answered complacently. 'With any luck she'll tell me I'm a very naughty boy.'

We laughed and then chatted a little about my day on the stunt team. He was all apologetic that things had not gone exactly according to plan on our honeymoon, but he didn't seem overly perturbed.

'Good night, love,' he said softly. 'See you tomorrow.'

When I got back to the bar, Michael was gone, and Geoff sat alone on his bar stool. 'He's flying back to the airfield tomorrow,' he said, 'and they have very strict rules about being drunk in charge of a chopper.' He leered cheerfully at his own pun.

'Good point,' I said, suddenly reminded that tomorrow would bring my biggest stunt challenge, and I didn't want to be facing it with a hangover.

'You're right,' said Geoff, seeing where my thoughts were leading, 'no more beers for us. I thought perhaps a little rehearsing instead.'

I was confused. 'Rehearsing what? More bike stunts?'

'No, nothing like that. There's another scene I thought you might enjoy doubling for.'

I could tell where this was leading – straight back to Geoff's room. But I wouldn't take much persuading. After my phone call to Kit, I was alive with desire, unresolved sexual tension quivering through me.

'What scene is that?' I asked.

Geoff could tell he was on home turf and, as he spoke, he put an arm around my waist and pulled me towards him.

'Well, after she shakes off the bad guy from the chopper, she escapes on the boat.'

'Mm-hmm?'

I knew this much already; it was in the scene I had read.

'Then, she has to go back to steal the secret file. From the castle.'

Standing between Geoff's thighs, I could feel the heat of his body soaking into mine.

'But before she can get out of the castle,' he said, so softly that I had to lean my face close to his to hear him, 'they catch her. And she is the helpless prisoner of the most evil, ruthless, foul and depraved man ever to appear in an over-the-top action movie.'

'And you want me to play the role of helpless prisoner?' I whispered back.

'That's right.'

'Sounds unmissable.'

Without another word, Geoff picked me up, put me over one shoulder, and walked out of the bar.

As soon as he had closed the door of his room I started to struggle like a real kidnapped heroine. It was futile, of course; Geoff was far stronger than me. He threw me on to the bed just roughly enough to add to the atmosphere and, before I could get up, he was kneeling astride me, his knees pinning my wrists to the mattress, his weight on my thighs. It was exciting to pit my whole strength against him and know that I had no chance of regaining control.

'Of course, in the film, our heroine wears an evening dress for this scene,' he said in a low voice that betrayed his excitement, 'but wardrobe have let me down on this occasion.'

Without letting me move more than an inch, he pulled my T-shirt over my head and off. Then, holding my wrists in one of his hands, used the other to unfasten my jeans. With one foot, he pushed my jeans down my legs till they bunched below my knees, restricting my movement still further.

He reached under the bed and produced a handful of rope.

'I think a little constraint is called for,' he whispered hoarsely. 'External, if necessary.'

He bound my wrists together tightly, palm pressed against palm, the thick cord biting into my hands. He knotted the end of the rope around a bedpost, so my arms were stretched out above my head. He sat back on his heels, one knee between my legs, enough to keep them locked in place, and looked down at me. He could have removed all my clothes, of course, but lying there in my underwear, jeans around my ankles, I felt more vulnerable, more humiliated, than if I had been naked.

'So,' he growled in character, 'now you find out what happens to those who challenge my power.'

He ran a rough hand over my arm, my shoulder, and under the lace of my bra. I squirmed, but couldn't move enough to escape his touch. His fingers pinched my nipple, and I felt the answering throb between my legs. Then he pulled down both cups so my breasts were exposed to the cool air. Both hands caressed me impersonally, their touch teasingly casual, so I tried to arch my back towards the sensation.

The heat and the visible bulge in Geoff's jeans told me he was also getting excited, but instead of pursuing his caresses he turned to sit sideways on the bed, still keeping enough weight on my legs to hold me down, and took out a small tin. I craned to see what new toy he would get out, but to my frustration he took out a packet of tobacco and some rolling papers. As I strained against the rope, he rolled a cigarette, apparently ignoring me.

'You bastard,' I said as he lit his cigarette and looked out of the window at the stars. Geoff raised his eyebrows as he took another drag.

'I'd keep quiet if I were you,' was all he said.

I was furious.

'How dare you! If you're not going to –'

I was cut off abruptly as Geoff covered my mouth with his broad palm, pushing my head back into the pillow.

'Enough,' he said, and continued to smoke calmly till he had finished his cigarette.

Without taking his hand off my face, he reached under the bed again. This time he produced a piece of white cloth.

'Don't say I didn't warn you,' he said as he rolled it into a thick twist. Then he pulled me on to my side, shoved the twist into my mouth and tied it behind my head. My tongue was pressed against the cloth, my mouth held wide open by the thickness of the gag.

'You like that?' he asked.

I tried to answer, 'No!' but all that came out was a muffled sound.

He laughed. 'I'll take that as a yes, then.'

Sitting athwart my legs, he pulled off my shoes and socks, still casual, and tossed them on to the floor. I couldn't see what he was doing; all I could see was his broad back, still in his work shirt. The faint smell of hard-earned sweat rose from him.

A sudden sensation made me jerk my leg in a vain attempt to free my foot from his grasp. There was a light touch on my instep, almost a tickle, but one that seemed to have found the direct circuit to my clitoris. He laughed again, and the touch retraced the same path. This time I was ready for it, and the surprise was replaced by pleasure. A third time the fingertip ran over my skin, leaving behind it a cold line this time, a wet signature.

Then Geoff's back bent away from me and I was overtaken by such an intense sensation that I cried aloud into the gag. My whole toe was in his mouth; wetness engulfed every tiny nerve ending, his tongue sending electric shockwaves up my leg and through my whole body. My pussy was as wet as his mouth. I could feel it.

As he sucked and lapped at me, his nails were scratching at the soles of my feet, so lightly that I felt I was walking on short grass. The powerful effect on my toes, combined with the subtle, barely pleasurable touches elsewhere, was hypnotic. I closed my eyes, unable to take in anything but what was happening to my feet.

Just as I was starting to lose myself completely, he stopped. I whimpered in protest, but he was already pulling at my jeans, shaking me free of them like tipping potatoes out of a sack. I opened my eyes to see him producing more rope. My legs were free for the moment, but I didn't have the presence of mind to do anything with them before my ankles were once more in his steel grip. I watched in a daze as Geoff tied my ankles to the two wooden knobs at the foot of the bed.

There I lay, legs spread wide apart and arms pulled straight above my head. Now I really was helpless, and Geoff could play the evil captor as much as he wanted. My black G-string felt like scant covering in this position, and my bra was already little more than punctuation, underlining my breasts that spilled out in full view. Geoff looked down at me with satisfaction and very visible excitement.

'Very nice,' he declared. 'If only that stills photographer was here now.'

He walked slowly round the bed, admiring me from

all angles. I was pulling at the ropes as best I could, desperate to make him touch me again, if only to tighten my bonds. It was hopeless; Geoff knew his knots too well. If he chose to go back to the bar and leave me here for hours, there was nothing I could do about it.

But he was going nowhere. He lay on the bed beside me, his head propped on one hand, and looked into my eyes. While his free hand stroked my defenceless skin, so I trembled and shook with an excitement that had no means of release, he held my eyes, drinking in each flicker of reaction. That roaming hand brought each part of me to vibrant life, awakening each nerve in turn: my arms, my shoulders, the delicate bowl under each arm; my throat, my chest, each breast, my belly; my legs from toe to thigh; every inch of my naked body got the same slow, dreamy treatment.

Only then did his hand venture under the flimsy triangle of black fabric between my legs. I was so aroused by now that at his first touch my whole body shuddered. He smiled into my face as his finger made its unhurried way through my bush of hair, flicked around my clit a few times, and glided down my cleft to slip into my pussy. I couldn't say what I wanted to – 'Yes, there! Now! Please!' – but he could see it in my eyes.

It had no effect. Slow penetration, a curiously detached exploration of my inner contours, was followed only by withdrawal. The finger continued on its downward path to the puckered muscle of my rear hole. My eyes must have widened in apprehension, because Geoff laughed softly and said, 'Oh, such a nice girl. Don't we take it up the wrong 'un, then?'

It was clear that the only rules here were the ones Geoff made. My heart beat faster in alarm, but at the same time it was exciting to know that I really was his plaything tonight, in any way he chose. Sliding through the wetness of my own excitement, the thick, rough-skinned finger pushed at the tight entrance.

'Come on, now,' he whispered, his face close to my ear. 'Open up for me. It'll be better for you in the long run.'

I tried to relax, knowing it would only hurt if he had to force his way in. The finger pressed harder, and I felt him inside me, the ring of muscle gripping his finger tight.

'Good girl,' he breathed, still pushing smoothly, moving deeper into me.

I felt the delicious touch of his skin on my deep-hidden pleasure centres, even as my hole protested at the rude violation. Geoff's hand pressed against the flesh of my buttocks. He must be fully inside me, I thought. Then I felt his thumb flicking at my clit, setting up ripples of response that made my muscles clench rhyth-mically at his finger. After waiting so long I was desper-ate to come, even like this, being fingered in such a humiliating way. I longed for him to speed up, but he kept a steady pace that left me hanging on the brink. Again, I tried to beg him to hurry, but only animal grunts came out.

Still he made no attempt to take his own pleasure but lay, fully dressed, working on me in that impersonal way, as if I were some kind of experiment. Every time I felt my climax nearing, and tried to buck against his hand to bring it on, he stopped moving altogether until I lay still. How long could he keep me here in this state?

'Would you like to come?' he asked me.

Yes! I cried inside, but a wordless grunt was all that escaped. I nodded frantically, but Geoff ceased his movements.

'Yes what?' he asked sternly.

'Please!' I tried. 'Yes, please!'

Though he can't have distinguished the words, Geoff gave me the benefit of the doubt.

'Well, why didn't you say so?' he replied.

He knew me well enough to get me there when he wanted to. At last his strokes built me towards the point of no return. My legs shook as I felt the coil of pleasure growing inside me, before exploding, and Geoff's finger pushed into me, echoing the beat of my climax. I shouted out with the long-awaited explosion of energy, biting on the cloth of the gag.

Geoff smiled with sly satisfaction and kissed me softly where my lips met the cloth of the gag. I lay, panting for breath, feeling my aftershocks pulsing against his finger. Then, abruptly, he pulled it out so I winced with the momentary pain.

I watched him stand and walk across the room. He took off his boots and left them by the door, then undressed slowly and deliberately, paying me no attention at all. The familiar landscape of his body emerged, tattoos moving like living creatures as his muscles flexed. My body trembled with renewed desire as he stood naked, his smooth cock standing out as big and stiff as I'd ever seen it.

I almost shouted with frustration when he turned away without looking at me and went into the bathroom. I heard the shower start and, after a few seconds, Geoff's voice cheerfully singing an old Beatles number. How long was he going to leave me here like this? Surely he wasn't planning to wank himself off without me? I tugged at the ropes holding my hands and feet, but it was hopeless.

The shower stopped and I held my breath, impatient to see him emerge and look at me. I could hear him moving around, but I couldn't tell what he was doing. I was starting to cool down and, as the night breeze moved over my damp body, I shivered. Geoff stepped out of the bathroom and laughed.

'Frightened?' he asked cheerfully.

I glowered at him, as much as I could with a soggy rag holding my mouth open.

Geoff was damp and glowing from the shower, but evidently still as horny as a few minutes before. My eyes followed him around the room to the foot of the bed, where he stood, hands on hips, and looked down at me. The faint, clean smell of shampoo rose from him. I tried to lift my hips towards him in a mute plea, and he smiled wickedly.

'Now, what was it I had to do?' he asked, rhetorically, since I could only grunt through my gag. 'I know I got undressed for something. Skiing? No, wrong time of year.'

Just to torture me, he started strolling around the room, rubbing his chin as he pretended to rack his brains.

'Christmas shopping? No, too early for that. Ironing? Was that it? Got to look my best for the shoot tomorrow.'

I whimpered my entreaty, and he turned as if seeing me for the first time.

'Of course! That was it.' He bounded on to the bed and held himself over me, looking down into my eyes. 'I had to fuck Emma's brains out. How could I forget?'

Without taking his eyes off mine, he pulled aside the damp strip of my G-string and entered me, fast and deep. I convulsed, wanting to move against him but held tight by the ropes, legs stretched so wide that I barely shifted with his thrusts. Each stroke rubbed against my pleasure spot through the shiny fabric. Unable even to rock my hips against him, I was a completely passive participant. Arms straight, Geoff looked down at my face as he pounded into me.

'That's what you wanted, isn't it?' he grunted. 'Isn't it?'

I nodded, but my head was already being tossed about by the shaking of the bed.

'Or was it this?' Geoff stroked my breast lightly, then pinched the nipple hard. I flinched, but couldn't escape his grip. Without slowing his thrusts, he pinched the other. Now I was at the mercy of two intense feelings: the waves of pleasure coming from between my legs and the sharp stings of pain on my breasts. There was nothing I could do to escape from either.

'That's right,' said Geoff. 'I'm the one in charge now, and if I want to give you pain, you get pain.'

Feeling his touch at my nipple again, I closed my eyes and tensed against the sensation.

'And if I want to give you pleasure,' he whispered, 'what you get is pleasure.'

The pinch never came; instead the finger found my clitoris and rubbed me expertly. I was on the verge of coming once more, but he seemed to be deliberately keeping me there.

'Pleasure,' he whispered, his face close to mine, 'but not till I'm ready.'

He was speeding up his strokes, pounding me so hard that my ankles tugged at their bonds. Beads of sweat stood on his tattooed shoulders. Still his finger played with me, held me teetering on the edge of the precipice, until he reached his own climax. Only when he came into me, shuddering with the whiplash of his orgasm, did he stop holding me back. Seconds after him, I came in my turn, straining against the ropes, taking the pleasure he had decided to give me at last.

6

For the first few seconds I lay blinking in the sunlight, aware of Geoff's familiar arm flung across me, but not sure where I was. Then I recognised his hotel room, the bed to which I'd been pinioned the night before, and remembered what I was doing there with him.

Geoff stirred and pulled me closer to him, but I was fully awake now, and too tense to stay in bed. I rolled away from him and slid out from under the covers, scattering ropes and abandoned garments. The needles of the shower jet on my skin brought the day into sharp focus. Under the force of the water I tried to work out whether or not I felt like a cheating slut for having fun with Geoff – and on our honeymoon, too! I knew that Kit wouldn't have been too pissed off; he knew as well as I did that needs must when desire gets the better of you. 'I wouldn't want to hold you back,' he had said. OK, he was talking about climbing, but last night's fun meant no more to me or Geoff than an afternoon on the rockface. My amorality dealt with, my stomach lurched in apprehension; I remembered that today was the day I had to really prove what I was made of as a stunt rider.

There was time for a light breakfast before we drove down to today's location on the shores of the lake. It was a glorious morning; a few wispy clouds strayed across a brilliant blue sky, and the air was already starting to warm up, even though the sun had only just cleared the wooded peak of the mountain. The coward in me longed to be off riding for pleasure again, setting my own pace and just enjoying the fine weather. Then I caught myself thinking about a carefree ride along the mountain roads, and smiled to realise how quickly I'd shaken off the ghost of Kit's crash; compared with today's stunt, a few blind corners seemed like child's play.

But I had no time for philosophising. Geoff was already supervising the completion of the ramp at the water's edge, checking it made a smooth, invisible join with the gravel. I paced the route I would have to ride; over the brow of the little hill, down over the grass, a little slalom on a patch of hard, dry earth – to make it look as if I was dodging bullets – on to the ramp and into thin air. I'd be landing on a pontoon, firmly anchored just out of shot of the shore, but I had to clear a couple of yards of water first.

I checked every inch of the ground; I didn't want to be surprised by a rabbit hole and come off before I'd even got to the hard bit, and I had to be doing something while the ramp was readied. It was little more than a solid take-off strip; speed alone would carry me over the water on to the safety of the pontoon. I knew I could do it; I'd spent two hours on the first day practising on the same bike and the same ramp. But that had been over solid ground. This time I was aiming not for a marker but for a dry landing point.

At last they were ready for me. At Geoff's suggestion, we were going to film every attempt, so this was no rehearsal, though it was the first time I'd tried the stunt for real. I warmed the engine up, listening to the comforting purr of the twin cylinders beneath me. I was going to depend on this bike, so each mechanical noise and vibration meant a lot to me. When I was satisfied that the bike was ready to go, I nodded to the clipboard-carrier beside me, and his walkie-talkie crackled into life. The answer came back, and he gave me the signal to go. This was it.

I clicked the gear lever down, released the clutch and felt the bike ease forwards. I was entirely focused on the machine and the path it had to follow. Slipping the clutch as I neared the top of the slope, I felt the bike slow and hang, almost suspended, on the ridge. Perfectly balanced, I had a moment to look down at the lake, to turn over my shoulder and see my imaginary pursuers, and bring my eyes back to the pontoon that awaited me. Then the momentum of the bike took it on to the downward slope and it began to roll again.

I wanted enough speed to take me through the slalom under control, not freewheeling, so I accelerated towards the marker stones. A sharp crack broke the silence, and dust scattered from the ground in front of me. Crouching low behind the fairing, I flicked the bike in a sharp turn, then back again, swinging the weight sharply from side to side. Around me, the small explosive charges in the ground crackled and spat like real bullet hits.

Now I was directly in line for the ramp and the pontoon, with nothing to do but prepare for take off. Smoothly, I pulled the throttle back until the engine was screaming, the needle on the rev counter edging towards the red line. I didn't want to hit the ramp so fast that I lost control, but I wanted to be sure I had enough momentum to carry the bike through the air. Five yards, four, and I eased the revs as my world narrowed to a ramp, a metal platform, and the shining surface of the water that separated them.

The front tyre found the solidity of the ramp, and I jerked the throttle open and felt the front wheel rise with the surge of power. The rear wheel threw me up the ramp and then I was flying, the engine suddenly shrieking as it revved against thin air. It felt like slow motion, as the landing strip marked on the metal deck of the pontoon moved towards me, beneath me. I focused only on preparing the bike for the impact, wheels perfectly in line, balance centred, clutch in so I didn't accelerate right off the end of the deck.

Then I felt the deck take the weight of the bike, back wheel a fraction of a second before the front, and the suspension sink as I braked fast and smooth and came to a stop right in front of the camera. My heart was pounding. I had done it.

My boot fumbled to find the stand, as the adrenaline washed through me. I tried to swing my leg coolly over the bike, but I was sure everybody could see me shaking. The director came towards me, grinning, and shook my hand.

'Nice one,' he said. 'That's a take. We don't need to do that again, it's perfect.'

I was smiling like a maniac, but I couldn't speak yet. Geoff appeared and hugged me tightly.

'That's my girl,' he said.

In the film, of course, Diana's character doesn't land on a pontoon. She flies through the air to land on a speedboat that is moving away from the shore. I had been afraid that Geoff would ask me to do that, but they'd decided to use wires for the landing on the boat, lowering the bike towards the deck in slow motion. Since Diana sat the bike so well, she'd bravely volunteered to do that shot herself, as well as the close-ups. So my work was done.

I felt a sense of anticlimax as I peeled off the PVC suit for the last time.

'I'll see if I can disappear it for you at the end of the shoot,' said Geoff, with a wink. 'I bet Kit would like to see you in that!'

Then he had to go back to work, supervising the suspension of the bike from the crane that would lift it across the water. One of the crew members offered to drive me back to the hotel, and as I got into the jeep I saw Diana sitting on the bike, high in the air. She waved cheerfully.

'Thanks for making me look so good,' she shouted. 'See you at the premiere!'

I could have stayed at the hotel another night, but there seemed no point; now I had done my part, I would have felt like a hanger-on. It had been terrific fun, and a huge challenge, but now I was ready to go back to Kit. Eagerly, I threw on my own leathers and got back on to my own bike, listening affectionately to the temperamental growl of the engine. Without regret, I swung out of the hotel car park and on to the road.

The stunt work had done its job, just as Kit had said; this riding on the road held no terrors now, and nor did I feel the need to prove anything. Enough daring and showing off for one day, all I wanted now was to get back to Jane's villa quickly and safely.

I knew Kit's bike would take some time to mend, so I was surprised to make out the shape of a bike in the shadow of Jane's courtyard. Even before I pulled into the drive, I had felt a quiver of shock and dark pleasure to recognise the machine. The long, low shape, the stark black and chrome colouring, were unmistakable. If that bike was here, then so was Max.

I tried to steady my breathing before I pushed open the door. The kitchen was empty, and I called, 'Kit?' My voice sounded thin and weak in the silence. Could he have gone somewhere with Max? I felt a rush of relief hearing his voice reply: 'In here!'

I followed the sound across the tiled dining room and up the big wooden staircase.

Kit lay in a white room, all sunlight and clean linen, propped up in a big canopied bed. His face, looking even more tanned against all the white, smiled warmly at me as I pushed the heavy door shut behind me. I smiled back and kissed him affectionately, then looked uncertainly at the dark figure standing at the window. Max, all in black leather as usual, stood unsmiling. With the daylight behind him, I couldn't even make out a twinkle in those ice-blue eyes.

'Hello,' I said. I had wanted to see him again since that last meeting in the biker clubhouse, of course, but now he was here – with Kit. I had both the men I wanted, but both at once in the same room, and I wasn't sure how to handle it. I decided to say nothing; to wait for them to set the tone and follow their lead.

Kit and Max exchanged a look, then Kit said – with an imperious gesture of his good arm towards the foot of the bed – 'Stand here.'

I moved to the spot and stood looking at him, no longer able to see Max at all.

'I know you feel guilty,' Kit went on.

I opened my mouth to agree, glad to have the chance to properly apologise, and to confess my guilt to Kit, but he shut me up with another gesture and continued.

'And so you should,' he said. 'Encouraging me to ride so dangerously. You've been a very bad girl indeed. And now you must be punished. Do you agree?'

'Yes,' I said, my mouth dry. Was Max to witness my humiliation and punishment? A shudder of arousal ran through me at the thought.

'Bend over,' said Kit, and I bent over the bed, pressing my face into the cool cotton sheet, my hands gripping the smooth wood of the bed. Of course, with Kit in bed and injured, Max himself would have to punish me. A ripple of fear and delight shook my body, and I pressed myself against the edge of the bed, trying to push my tingling clit against the wood.

The room was silent; then I heard the creak of leathers as Max moved towards me. I didn't know what I wanted him to do to me – touch me between the legs where the heat throbbed so urgently, or rub himself against the leather stretched over my upturned rump for his own pleasure. Or, darkest of all, to give me pain, inflicting corporal punishment to assuage the guilt I felt inside.

My buttock felt his hand, a firm but gentle stroking that, even through the thick leather, left a fiery trace on my skin. I wondered what Kit was thinking, lying there watching me under Max's hand. Was he too waiting eagerly for the first blow? Was he aroused by the sight of me bent so submissively before him?

Then sharp pain cut through my thoughts. A stinging blow landed across my rear with a sharp thwack. The skin glowed with soreness as I tried to work out what was happening. Surely his hand could not hurt so much through my leathers? Another wallop came, and another. I had just enough time to recover from the impact of the previous blow before the next caught me.

I thought I was starting to know the timing, but then Max changed the rhythm, so each impact took me by surprise. I was reeling between the pain of the stroke and the warm glow that followed. The heat was spreading, as each time he found a new part of my skin: bottom, flanks, thighs. I was only aware of my skin, of the pain, and of the anticipation of the next blow. It took me a second to realise that he had stopped.

'Stand up,' said Kit.

I straightened up and looked at his face. It was clear that he had enjoyed watching my punishment very much.

'Now take off your leathers,' he ordered.

Unsteady from arousal and intense sensation, I unzipped my suit and stepped out. My T-shirt and pants were soaked in sweat from the day's riding, and the cool air from the window chilled me.

'Take everything off,' said Kit.

I obeyed, still facing him. Max was standing behind me, and I couldn't turn to see him. I knew that Max would read in my eyes how deeply I had enjoyed his punishment, and I was ashamed. Instead, I stood naked before him, exposing to him the skin he had roused to sharp tingling. But Kit gestured with his hand, small circles that told me to turn round where I stood.

Suddenly bashful, I kept my eyes on the floor as I turned, but I could still see Max's eyes roaming freely over my naked body. In his hand he held the belt from his leather jeans, the one with the silver eagle and snake buckle. No wonder I'd felt him through my leathers. I caught sight of myself in the bedroom mirror and wasn't surprised to see bright pink stripes across my skin where the belt had landed.

'Good.'

Max spoke for the first time and, hearing his voice, I raised my eyes to his. There was no smile on his face, but a look of approval that filled me with irrational pride. No matter that I had done nothing but hold still beneath his punishment. Max was pleased, that was all that counted. With the hand that still held the belt, he pointed towards Kit on the bed.

'Now, service your husband,' he said.

I must have looked blank for a moment, then I felt the belt flick sharply across my naked legs.

'Suck his cock,' said Max.

Dazed, I lifted the sheet from Kit's body and bent over the familiar column of his penis.

Kit smiled in pleasure and closed his eyes as I took him into my mouth and worked my tongue over him. I knew how to please him, but this felt strange, as if I was doing it not for Kit but for Max.

Deliberately, I angled myself so Max could see exactly what I was doing. I hoped that seeing Kit's cock sliding in and out of my wet lips would arouse Max too, make his cock swell and push against the leather of his jeans. I hoped that Max would undo the buttons of his fly, take out his own cock and play with it as he watched. I hoped that he would come behind me as I sucked, grip my hips with his strong, dry hands, and push himself into me from behind, fucking me while I sucked off my husband.

As hard as I worked, Max stood, impassive, watching. I ran my tongue up and down Kit's shaft and around the head; I bobbed my whole body up and down, so my breasts swung below me. He might have been carved from black basalt, so immovable he stood. Kit rolled his head in pleasure. He was reaping all the benefit of my performance. At last, despairing of having any effect on Max, I quickened my pace and brought Kit to his climax. He came, hot and salty, into my mouth and lay, breathing heavily.

'Good girl,' Kit said.

I looked to Max, awaiting his approval. Not so much as a nod from him, though still his eyes flicked over me.

'You find that arousing, to give your husband a blow job while I watch?' he asked.

I blushed hotly to hear it stated so baldly, but I nodded in reply.

'You want to be fucked?' he went on.

I glanced at Kit, but he didn't come to my rescue; he lay on the bed and raised his eyebrows, echoing the question. I nodded again, too embarrassed to speak the words, but too excited to lie.

'You have to do better than that,' said Max. 'Ask nicely.'

I forced myself to say the words: 'I want to be fucked.'

Without warning, the belt found my buttock again.

'Nicely,' Max rebuked me.

'Please,' I mumbled. 'Please may I be fucked?'

Max and Kit looked at each other, and Kit shrugged.

'She doesn't sound that bothered to me,' he said to Max.

I was squirming with humiliation, but I was also quivering with arousal.

'On your knees,' said Max, pointing at the floor.

I knelt down, the wood hard against my bare knees.

'Please may I be fucked?'

I wasn't even sure who I was asking now, or whether I was asking for permission or for servicing.

Max walked around me, looking down at me, so I addressed myself to him. 'Please, Max, please fuck me.'

'Why?' he asked.

'Because you have brought me to such a state, with your beating and watching me service Kit, that if I'm not fucked soon I will die of frustration,' was what I wanted to say. But I was starting to pick up on the rules of the game.

'Because I am a dirty slut that needs your cock,' I answered. 'I need you to fuck me.'

There was a moment's pause, as if Max and Kit were exchanging looks over my head, and then Max pointed across to the window.

'Stand there,' he ordered me.

I obeyed.

Max walked slowly over and stood in front of me. From here, I could see Kit's face, watching with fascination.

'Undo my trousers,' said Max.

I fumbled to find the buttons in the stiff leather, and to pull open the fly. Underneath, he was naked, his cock already springing out into my hand.

'Turn around,' he told me.

I leaned over the windowledge, my naked breasts exposed to the outside air. If anyone arrived back at the villa now, they would get a right old treat, but that didn't matter to me now. I was actually going to feel Max inside me. After imagining for so long how it would feel for him to take me for his own pleasure, at last this enigmatic Dutchman was about to plunge into me.

'Now,' he said, 'what do you want?'

'Please, Max,' I said, not caring who might hear me. 'Please fuck me. Please ram your cock into my cunt.'

I was shaking with anticipation, waiting to feel the rod of his flesh push into me and relieve the sexual tension I felt.

'Please?' I heard myself cry.

At the first touch I twitched with pleasure, but it was only a finger, running casually down the cleft of my buttocks and over my slippery sex.

'So wet,' said Max. He pushed the finger into me and flicked inside me, each movement setting off ripples of pleasure that ran right through me. I tried to push back against his hand, but a sharp slap in the flank stopped me. Nearly bursting with frustration, I kept still as Max withdrew his finger and held it to my mouth. Eagerly I sucked it, tasting my own sour juices on his skin, but still he denied me the other penetration I wanted.

'Ask me again,' Max said softly in my ear, 'but this time call me Sir.'

'Please, Sir,' I moaned. 'Please fuck me, Sir.'

At once Max grabbed my hips and held them tight as he thrust deep inside me. He braced me against his strokes, plunging deep into me every time, turning me inside out with pleasure. I gripped the edge of the windowsill, wondering if Kit could see this, if he was watching Max's cock disappearing into me and emerging, shiny with my arousal.

I wanted Max to move his hand in front of me, to rub me as he thrust, but his fingers kept their hold on my hips. Only when I moved my own hand towards my clit did he release his grip, and then it was only to grab my wrist in mid-air.

'Did you ask permission?' he whispered.

'Please, Sir, may I touch myself?' I panted.

'Only with your left hand,' he answered, and resumed his position.

After waiting so long, I was desperate to reach my climax, but my left hand felt clumsy as I rubbed at myself. I arched towards Max, feeling myself close to the edge, straining to reach the point of no return. Then I felt him take hold of my hand and take control, rubbing me with my own fingers in time with his cock. Inside and outside, he rained blows of pleasure on me, just as earlier he had rained blows of pain.

'Come now,' said Max, and I came on command, bucking between his hand and his prick, even as I felt his own climax shudder through him, through both of us. I was no longer thinking about Kit watching, or about somebody arriving and seeing me there, being fucked by Max. I was beyond thinking about anything. I was a creature of pure sensation under Max's complete control.

7

As I showered, I tried to make sense of what had just happened. It wasn't the first time Kit had got off by sharing me with another man, but it was the first time the other man had taken control of the situation so completely. My mind ran round in circles, but I was too tired and drained to get a handle on anything, so I focused on my body instead, slathering on a richly scented lotion I had found in the bathroom, rubbing at my tired limbs. My skin smarted where Max's belt had caught me.

I craned my neck to see the sore parts in the mirror. The pink weals clearly showed where the leather strap had hit me, their criss-cross pattern marking my rump. I ran a fascinated finger along the skin, feeling the heat where the blood still pumped harder. Since we met on the ferry, I had worn Max's badge on my leathers; now, for an hour or so, I would wear his marks on my skin.

Too sore to wear trousers, I pulled on a light silk dress and went back into the bedroom. To my surprise, neither Kit nor Max was there. As I descended the staircase, I heard their voices, and Jane's, from the terrace outside. Kit was reclining on a lounger, and Jane was refilling his glass from a jug of something cool. Max sat in his T-shirt, the first time I had seen him wearing less than a leather jacket.

Jane greeted me warmly, asking lots of questions about the film and a few about Geoff. I'd often wondered whether she had designs on him. The thought suddenly crossed my mind that Max had come here not to see me, but to see more of Jane. Ridiculous under the circumstances, of course, but a pang of irrational jealousy bit through me as she refilled Max's glass. His eyes met hers in a smile, then turned back to me. I relaxed a little, then pulled myself up.

What was I thinking of? True, I had finally got what I had, at heart, wanted ever since I first saw Max on the ferry. But what of it? Where could we go from here? I loved Kit, who was going to be convalescing here for some weeks. Max was not local – nor did he live in Britain. It was very unlikely that I would see him again, once he had got what he came here for. Perhaps he already had and, now he could notch me up as another one of his conquests, he would be off.

But for now he showed no sign of getting ready to depart. We sat watching the sun sink towards the horizon, the reddening sky reflected in the lake, and talked about motorbikes and travelling, like any bunch of friends who have met on holiday.

Max told us he lived in Amsterdam, but he liked to spend as much of the summer travelling as he could. He knew England well, and had ridden many of the same roads that Kit and I had enjoyed. It all seemed so normal that I had to run a discreet finger over my own thigh to remind myself that I still bore the evidence of the extraordinary scene that had just taken place upstairs. As I did so, I looked up to find Max's pale-blue eyes on me, shining with amusement. I flushed, embarrassed to be so caught out.

Jane went into the kitchen and crashed pans about in her usual chaotic fashion until appetising smells started to float out: garlic, olive oil and wine, and aromatic herbs she had picked up in the local market. As the sun began to melt into the crimson water, she piled the table with dishes of chicken, pasta, salad and cheese, and we all ate with gusto. I had forgotten how many hours ago I took a hasty lunch on the road. It was amusing how quickly we emptied the dishes and sat back, replete.

Kit pulled himself up to standing. He was recovering fast, it seemed, already able to walk around with a stick.

'What about this evening out, then?' he said.

Lying around was not his style at all. Max and Jane nodded to each other; they must have planned this before my arrival.

'I'll drive,' said Jane. 'You can lie across the back seat, Kit.'

We helped Kit arrange himself across the back seat of Jane's car, propped with a rug and some cushions.

'Where are we going?' I asked, but Max just smiled.

'Follow me,' he said, more to Jane than to me.

I had half-guessed that we were going to another club-house. Max sat like the Black Knight on his bike, and we followed the silhouette, and the threatening rumble of the engine, through the darkening lanes. In daylight, these were probably scenic roads that wound through olive groves and cornfields; now, they seemed sinister and mysterious. Even the sky was deepening from blood red to purple overhead. Jane's eyes shone; she loved an adventure. As we pulled up in front of a high wooden gate, I wondered if she had any idea what she was heading for.

As before, the gate swung open at Max's approach. Jane drove in behind him and let out a low whistle as she pulled up in front of the whitewashed building. All the wooden shutters were closed, and loud rock music came from behind them. The doorkeeper looked us over then, on Max's nod, held open the door for us to go in.

Kit led the way at his own careful pace, then Jane. As I stepped over the threshold, I felt Max's hand on me, this time a gentle touch on my behind, a thumb feeling the edge of the sorest welt. I couldn't meet the door-man's eye.

This clubhouse was bigger than the one Max took me to before, with proper chairs at round tables, and a stage at one end, like some primitive cabaret. Most of the tables were already full, but Max propelled us to one close to the stage that seemed to have been kept for us. Jane was round-eyed, looking around at the men and already courting their attention. Dressed to kill as usual, tonight she had on a figure-hugging blue satin dress and strappy sandals. Knowing how much of a stir I had caused at the other clubhouse, simply by being female, I knew she would be getting all the attention she wanted before the night was over.

Four beers arrived on our table. The music changed, to a slower, sleazier beat that we could feel through the floor. A single spotlight lit up a circle on the red curtains at the back of the stage. The men in the room were suddenly quiet, expectant. I looked at Max. He sat, his face a mask as usual, his eyes fixed on the stage.

Through the curtains a hand appeared, pale fingers waved in a coquettish gesture of greeting. The audience responded with a low noise, something between a hum and a growl, and the hand disappeared. Now a foot emerged, arched in a clear perspex shoe, painted toenails sparkling silver in the spotlight. Again, a wave of teasing hello was met by a vocal response, but this time the foot did not retreat. Slowly, in time with the heavy music, a leg slid out, calf followed by knee and thigh, till its whole length was twisting and waggling with the bass beat.

A slow handclap started, and a chant that I couldn't make out. The leg began to kick in time with the clapping then, as it reached a climax, shot out in a dramatic lunge, followed by the whole woman. She stood grinning, dressed only in a silver basque and matching hotpants, hips thrust forwards, as the men erupted in applause. The basque was laced up the front, bare skin showing between the bows, and the hotpants showed bare flesh at the sides where they too laced up. She wore a silver wig, a bob that swung as she cocked her head from side to side.

Then she was off, dancing around the stage, lithe and amazingly agile in the high perspex shoes. Every move was designed to tease and provoke, as she kicked her leg so high that the narrow strip of the hotpants barely hid her sex, or arched her back to push her breasts out against the basque. Kit watched with interest, a bulge already visible in his jeans, but Max was impassive.

The dancer put her hands to her breasts and squeezed them together, to a roar of approval from the audience. She jiggled them together, wiggling her hips at the same time. She certainly knew how to tease this crowd with her burlesque repertoire. Then I saw her pull at the bow between her breasts, tugging delicately at the ends to release the fastening. Feigning coyness, she held the two sides together while she danced a full circuit of the stage.

The crowd was howling with protest by now, so she stopped moving and slowly undid the front of the basque, releasing each bow in turn till only one held the two sides together against the pressure of her full breasts. Then she beckoned to a man on the table next to ours. To gleeful shouts from his friends, he got up on to the stage and held the ribbon the dancer offered him.

She did an elegant pirouette away from him and he was left holding the empty garment. A metre or so away, she stood wearing only the hotpants, back turned coyly to the audience. His face a mixture of disappointment and pleasure, he went back to his seat, still holding the basque.

The audience clamoured to see more. For once I didn't need to speak Italian to know exactly what they were asking for. The silver wig flicked over each shoulder as the dancer offered little sideways glimpses, working the men into a frenzy of anticipation, letting the music build towards a climax of its own. Legs apart, she bent to look between them, but kept her hands over her nipples to boos of disappointment. Then, as the music peaked, she spun around and stood gloriously exposed. The crowd went wild at the sight of her silver-painted nipples.

Now she shimmied around the stage in earnest, shaking her tits and spreading her legs to give anyone watching a pretty clear picture of what she would look like in the act of sex. I was starting to be turned on myself, aroused by the very shameless way she was using her body to turn on a roomful of men. I glanced at Jane, whose shining eyes told me she too was involved in the spectacle.

Now the dancer tucked her thumbs into the top of the hotpants, pushing them down a little further to show her hipbones. A low noise of encouragement came from the audience. Starting at the bottom this time, she slowly released the first bow and let the straining fabric gape at her thigh. She worked her way from side to side, alternating top and bottom, till only one bow at the crease of each hip held the hotpants in place.

Now she beckoned two men on to the stage, one from each side. The suspense was impressive; nobody in that room, including me, could wait to see what was under those shorts. Each man held a ribbon in his outstretched hand, as the dancer stood between them with a knowing smile. She gestured, and the music stopped. We all sat and listened to our own breathing, waiting for the moment.

With her hands, the dancer mimed a drumming

movement. Taking the hint, we all began to drum on the tables with our hands. All except Max, who sat as still as always, watching the stage. As the drumming of our hands rose to a crescendo, the men began to drum on the floor with their boots, filling the whole room with a sound that echoed our racing pulses. The dancer stood with her hands resting on the shoulders of her two assistants.

The drumming reached its peak and suddenly she threw herself backwards, into the air. Her long legs flew in a graceful arc, above the heads of the two men, and landed behind them. She stood, naked but for her shoes, as poised as a gymnast. Between the men, her silver shorts swung, abandoned, a mere strip of fabric.

Wild applause greeted her finale. She blew a few kisses, caught her costume as it was thrown back to her, then ran off the stage. Kit blew a kiss at her back, then turned to us all, eyebrows raised in an expression of approval.

'Very impressive,' he said.

'You want a private dance?' asked Max.

Now it was my turn to raise my eyebrows in surprise.

'You think that's the show?' he asked me. 'That's just the trailer, to make you want to see the show. The real show happens in the back rooms.'

I felt foolish and unworldly, but a frisson of excitement ran through me as I imagined Kit sitting in a back room, the lithe and flexible dancer performing who knew what tricks to arouse and entertain him.

The lights came up in the room, and there was a general stir of movement, some towards the bar, a few between the tables as the men went to talk to their friends, and a couple towards a door near the stage that led, I guessed, to the back rooms. Taking the opportunity to flirt with some of the handsome bikers she'd been eyeing up, Jane went to the bar.

Max stood up. 'Come on,' he said to me, 'time to get ready.'

I rose and followed him, not knowing what he meant, but knowing better than to argue. He led me through the door by the stage, and into a brightly lit room with a big mirror. Make-up and clothes were scattered around. It was a dressing room. Fear and delight fought inside me; did Max intend me to strip for this room full of bikers? What on earth would my architect friends back home make of it? Part of me was appalled at the idea, but I could not resist, nor could I deny that part of me longed to rouse the animal desires of that audience, just as I had seen the cute, silver-wigged dancer do just now.

Max lifted the hem of my dress with one hand and looked at the simple white pants I wore.

'They're no good,' he said. 'Take them off.'

I obeyed silently, wondering what he intended me to wear instead. He picked through a wooden crate, examining and discarding scraps of fabric, leather and PVC.

'Try these on.' He held up a pair of long leather boots. As I laced them up, he threw across the rest of the outfit – a leather miniskirt and bikini top, long leather gloves and a tiny leather G-string. As I dressed, he gave me instructions for my act.

'Start with the bikini top, but don't rush it; you've seen how it should be done. Show the knickers next, but don't take them off too soon. Do the gloves first. Then take the knickers off, but keep them waiting a while before you show them what you've got. Keep the skirt and the boots on.'

I nodded dumbly. It felt unreal – could I be about to perform a striptease in this place, in front of this gang of bikers? I struggled with the waistband of the skirt, which laced up at the back.

'Come here,' said Max. He pulled the laces tight,

cinching my waist in like a corset. I couldn't take it off unaided if I wanted to. I saw myself in the mirror, every inch an exotic dancer preparing to tease a leather-clad audience. Over my shoulder Max met my eyes.

'Put some make-up on,' he said, 'and wait here till you're called.'

He was gone, and I stood alone in the dressing room. In the mirror was a figure from a fetish magazine, all shiny black leather and tight, constraining clothes. The two black triangles of the bikini emphasised the dark slash of my cleavage, and the curve of my buttocks was just visible below the hem of the skirt. I practised a couple of moves, thrusting my bust towards the mirror, and shimmying my hips. It was harder than it looked to be sexy in such a self-conscious way. I needed a little help – some glamour was required.

I picked up some dark eyeliner from the counter, and found some bright red lipstick. Now a real showgirl looked back at me from the mirror. This was better; now I felt anonymous. I pouted, ran my gloved hands over my body, squeezed my tits together. I could do this, and I wanted to do it – for Max, to show all those men that he had brought them something worth watching.

It felt like hours that I was left sitting there, listening to the music that came faintly through the wall from the main room. Doors opened and shut, more men coming into the back rooms for their private dances, perhaps. I should run through some ideas for the dance, I thought, but I just sat staring at the woman in the mirror. Was this really me?

A door opened, and a man stuck his head through. Even as he jerked his head, summoning me towards the stage, I heard the music change, loud insistent beats heralding my approach. My heart thumped against the thongs that held the bikini together, but out of the corner of my eye I saw in the mirror that other girl, the professional showgirl, slinking out of the room full of confidence.

This time I was in the darkness on the other side of the curtain, a slit of light falling across me from the spotlight. I slid my fingers through the slit and felt, rather than heard, the expectant hush that told me all eyes were focused on that flash of black leather. No coy wave for me; I slid the gloved hand up the edge of the fabric like a pole, knowing every man in the room could picture it sliding up his cock.

Now the boot. Without withdrawing my hand I lifted my leg and kicked through the gap between the curtains, my leg punching through on the beat of the music. I heard the response of the audience. Yes, I thought, you like these boots, don't you? I let my free hand stray down my leg into view, leather stroking leather, till I could grasp my ankle. The growl of approval from beyond the curtain reassured me – I was on the right lines. I pulled my leg higher, steadying myself on the curtain, till my leg was straight and my foot was higher than my head.

Then I took hold of the other curtain and pushed them apart. Slowly I lowered my leg in front of me, arms raised triumphantly, and looked out at the crowd. A hundred pairs of eyes stared back, already captivated by the spectacle I was creating. There in the centre were Kit and Jane, looking on with a curious mixture of pride and lust. And between them, blue eyes as piercing as ever, sat Max.

A moment of panic overtook me, as expectation filled the room. What did I do next? I looked to Max, and let his calm attention steady me. I couldn't let him down by bottling out now. Fighting the urge to turn and go back the way I had come, I let my hands slide down the curtains and let go of them, then stepped forwards on to the stage, my hips swaying in time with the music. I kept my eyes on the audience and felt their heads follow me around the stage.

My confidence grew as I felt the power I was exerting on all those men. Without removing a single garment, I had already captivated them. I placed my hands arrogantly on my hips and stood centre stage, flicking my long hair to and fro to the beat of the music. I expected them to start the slow handclap, impatient to see me undress, but they sat docile, awaiting my next move.

The other dancer had been playful, but I was finding a different style – more challenging, more dangerous. I ground my hips, holding eye contact with a man in the front row. He stared, open-mouthed, his beer forgotten halfway to his lips. Only when I moved on to another table did his friends jostle and jeer at him.

I was starting to enjoy myself now, and ran a lascivious tongue over my lower lip as I shimmied across the stage. My leather-gloved arms were pressed into my sides, squeezing my breasts together so they nearly pushed out of the tiny bikini. I thrust them towards the men at the nearest table, bracing my hands on my parted thighs.

This was good. The audience was getting more vocal and, though I still didn't understand any of the words, I was getting the gist. They wanted to see more. Sliding my hands down the leather of the boots, I turned slowly around, still swaying to the beat. Hands on my ankles, I twitched my butt at the audience, seeing between my parted legs that a few at the back were standing for a better view.

I arched harder, and made a few mock thrusts towards the watching bikers. The response was instant, animal baying that was unequivocal in its meaning. I flashed a dirty smile over my shoulder, and stood up as I turned back to face them. It was time to start delivering the goods, if I was to keep this momentum going.

The bikini was held together by thongs, tied at the back with a bow. I returned to the man I had transfixed with the first hip-grinding, and beckoned him towards the stage. Before he could climb up to my level, though, I stayed him with a hand gesture. He stood, blinking, awaiting my command. I took his hand, turned my back on him, and placed the business end of the thong between his trembling fingers.

Again I looked back over my shoulder at the room full of men. As if in answer, they bayed their approval. Making sure I swayed my hips extravagantly from side to side, I sashayed away from my assistant, and felt the thong grow taut. Just before it gave way I paused, just for a moment, and shot another seductive look at the crowd, tongue to my top lip. They were frantic, shouting and gesturing, shouting at the man to pull it (I think) and at me to keep walking.

Instead, I threw my head back, flicking my long hair over the bikini fastening, and then threw my upper body forwards on the return stroke. The knot slipped, the fastening gave way smoothly, and before the leather triangles could fall to the ground, I clasped my hands to my breasts and grinned between my legs at the crowd. This time I knew exactly what they were saying. 'No!' went up the cry of a hundred men cheated at the last minute of the sight of my breasts.

My assistant sat down abruptly, feeling perhaps that he might be blamed for the last-minute disappointment. I let the crowd wait another few seconds, time for the disgruntlement to turn to suspense again, then I simply turned to face them, naked to the waist, the redundant bikini cast aside. They went wild.

Now all I needed to do was shimmy, and the audience

quivered with every shake of my breasts. Even as I revelled in my sexual power, I was remembering Max's instructions. Gloves next. But don't rush. I passed lazy, sensual hands over my own body, enjoying the coolness of the leather and the friction on my skin. The drag across my nipples was just rough enough to send darts of pleasure through me, and to leave them standing out in the warm smoky air.

Remembering Rita Hayworth's famous striptease in *Gilda*, I began to play with the fingertips of one glove, loosening them as I did so. I raised my arms above my head, so that pulling on the glove would make my breasts bounce and swing. The glove was sticky with sweat now, so each tug shifted it only an inch or so. I was worried that this was going too slowly, but to my amazement the watching men took this as part of the tease. They started the slow handclap, following the rhythm of the slow-sliding glove.

Taking the hint, I raised my elbows to emphasise the side-to-side motion, swinging my hips with each pull on the glove, and speeding up with each tug. By the time the glove was sliding over my wrist, the men were stamping and shouting with enthusiasm. I let the glove slide off my hand and over my chest, like a languid hand slipping across my pert nipples.

I still had the other glove to remove, but I didn't want to push my luck by taking that long again, so I decided to leave it on after all. Instead, I swung the empty glove around my head and then between my parted legs. Catching the other end, I rubbed it lasciviously backwards and forwards, thrusting my hips against it. The friction between leather glove and leather G-string set up agreeable vibrations, and I let my real pleasure show on my face.

I let the glove fall free, lifted it to my nose and sniffed. In fact, I could smell nothing but leather, but the clamour and the outstretched hands told me that suggestion was stronger than reality in this case. I strolled to the front of the stage, whirling the glove around like a tassel. Ignoring the eager hands, I dangled it in front of a few rapt faces, then threw it high into the air. A near scrum gathered where it had landed.

Now I began to lift the hem of my skirt, inch by inch, revealing a greater stretch of thigh above the high boot. This regained their attention fast – they could tell where this was headed. I slid my feet farther apart and bent my legs, so the skirt rode up to the top of my thighs and the enrapt men caught a glimpse of the black leather G-string.

I slid my gloved hand into the top of the G-string and gyrated against it. Then I took hold of the leather thong that held it together at one side and, with a sharp tug, freed the knot. A collective growl went up from the audience. With a cheeky grin, I transferred my hand to the other side and released the knot, then pulled the slip of leather free and swung it in front of the whooping audience.

Now what? I couldn't have got the skirt off, even if Max hadn't told me to leave it on. The stripping was over, but I had to have a show-stopping number to finish with. More important, I had to leave them wanting more – wanting it so badly that they'd pay for a private dance. I didn't know what I'd do if one of them did come backstage, but I'd be disappointed if nobody did, after the performance I'd just given.

Thinking on my feet, I sashayed to the front of the stage, still swinging the scrap of leather that had been my G-string. Again, outstretched hands told me that it would be a prize for any of them. My mouth was dry. I gestured towards one of the beer bottles on the nearest table, and it was handed to me at once. I took a swig. Then I had an idea.

Placing the beer bottle on the edge of the stage, I bent my knees low, bringing my body down close to the bottle. Suddenly my audience caught on to what I was doing. Every man was on his feet in seconds, yelling for me to do it. This was perfect. I licked my lips as I slowly swayed lower, the hem of my skirt just touching the rim of the bottle. Then the neck of the bottle disappeared behind the leather curtain.

I lowered myself carefully, feeling the cold glass touch my clit as it made contact. Delicately, not wanting to knock the bottle over, I slid forwards on to my knees and felt the bulge of the bottle's lip push between my lips. It was not far in, but it was enough. The slightest rotation of my hips caused a hollow grinding as the bottle swivelled below me. The men were going nuts. Time to cash in my chips and leave the table, I thought.

I squeezed against the bottle, gripping it tight enough to pick it up from the floor as I stood, and released it into my hand. One thumb over the top, I shook it and let it erupt in a torrent of foam that scattered bubbles over me and ran down between my breasts. I could picture myself in their eyes, standing in thigh boots and the tight-laced skirt, one leather-gloved hand rubbing in the white foam that covered me. If I didn't get asked for a private dance now, there wasn't a real man in the room. I stalked off the stage to wild applause, without a single backward glance.

The little dressing room was deafeningly quiet after the clamour of voices and the pounding beat of the music. I sat in the solitary plastic chair, still buzzing with excitement. What now? Would the stage manager come back and tell me where to go? I looked at myself in the mirror, eyeliner streaked, naked body wet with beer. I felt no shame, only pride that I had brought a hundred men to such a pitch of lust.

The door opened and I looked up, expecting the stage

manager, but it was Kit. He smiled strangely at me as he came in, followed by Max. It was Max who looked at me with his cold gaze and said, 'Very good. A natural.'

Kit was looking at Max, not me, and it was to Max he said, 'So we have a deal?'

'We do,' Max replied, taking a large bundle from his jacket pocket. I sat stupefied as he counted out a huge pile of Euro notes into Kit's hand. Was this some kind of bet? Kit put the bundle into his own pocket and shook Max's hand.

'Enjoy your purchase,' he said, and turned to me.

'Since I'm in no physical state to get full use of you,' said Kit, 'I've sold you to someone who can. I had to knock something off the price, since you lack discipline and training, but I'm sure Max can rectify that.'

I tried to protest but it was futile. It was one of Kit's surprise sexual jokes. He loved me, I was sure. But we were on our honeymoon, for goodness sake! He couldn't abandon me to Max for money – could he? Before I could make up my mind what was happening, Kit was leaving the room, flashing me a broad grin before closing the door. And I was alone with Max.

8

I stood silent while Max sat in the only chair and looked me up and down, his expression a blank as always. I could see his fine profile reflected in the mirror behind him, the light through his blond hair turning it to fine gold. I was shaking with nerves. This was what I had wanted, yes, but now it was being thrust upon me I wasn't sure I could handle it in reality. Max just looked. Perhaps he was expecting me to go after Kit, but I wasn't capable of movement.

He put a hand into his inside pocket and brought out a narrow strip of black leather. He held it out to me and I took it from him. The centre was adorned with a silver eagle that seemed to be holding the leather in its talons, like the snake on Max's belt. Four D rings were stitched into the leather at intervals, and it fastened with a plain buckle. But it was much too short to be a belt. I looked dumbly at the silent man before me.

'That is your collar,' he said. 'It shows that you belong to me. And from now on you will address me as "Master" or "Sir".'

It sat, cold and heavy, in my hand. My rational mind cried out in protest – what kind of charade was this? In the twenty-first century, why should a professional, intelligent, independent woman like me submit to this kind of archaic ritual?

And yet a serpent of desire shifted its coils inside me as I imagined myself wearing the collar, obeying Max's orders. I remembered how shame and arousal had mingled within me as I had called him Sir and Master for the first time and had begged him to fuck me. I recalled the intensity of my climax when, at last, he had commanded me to come. What new extremes could he push me to if he truly became my Master, and I his slave?

I lifted the collar to my throat. The hard leather wrapped around my neck as I slipped the end through the buckle and pulled it to. There was just enough pressure, with the pin snicked into place, to remind me that I was wearing it. The silver of the eagle's talons pressed, cold, into my soft skin. I dropped my hands to my sides.

Max smiled – that rare, radiant smile that lit up his face like sudden sunlight. I saw myself in the mirror behind him, the single glove only emphasising the nakedness of my body between the collar and the tight waistband of the skirt. Make-up smudged, my hair in disarray and my breasts still shiny with the spilt beer, I looked as if I had just been dragged out of an orgy.

Max stood up. 'Come with me, slave,' he said, and I followed him out of the room. I imagined any of my friends witnessing this scene – smart sassy Emma letting a man call her 'slave', and I burned with shame, but still I followed him like a well-trained dog. He led me across the corridor and into another small room, mirrored on three walls like the one in the other clubhouse.

Again, there was only one seat, a generous leather armchair in which Max sat as I closed the door behind us. Opposite the chair was a steel pole, chromed to a finish that reflected the three coloured spotlights into a dazzling lightshow. It seemed I was being asked for a private dance, as I had hoped. The music from the main room came faintly through the walls, and I began to sway in what I hoped was a sexy way, trying to pick up the beat.

Max shook his head.

'Not yet,' he said.

A simple gesture of his hand told me to kneel before him, and he held out his hand for mine. I knelt and made to take his hand, but as before he took hold of my wrist and, so swiftly I was hardly aware of what he was doing, buckled a leather strap around it. As I gave him my other wrist for the same treatment, I examined the cuff – a simple band of leather with a D-ring like the collar and a clip like the one on a dog's lead.

He nodded for me to go back to the pole, but before I could resume my attempts at sexy dancing Max took hold of both my wrists and brought them behind me. The dog clip clicked shut, fastening my arms together around the pole. I was free to move, but only within an arm's length around the pole.

Max sat back, legs apart, in the armchair, and hit a button that started heavy rock music pounding through the small room.

'Now dance,' he told me.

Unable to use my arms, I began to grind my hips in time with the dirty guitar sound, sliding the back of the leather miniskirt to and fro across the pole. It was hard to balance on the high-heeled boots, with my hands cuffed behind me. I tried to hold on to the pole for support, but could only rest my hands either side of it, pulled tight against the clip which rattled, steel on steel, as I moved.

Max sat, coolly observing my efforts with no obvious sign of arousal. I tried to remember pictures I had seen of professional pole-dancers, how they had rubbed themselves against the pole and swung around it with gymnastic aplomb. I couldn't do any of that, constrained as I was. Improvising wildly, I slid my feet backwards so I was gripping the pole between my legs, my balance more precarious than ever. I wriggled my hips, hoping to give the impression that I was using the pole as a sex toy.

In fact, of course, with the pole behind me I was finding it impossible to reach the important spots at all. I saw myself in the mirrored walls, multiple reflections of me rocking with the music, breasts swinging above the narrow-waisted skirt that gave me an hourglass figure. I saw Max's mirror images sit, expressionless, waiting for me to pole-dance for his pleasure.

The image was sleazy, anonymous, like something from a late-night documentary, the kind that masquerades as an exposé as an excuse to show titillating pictures. I was that anonymous woman, and the idea made my skin prickle with excitement. I could see my nipples swell and stand up, as my situation stoked a slow fire within me. It was frustrating, not being able to add physical stimulation to the visual, and I writhed against the pole with genuine hunger.

I arched forwards as far as my pinioned arms would allow, and managed to get the pole further between my legs. It felt slightly pathetic, rubbing myself against it like a cat, but I had to scratch the growing itch somehow. I licked my lips at Max, hoping that he would take the hint and let me turn my attention to his pole, but still he sat without any sign that he shared my need. I could feel the leather of the skirt getting wet where it was stretched against the cold metal of the pole.

I slid my feet out again and sank down towards the floor, knees wide apart in the high leather boots. I was sure Max could see, in the dark shadow of the skirt, the copper shadow of my bush and, below it, the shiny flash of my sex. I worked my thighs and waist, trying to show him how good it would feel to be inside me, how well I would perform for his pleasure. The pole was cold between my shoulder blades. I let my head fall back, the leather of my collar squeaking on the chrome as it brushed over my cheek. I forced my head back so the metal touched the corner of my mouth, and let my tongue run over the tiny section it could reach.

At last I saw a tiny movement in Max. He shifted slightly in his seat, the only clue that he was swelling inside the scuffed leather jeans. I pursued my oral attention to the metal pole, shifting my weight so I was sitting on the floor, legs curled sideways. I had the pole in the crook of my elbow now, and in my knee. Turning my head, I licked and sucked at the unresponsive chrome, knowing that Max had a perfect profile view.

As I ran my tongue over the smooth, hard surface, and opened my mouth wider to take the thickness of the pole into it, I imagined it was Max's prick that I was servicing. I could see the girl in the mirror, body arched and twisted above the black leather skirt, shiny black boot and gloved arm hooked around the pole. She looked like a desperate slut, deprived of a human partner and turning in her degradation to the nearest inanimate object. And I was her. I moaned as I struggled to get more of the pole into my mouth.

Then I felt Max's hands on me, and nearly fell as he released the dog clip that held my arms around the pole. He sat back in his chair as I stretched my aching shoulders, and pointed to the floor between his legs.

'Crawl to me,' he commanded.

Trembling with arousal, I obeyed.

'Now undo me.'

He pointed to his crotch. Awkwardly, my gloved fingers clumsy, I undid the buttons of his jeans and released his cock, already huge and hot.

I needed no prompting to take him in my mouth, to feel his flesh at last and taste the first salty drops that already gleamed at the tip. Kneeling between his thighs, I sucked him deep into my throat, working my tongue over the ridge that ran its length. I was his sexual subjugate and I wanted to show him how well I could please him. My cuffs jingled as I put my hands between my own legs. I looked up at him, wet-faced, and asked, 'Master, please may I touch myself?'

'No,' he replied. A flash of resentment ran through me. I was playing by the rules, after all. Max should play fair and let me enjoy myself as well as pleasing him. But obediently I bent my head and filled my mouth again with his length. I was almost as excited by his responses as he was. Normally Max was such a closed book, that any sign that I was making an impression on him felt like an achievement.

He must have been more impressed by my perverse pole-dancing than he had let on, because I could tell from the subtle changes in his expression that he was already getting close to his climax. I worked him harder and faster, eager to give him satisfaction, and hoping that he would then allow me to take mine. His legs shook, but his glacier-blue eyes remained fixed on me, watching my wet mouth working on his shaft. A slight frown was all that betrayed how close he was to coming.

And then he jerked into me, shooting his climax wet and sticky into my mouth. A gentle breath, the nearest thing to a sigh I had ever heard him give, and he closed his eyes at last. I saw myself, reflected, a half-naked woman kneeling between the legs of a man, face shiny with his come, her job done.

I was burning with arousal, but this time he gave me no command to come; he seemed oblivious of my presence. Furtively, I rubbed myself with my gloved hand, enjoying the roughness against my clit, slipping a leather-sheathed finger inside myself. I was on the verge of my own climax, biting my lip to avoid betraying myself to Max with a cry of pleasure.

I didn't see Max's hand move, but I felt my head jerk up as my collar was pulled sharply towards him. A squeak of alarm escaped my lips. His eyes were still closed, but he spoke.

'Did you ask me for permission to touch yourself?'

'Yes, Master,' I replied, slightly indignant.

'And what did I say?'

I felt like a naughty schoolgirl.

'No,' I muttered. Now his eyes opened and stared coldly into mine.

'Speak up,' he said, 'your master can't hear you. What did I say?'

'No, Master,' I said.

A cold breath of apprehension made the hairs on my neck stand up.

'You said no.'

'So you wilfully disobey me? Stand up.'

My heart beat faster as I did as he ordered. What had I brought upon myself? Another beating? I was afraid to face more pain at his hands, but I was more afraid to think that I had displeased him already, and that he might have decided I was unfit to belong to him. It was one thing for me to decide that I didn't want to be his plaything, that I was a free woman. But for him to reject *me* – that would be unbearable.

He clipped my hands behind me again and I stood and watched him do up his trousers. Then, with that pre-emptory flick of the head, he summoned me to follow him out of the room. I paused behind him at the door of the main hall, suddenly aware that my face was still sticky with his seed. I had made a triumphant exit from this room, my body in my own control, my sexual power a weapon I had used to take control of the audience. To re-enter like this, hands fast behind me and obviously fresh from giving Max a blow job, would be a complete reversal.

But I didn't want to give Max any further reason to be dissatisfied with me, so I lowered my eyes to the floor and followed him into the room. A hush fell as he moved between the tables to the stage, but I heard behind us a low buzz of whispered comment. My eyes flicked up once, aware of a man's eyes staring. He was looking, not at my smeared face or naked breasts, but at the collar with its eagle insignia.

With one easy stride, Max stood on the stage. All eyes were on him. Without my arms for balance, I struggled to follow him, using my knees to scramble up. Max put a finger through one of the rings on my collar and steadied me to my feet. He spoke in Italian to the attentive audience. I made out a couple of obscenities, but apart from that I knew only that he was talking about me. I felt utterly vulnerable. What was he saying? Could he be offering me to the room for hire, or worse – for sale?

Something black flew through the air and Max caught it with his free hand. It was the bikini top I had taken off during my striptease.

'*Grazie,*' said Max.

I expected him to release my arms so I could put the top back on, but instead he pulled the leather thong free of the bikini top, then took hold of my wrists and pushed them up my back as far as my shoulder joints would allow. I heard the dog clip rattle as he did something with the thong, and then felt a slight pull on my collar. Max stepped back, and I found my wrists were tied to the collar. With my shoulder blades forced together, almost to the point of being painful, my elbows stuck out sideways, and my chest was pushed forwards.

Max ran a proprietorial hand over my breasts, eliciting whoops from the audience. Then he said something else in Italian. At the back of the hall, somebody waved the glove I had thrown into the audience, as if to throw it back. Max said something else I didn't understand, then turned to me.

'Fetch,' he said, and dealt me a slap to the behind that could be heard at the back of the hall.

Humiliated, but nevertheless aroused, I climbed awkwardly off the stage and made my way between the staring men to the waving glove. Nobody dared touch my naked flesh, but their eyes roamed over me shamelessly.

The man holding the glove was a heavily built biker with a beard. He looked me over as I stood before him, his expression telling me clearly what he would do to me, bound and helpless as I was, if I were not Max's property. I expected him to pass the glove behind me to my cuffed hands, but instead he dangled it before my face. Blushing with the degradation, I leaned forwards to take it in my mouth. As I bent over, he held the glove further away, so I nearly overbalanced as I caught the swinging leather between my teeth. My nipples grazed his knees, and I knew the men on the next table had a direct view up my skirt to my damp, naked sex.

Two of the men in the front row were putting a chair on to the stage as I returned, and one of them lifted me up, his hands on my waist as impersonal as if I too were part of the furniture. Like a good dog, I offered the glove to Max, head tilted up to his. He didn't take it out of my mouth, though. Instead, he gestured to me to turn around and, when I obeyed, tied the two ends together at the back of my head, pulling the leather deeper into my mouth as he did so. The glove sat thick across my tongue, forcing my mouth open.

Max said something to the crowd, and they all shouted back in Italian. He nodded, and sat on the chair facing the audience, gesturing for me to kneel beside him. I could see what was coming, but it was still a shock when Max grabbed the front of my collar and pulled me across his lap. Arms held so tightly behind me, neck held in place by the collar, I couldn't move.

His hand moved under my skirt and over the sensitive skin of my buttocks, awakening each nerve and making me long to squirm against him. Then I felt him fold back that modest flap of leather and expose my rear to the gaze of the crowd. I expected some more lewd shouting, but they were quiet, tense with anticipation. Knowing what they were waiting for, I whimpered with apprehension, but the leather glove muffled the sound.

Again, Max's hand strayed lazily across my skin, sensitising it to the point where I could feel the warm current of his out breath across my flank. Then the contact was broken and I braced myself for the first blow. Less than a second felt like hours, before the sharp sound of a slap was followed by hot stinging pain. I gasped with shock, but even as I winced I felt the heat of arousal flood through my sex. I was being spanked in front of all these men, and the idea was darkly exciting.

Even as one cheek burned, the other was responding to the gentle touch of his caress. Pain and pleasure were being delivered in the same package, and I was actually groaning with enjoyment when the second smack hit me. Max's hand stroked and slapped, stroked and slapped, till I was reeling with the unpredictable onslaught of sensation. Then his hand slipped into my cleft and his fingers worked on my clitoris as delicately as they had played over my bottom.

I wanted to rock against his hand, to set the rhythm that would bring me to the climax I needed, but I was learning fast. I lay still and passive, willing him silently to have mercy on me. My nipples, crushed against the leather of his thighs, answered each electric spark from my clit. I bit on the leather glove. I didn't care that a hundred bikers would see me squeal beneath his hand, trussed like a game bird. All I cared about was finding the release that had been withheld for so long.

When Max's hand withdrew, I almost sobbed in protest. He was determined to punish me, it seemed, both by inflicting pain and by teasing me with the denial of pleasure. If he had invited every man in the room on to the stage to fuck me I would have welcomed it; anything to bring this drama to its denouement.

Max pulled my skirt down and then released my collar, pulling me up with a hand on the thong behind my back. Unsteadily, I stood up. Max addressed another question to the crowd, and they bayed a dozen answers. Though I still didn't understand the words, I guessed that they were offering suggestions, and even their own services, as to what should be done with me. Max smiled slightly, a cruel twist of the mouth that made me shiver.

He took a dog lead from his pocket and clipped it on to my collar. I had to bend down slightly to follow him out through the curtains behind the stage, taking quick steps behind him to keep from falling over. He didn't turn left into the dressing room – instead he pushed open a door that let the cool night air billow the curtains behind us.

We stepped out into the yard. Max's bike stood in the shadow by the wall, the light from the door behind us gleaming in the chrome. He led me over to it and my heart pounded in expectation. Kit had fucked me on a motorcycle once, mounted on it as if I was riding the bike. Max, the ultimate biker, would surely want to combine his pleasures in the same way.

I should have known better than to think I could anticipate Max's intentions. He stopped by the bike, yes, but only to pull my face closer to the machine.

'You see,' he said softly, 'how much care I give my motorbike?'

I nodded my assent. It was easy to see; every inch of it gleamed, there was not a speck of rust anywhere, and the sheen of fresh oil showed that he took the engine maintenance as seriously as the cosmetic finish.

'It is a beautiful machine,' he went on. 'As soon as I saw it I knew I would not be happy until I owned it. I paid a lot of money for it, far more than it is really worth. I spent many weeks making it exactly as I wanted, moulding it to my needs and desires.'

My eyes wandered over the machine. It was true; I had never seen a Harley like it. Max walked all around the bike, and I followed, looking at the magnificent work. The leather of the seat was sculpted, made to fit Max's body like a glove. The chrome handlebars curved back to where his hands would naturally sit on the black leather grips. Each of the twin exhaust pipes, I saw, was a sinuous form that ended in a serpent's head. Mouths open to belch smoke, they stuck slivers of silver into the dark like two forked tongues. In front of the fat black circle of the rear wheel, two silver eagle's talons gripped the pipes, squeezing so tightly they bulged between the claws. Every detail screamed that it was Max's bike and nobody else's.

'But it rewards me with absolute obedience,' said Max. 'It answers my every command, meets my every need at once, as if it read my mind. If not, why should I lavish so much care on it? If it turned left when I wanted to go right, why would I keep it? I would let one of my men take it and use it as he wished, or I would give it to the first stranger I passed in the street. You understand?'

I nodded again. Max reached behind me and undid the thong that held my wrists so high. Even as my arms straightened in relief, he pulled me forwards over the low seat of the bike and looped the lead around the footrest. My breasts pressed against the cool, smooth leather of the seat. Kneeling against the engine, I could feel the hard stone of the yard through the thin leather boots. The cold air found my sex, raised provocatively behind me. I heard the soft noise of Max undoing his trouser buttons.

'Now, learn from the bike,' said Max. He pushed the skirt up and entered me with a single stroke. I imagined myself as a machine, bought and customised by Max for his own pleasure. I tried to ignore the urgency of my own needs, the hunger that rang through me, the discomfort of my knees being rocked against the stone. I focused on his desire, bracing myself as well as I could against his thrusts.

He pushed his hands underneath me and found my breasts, squeezing them so hard I groaned in pain. Then he pinched my nipples between finger and thumb, so hard that tears sprang to my eyes. Still I tried not to flinch, but to follow the rhythm of his thrusts and meet them with my own, like a well-tuned engine following piston with piston.

'Good girl,' he grunted, and his hand, at last, moved down to where the front of my skirt was riding up against the cold metal of the cooling fins. My clit was already slippery with my excitement, and he had only to hold his fingers still and rock me against them with each stroke. As his cock plunged into me, the force pushed me against his quick-moving hand, and my long-pent-up tension drove towards its release.

His other hand still pinched at my nipples, but that only added to the intensity of what I was feeling. Unable to move away, to use my hands or to speak, I could only respond to what Max was doing to my sexual parts. I was nothing but my desire, my need and my sexuality. The waves of excitement that were building within me were obliterating everything else from my mind.

I felt Max tense, tremble, and as he commanded me: 'Come now,' he came, throwing himself into me with complete abandon. I could not have held back if I had tried; my climax shook me with violent waves of release, and I heard my own voice shouting incoherently through the gag. As Max stood and fastened his clothes, I lay over the bike, shaking with exhaustion.

He bent down and undid the knot that held the glove in my mouth. My jaw ached, and I felt my cheeks wet with my own spit.

'What do you say?' he asked.

'Thank you, Master,' I replied. I heard him walk off, but I was too drained to move, and in a minute his footsteps returned. He held a glass of beer to my mouth and I raised my head as far as the lead would allow, and drank thirstily. When I had drunk enough, he took the glass away and unwound the lead from the footrest.

Then he seemed to think again.

'Open your mouth,' he said, and obediently I gaped for him to replace the gag. This time, however, it was the end of the lead he placed between my teeth.

'Hold this,' he ordered me, and I bit on it. I felt something warm and heavy being placed across my back.

'Stay here,' he said, and walked away again.

Gradually the experience receded from my body. It seemed unreal: that I had bent submissively over this bike at Max's command; that bound and gagged and humiliated I had enjoyed such an extreme orgasm. But the collar still sat around my neck, and my hands were still held behind my back by the leather cuffs. As the sweat cooled on my naked legs I shivered, glad of the covering on my back. He must have left me with his jacket.

Still he had not returned, and I waited patiently as he had told me. Then the door of the clubhouse opened, and I heard a burst of raucous conversation. Footsteps came towards me, but they were not Max's; they were too quick and light. Two men walked past me and out through the small gate. I was alone again.

I waited. More men left the building, walking past me as if I didn't exist, as if the sight of a woman leashed and tethered to a motorbike was an everyday event. Perhaps it was, here. I had already seen enough to know that normal rules did not apply in this world. For all I knew, I was no more than this week's entertainment.

I began to worry. Had Max forgotten me? How long did he intend me to stay here, helpless? But, thinking seriously about my situation, I realised that I was not as helpless as I had assumed. I ran a curious finger over the clip that held my cuffs together. Sure enough, it was a simple device that I could unclip myself with a little bit of fiddling. As for the lead, it was held only in my own mouth. I had only to open my teeth to stand up.

So this was why Max had left me here. I was, in reality, free to go. If I unclipped my hands and let fall the end of the lead, I could easily shed the collar and cuffs, pull his jacket on and walk out of the gate. There was bound to be enough money in his jacket pockets to hail a cab back to Jane's villa and rejoin Kit. Max was giving me the chance to bale out.

A flood of relief ran through me at the idea. All this strangeness could be over, like a weird dream. I could be back among familiar people, back in control of my life as I always had been. I was Emma Fowler, after all, a respected young architect, a modern, liberated woman. I didn't have to put up with this kind of degradation. Why wasn't I freeing myself, even now, and walking back to normality?

The answer was because I was motionless, just as Max had left me. Though my back ached from leaning forwards, and my knees were stiff from the cold stone, I was obediently staying where I was told. I was telling myself how much we owed Max for all his help with the bike, how little we could afford to repay him the money I had seen Kit take from him in the dressing room. I was telling myself that I was afraid of Max coming after me, that he might hurt Kit or Jane in his determination to get me back.

But even as I thought it, I knew this was all nonsense. Only one thing was holding me there – my own desire. I wanted to belong to Max the same way the bike did; to be his prized possession, his precious object. I wanted him to mould me to his will the way the bike had been customised to reflect his every whim. Geoff was right; I could never say no to an adventure, no matter how dangerous. To relinquish all control over my own life, to be the plaything and slave of a biker gang leader – this was an adventure I could not refuse.

9

The sky turned from black to deep blue as I knelt on the stone. If Max was testing me, I was testing myself too. My wrists protested at the leather that pressed against my flesh, and my bare thighs grew goosebumps and then turned numb with cold. From the corner of my eye, I saw a pink glow spread across the sky above the high gate, and heard the first bird joined by a second, a third, and a clamorous chorus that heralded the coming day.

In my student days I had worked as a life model for the Fine Art department a few times, sitting nude in the dusty art room while serious-faced students tried to immortalise me in charcoal or clay. I had learned then that a pose that seems comfortable for a few minutes can quickly become downright painful if held for longer. If those simple poses, sitting or standing with one hip outflung for visual interest, had turned to agony within the half-hour before the first break, how much more did my body protest at this position.

I let my head fall forwards to relieve the aching of my shoulders, but my arms were still pinioned behind me, so it was impossible to relax my back completely without the leather cuffs cutting into my wrists. Nor could I entirely let my weight rest on the seat, because my weight tried to fall backwards and left my chin resting uncomfortably on the lead, stretched around its tethering point. I quickly gave up trying to shift to a more comfortable position, and focused instead on accepting the discomfort as part of the experience.

By the time I recognised Max's sure, even steps coming across the yard, the sky was ablaze with golden light. He put out a hand to take the leash from my mouth, and I was surprised to find my jaw almost too stiff to let it fall into his fingers. Gently, with his other arm around my shoulder to steady me, he guided me to my feet. I stood, aching from the sudden release of back, legs and neck from their hours of stillness, waiting in silence. He smiled, a new kind of smile, almost shy, almost tender.

'Well done,' he said quietly, and kissed me on the lips for the first time.

I blazed with pleasure. Never had a kiss been so hard-earned. It felt like a gift, like the most precious, delicate thing he could have chosen to give me. His lips pressed on mine as softly as sunshine on bare skin, but all the passion of his lovemaking was in that kiss. The rush of emotion that went through me was more than just physical desire. I was giving myself to him, but I was also receiving his gift of himself to me. If I could, I would have flung my arms around him and held him tight, but all I could do was to open my mouth to his tongue, to press my lips on his to express my willingness to give him all that I was, all that I might be under his command.

Max released me, smiled again and slipped a hand under the leather jacket to unclip my wrists.

'Go in and freshen up,' he told me. 'Come back when you are ready to leave.'

I didn't even bother to ask where we were bound, or if I needed to bring anything. Max would provide anything I needed. I stumbled indoors, glad of the chance to get the blood moving in my legs again.

We rolled out of the gate before the sun rose above it. The air was still cool over my bare thighs and the wind in my face made my eyes stream. I had never worn an open-faced helmet before – but then, I had never sat on a pillion seat wearing nothing but a leather skirt and high boots, either. Under Max's jacket I was still naked, though he had replaced the single long glove with a pair of short gauntlets that covered the cuffs. I also had his scarf to keep the chill from my neck – and to hide the collar from passers-by.

I had a little seat behind Max, complete with a padded leather back, so I was able to sit back, holding on to the grab bars, and enjoy the view. We rode an unfamiliar route through rolling hills planted with maize and grapevines. The sweet smells of the countryside blew into my face. After the extraordinary night I had just been through I was reeling with tiredness and happy to sit up, warm and relaxed, with nothing else to do.

It didn't occur to me until we'd been riding for an hour that Max had no luggage with him. He must have been travelling for weeks since we first encountered him on the ferry, without so much as a washbag. Or did his henchmen carry his baggage as well? Were we going to rejoin the men I had seen with him the first time we met? I was starting to get hungry; the previous night's pasta seemed a million years ago, and I was grateful when Max turned off the road by a small café.

I dismounted and stood by the bike, waiting as I was told to till Max came out with a coffee and a large pastry. He laughed to see me devour it in a few seconds, gave me his own as well and went back indoors to get another. The hot bitter coffee woke my mouth and warmed my throat. Max had not asked how I took it, so I drank it as he gave it to me – strong, black and sweet. Then we were back on the road.

I couldn't say how long we rode for, because my head was nodding with tiredness. Certainly, the sun was high above us when we pulled up at a pair of wrought-iron gates, and I was glad of the wind over my bare skin to keep me cool.

Max spoke into the intercom, but his voice sounded strange. My befuddled mind worked slowly, and as we rolled up the sweep of tarmac I worked it out – he wasn't speaking Italian. It sounded like a Scandinavian language. Whoever he had spoken to, this was no bikers' clubhouse. A renaissance garden, dotted with classical statues, surrounded a white stone villa. An ornate fountain played in front of the pillars that adorned the front entrance.

A slender young man dressed in black walked towards us as we approached the front door, but Max shook his head and rode straight past. We went under an arch into a stableyard, and into an open doorway. Max pulled up in a stall that had once housed a thoroughbred horse, and I got off. The young man appeared in the doorway with a cloth in his hand, and Max nodded his consent. Nobody but Max could ride his bike, but he didn't mind sharing the cleaning, it seemed.

As the youth bent to wipe the dust off the serpentine pipes, I saw that he too wore a collar: a plain black band of leather with a flash of silver at the front. I glanced at Max. Was this his home? And was I just the latest addition to a stable of slaves? I shivered inside, thinking that I might be nothing more to him than a new acquisition. The boy with the cloth had given no sign of surprise or jealousy at my appearance, or of pleasure at Max's arrival. Then again, he might just be a well-trained slave.

'Come on,' said Max, 'it's time for you to meet Alexandra.'

I followed him out into the sunshine, feeling ready to cry. I was worn out. I had given all I could to be worthy of Max; was I now to meet the woman he had already trained to be his ideal? I walked behind him, eyes down to hide the tears welling in them, seeing nothing of the entrance hall except the obscene mosaics that decorated the floor.

Writhing bodies intertwined together, male and female, human and animal. Normally their explicit depictions would have stirred me: the hairy satyr plunging his enormous member into the lush pink gash of a voluptuous nymph; two women with the dappled flanks of deer, running generous pink tongues over one another's breasts. Today I could only look glumly at them, dreading the scene of humiliating rejection that I was about to face.

Like an automaton I kept in step with Max's black boots across the colourful floor and into a bright room with a marble floor. Aware of someone standing before us, I forced myself to look up, and saw a magnificent woman at the French windows. Long black hair draped over her shoulders, and a tailored black suit, narrow-waisted jacket over a full skirt, fell to the floor. As Max walked forwards and kissed her on both cheeks, I registered that she was not wearing a collar. Indeed, there was nothing about her that suggested she could submit to the will of another.

'Alexandra,' Max was saying, and she answered, 'Max, welcome, it's good to see you.'

'No Otto?' asked Max, and she shook her head.

'Sadly, Otto is still in England.'

He flicked a finger at me and said, 'This is my new slave.'

I stepped forwards and held out my hand.

'Emma,' I said, 'How do you do?'

Alexandra stared at me then raised an eyebrow at Max. I dropped my hand in embarrassment, keenly aware that I had done something wrong.

'New,' said Max, 'and largely untrained.'

Alexandra turned to me a little more kindly.

'Slaves do not speak unless they are spoken to,' she told me. 'Slaves do not have names unless they are given them by their Mistress – or Master.' She smiled at Max. 'And slaves do not address their betters as equals.'

I blushed deeply and looked at my feet.

'However,' she went on, 'since you acted out of ignorance, perhaps your Master will be lenient with you.'

Max looked at me, unsmiling. 'Perhaps,' he said, 'but for now she needs food, drink and sleep.'

Alexandra picked up a small bell from the mantelpiece and rang it. The young man who had cleaned Max's bike appeared in seconds. While Alexandra gave her instructions I was able to study the insignia on the front of his collar, a serpent coiled into a figure 8 laid on its side – the mathematical sign for infinity.

He was clearly better trained than I, since he said nothing at all as he led me upstairs to a room where a bath was run, food laid out and a bed turned down ready for me. I was almost too tired to get out of my clothes, but the bath was too tempting, and I soon had a pile of crumpled leather beside the tub. I thought back to my first night with Kit in the chateau, and how we had enjoyed our historical costumes. There was to be no such frivolity here.

I had my fingers on the buckle of the collar when I hesitated. What if Max came in while I bathed and saw me without it? I looked around for Alexandra's slave, hoping to ask him for guidance, but he was gone. So I sat in the bath wearing my collar, looking down at the marks on my body from the tight skirt, the cuffs and the boots. Hungry as I was, I could only manage some bread and fruit, and a glass of water, before I climbed gratefully into the bed and slept deeply between clean white sheets.

* * *

When I awoke I was aware of two things. The sun was low in the sky, painting the wall in front of my eyes a rich golden red, and a man's silhouette told me that Alexandra's slave stood at the window. I rolled over, expecting to find him looking out at the sunset, but he stood, hands behind his back, watching me. I had no idea how long he had been standing there, but his silent patience unnerved me.

When he saw me move, he stepped forwards at once and handed me a glass of water. I drank, as much to give myself time to wake up as because I was thirsty. I gave the empty glass back into his outstretched hand, and he replaced it on the tray. Then he told me to follow him. He moved towards the door and looked back.

I lay in the bed, acutely aware that I was naked except for the collar.

'Come,' he said, a little impatiently.

I glanced about the room, but saw nothing I could wrap around myself, not so much as a towel. I slipped coyly out of the bed and moved towards the bath, but the pile of clothes had gone. I was caught, bare and defenceless, between bath and bed.

The youth looked at me as if I was a difficult child. My body did not appear to spark the slightest interest in him.

'Come now,' he said and, naked as I was, I walked behind him out of the room and down the stairs. The air was warm as we walked across the marble-floored room, and out into the stableyard. I enjoyed the warmth of the sun on my skin, but my escort walked straight across the yard and I followed him into the darkness of a barn.

A young woman stood in the barn, wearing the same collar as my guide, and a tight trouser suit that emphasised her curves. The man nodded to her, and she walked out without a look at me. I was starting to resent the way they were treating me so anonymously. Max might mix cruelty with his attention, but at least he showed some interest in me.

The man turned to me, holding out the leather cuffs I had taken off to get into the bath. I stepped towards him and allowed him to buckle them back on to my wrists. As my eyes adjusted to the gloom, I could see that the barn was far from empty. Most of the walls seemed cluttered with strange shapes, the gleam of metal and the brutal bulk of dark wooden structures looming in the shadows. The wall nearest me was mirrored, and I saw myself, collared and cuffed, ready to be attached to anything for my master's pleasure. I shivered. What did Max, or indeed Alexandra, have in mind for me?

The man took my wrists and attached them to a rope that hung above my head. He walked over to the door and pulled another line that ran through a pulley and over the beam above me. My wrists rose above my head till I could barely keep both feet flat on the floor. He turned to look at me, dispassionately checking my position, then tied off the rope and walked out into the yard. I was alone, exposed and helpless.

The yard was silent. I strained my ears for Max's footsteps, but all I could hear was birdsong. The cuffs bit into my wrists and I strained upwards to give them some rest. I saw my reflection, the archetypal bondage pose, arms stretched up, breasts lifted and exposed. The warm afternoon breeze moved over my skin, and I closed my eyes, enjoying the delicious feeling of my naked skin in the mild air.

Quick, light steps approached, and I opened my eyes as Alexandra walked into the barn, followed by the female slave. Alexandra stood in front of me and surveyed my body coolly. I felt self-conscious, but there was nothing I could do to cover myself so I stood with my eyes respectfully downcast. Alexandra gestured with a lace-gloved hand to the slave, who handed her something. It was a riding crop.

'Since you are inexperienced, I should warn you that the slightest blow from one of these is extremely painful,' she said to me. 'However, since you will obey me in everything, you have nothing to fear. Have you?'

'No, Mistress,' I answered, feeling strange to say this for the first time, looking warily at the crop. It did look vicious. The female slave stepped towards me holding something made of black leather, which she wrapped around my body and buckled together at the front.

It appeared to be some kind of corset, boned and stiff, that sat on my hips and rose high enough at the front to push my breasts together and up, but not high enough to cover them. The effect was more obscene than nudity, and I looked, fascinated, at my silhouette in the tight leather binding. 'Comfortable?' asked Alexandra, walking around me. I took in a deep breath, feeling the leather give slightly as my ribs expanded. 'Yes, Mistress,' I answered.

'Then you must be laced a lot tighter,' I heard her say as she took hold of the laces behind me and began to pull. The boning pressed into my ribs, the leather creaking as Alexandra tightened the corset mercilessly. Though my lungs fought in vain against the restriction on my breathing, I was hypnotised by my changing shape in the mirror. My waist was being pinched down to a caricature of my normal shape, a true hourglass with wide, curvy hips and bust bursting upwards and outwards. This explained the female slave's extraordinary shape. Did her mistress keep her laced this tight all the time, day and night?

Alexandra stood back and surveyed her work. She seemed disappointed that my body refused to force itself into the exact form of the corset. I was working hard to breathe, and my bosom was rising extravagantly above the corset. Alexandra ran a hand over my breasts, the lace surprisingly rough on my nipples. Then she gestured to the slave.

I could scarcely see what was happening at my own feet, so far were my breasts thrust forwards under my chin. I felt the light, quick hands of the girl placing my feet into boots, lacing up the legs as I swayed unsteadily on the stiletto heels. They were so high that my weight rested entirely on the ball of my foot, and I was glad of the support my suspended wrists gave me. In the mirror I saw how long they made my legs look, the elongated foot and the tight-laced leather sheath that rose above the knee. I was a fantasy woman: waspish waist, huge, high tits and long slim legs.

I watched the slave in the mirror, as she strapped ankle cuffs around the boots. She clipped one to the end of a metal bar, then pushed my legs apart so I lost my footing and hung, briefly, from my wrists. My feet were pushed far apart by the bar, but I regained my balance and teetered on the high boots. Now my bush of russet pubic curls was spread out to view, a flash of pink flesh visible beneath.

I heard light footsteps entering the barn, but dared not risk turning to see who it was. The male slave came into my field of vision, carrying a jug and bowl that looked as if they belonged on a Victorian washstand. He placed them on the floor at my feet, and I felt the warmth of the steam rising to my bare skin. The girl knelt between my legs, her weight on the metal bar stabilising me so I relaxed slightly into the boots. She put her hand into the bowl and took out a cut-throat razor.

I jerked against my bonds, instinctively recoiling at the sight of the blade, but all I did was sway backwards, lose my balance, and hang painfully on the wrist restraints. A sharp line of pain landed on the back of my thigh, and I gasped with the shock of it. Alexandra's voice was soft in my ear, low and full of menace.

'A slave must be clean,' she said. 'Clean and smooth for her master's pleasure. Have no fear. I always train my girls well to shave each other for my delight.'

She nodded to the girl, who pulled a cloth from the jug, dripping with hot water, and a bar of white soap from the bowl. Fearful of provoking another blow from the riding crop, I tried to keep still as she rubbed the soap on to my bush and down between my legs. Her light touch – and the warm slippery soap – sent ripples of guilty pleasure running through me.

The cloth, warm and wet, ran over my sex like a big rough tongue, lathering up the soap till thick white bubbles concealed everything. It was maddening, the way she rubbed my most sensitive parts in that impersonal way, arousing me carelessly, not even bothering to tease me as she brushed the soft towelling between my sex lips.

Then she dropped the cloth and soap into the bowl and took up the razor. I watched in the mirror, not entirely trusting her with that glittering blade in my most vulnerable area, but powerless to escape. She took hold of the proud thicket of hair at the front and, with one expert snick of the blade, left a bare pink strip in the white bubbles.

I was amazed; not only at the speed and skill with which she worked, but at how the shaving transformed me. In a few seconds there was nothing to see below the corset but a naked pink triangle of flesh with a demure crease that showed where my legs divided. As she worked her way down, the razor slipping cold and smooth across my skin, my sex lay exposed to the eye. Every fold and dimple was there, no longer masked by hair, glowing pink in the steam from the jug.

She finished her work and stood back, razor in hand. I

hung in the mirror, a pink doll ready to be looked at, touched and penetrated with a finger, a cock, an object. I looked at myself so objectified, and felt a dark current of guilty desire. I wanted to be used, to have that naked pink pussy probed by a rough hand, ploughed by a cock. Where was Max? I felt my sex contract at the thought, and heard Alexandra's dry laugh behind me.

'Thinking about your Master?' she asked. I saw my face flush with shame in the reflection. Could she really see every twitch of my flesh that betrayed its longing? A lace-gloved hand stroked my buttock and pushed at the puckered entrance of my rear hole. Sharp as the lace was against my tenderest skin, I had to fight the urge to push back against that finger. It was a slave's place to be still and submit, not to seek her own pleasure: I was learning that.

The lace-clad finger strayed forwards into the naked cleft of my sex and found it already moist with desire. Alexandra rubbed my clit a couple of times, then held her wet finger out. The female slave stepped forwards at once and took the finger between her pink lips. She sucked on her mistress's finger. The sensations were vivid in my imagination: the taste and scent of my own juices, mingled with the scented bitterness of the soap; the intimate pleasure of feeling the slave's mouth through the web of lace. I convulsed with imagined pleasure, and again Alexandra laughed at my futile excitement.

'Clean her,' she said to the female slave, who knelt again between my legs. I flinched in readiness; I was already washed and shaved. What else could I be subjected to in the name of cleanliness? I was completely unprepared for the soft touch of her tongue at the top of my thigh. With no hair to get in the way, every touch of her mouth went straight to my sensitised skin, already aroused and glowing with the hot blood of desire.

I couldn't stop myself from moaning in pleasure as her tongue found the tender valley that ran between my lips and flicked into the wet mouth of my cunt. She teased me, working only at the very entrance, only once pushing her tongue deep into me to let me know how good it would feel, then returning to the surface. Her nose brushed against my clitoris as she worked, too skilfully to be accidental. I forced myself to hold still, not to grind myself against her mouth and hurry myself towards the inevitable climax.

Slowly, agonisingly slowly, her tongue worked its way back up the valley towards my hot spot. At the first flick against my pearl, I arched back against my bonds and swung helplessly from my wrists. The pleasure was too intense and, stretched open as I was, there was no escape from her questing tongue. I felt overwhelming tides of orgasm building in me, too strong to resist. No matter if, breaking some unknown rule, I incurred the wrath of Alexandra and her riding crop. No future pain could deter me from this pleasure.

But as I hung on the brink, Alexandra's sharp voice said, 'Stop,' and in instant obedience, the lapping tongue withdrew. I gasped in indignant shock and felt the burning stroke of the crop across my buttocks.

'Dirty girl,' hissed Alexandra. 'Who told you that you could come?'

I whimpered in pain and frustration.

'Nobody, Mistress.'

'Then you had better not come,' she said, and walked out of the barn, followed instantly by her two slaves carrying jug, bowl and razor.

I was alone again, roused to a frenzy by that well-trained tongue, but with no way of finishing the job she had started so well. Legs stretched so wide apart by the metal bar, I could not even squeeze them together and find some stimulation that way. I looked up at the wrist cuffs. The dog clips were out of reach, held taut by the rope that rose into the darkness. There was nothing close enough even to rub my bare nipples against.

Nor could I free myself of this arousal. Even if I closed my eyes to the image of myself, bound and waiting to be fucked, it was burned into my mind. I shut my eyes and tried to think sane, normal thoughts – to list my top ten buildings in Europe, or something. The corset pressed against my breasts, constrained my ribs, like a lover holding me tight. The evening air blew cool across my bare sex, making my damp flesh quiver.

I fantasised about somebody, anybody, coming into the barn and finding me here. A farmhand, perhaps; even a motorist who had broken down and wandered up the long drive. Somebody would come in, see me here, and want to take advantage of my helpless state. Somebody would use me for their relief and, in satisfying their own urge to plunge into my open, waiting sex, would give me the release I craved.

I was suddenly alert, eyes open, body poised in my bonds. Max's unmistakable steps came across the yard and into the barn. My eyes met his in the mirror as he stood in the doorway. Burning as I was with unfulfilled sexual yearnings, I forgot to hope that he would meet my needs. My first thought was simply to hope that he liked what he saw.

He stepped into the barn and walked around me, his eyes moving over my body, drinking in every detail. I looked anxiously at his face, dreading a look of disapproval. Though I had no say in any of this, if Max didn't like anything I knew I would feel his disappointment keenly, and might even suffer for it physically. There was no rule saying that punishment had to be fair, I feared.

Max ran a hand over my skin, straying over my back and breasts. Then he placed it between my legs, feeling my naked folds and creases with almost medical detachment. I tried not to shudder under his fingers, but the mere touch of his skin on mine was stoking the fires that Alexandra and her slaves had lit in me. Max nodded, apparently satisfied, and relief must have shown on my face, because a glint appeared in his blue eyes as he said, 'An excellent job. I must congratulate Alexandra.'

Perhaps my face betrayed something, because he said, 'You are wondering what my relationship is with Alexandra?'

'Yes, Master,' I replied honestly. I was afraid to hear the answer, but I was more afraid to lie to a man who seemed able to read my mind.

'It is not the business of a slave, who else shares her Master's favours,' he said, his blue eyes stern.

'No, Master,' I replied, my heart sinking.

So it was true; he and Alexandra were lovers. Cold, unreasoning jealousy trickled through me.

'However,' Max continued, 'you should have noticed that Alexandra, like myself, submits to nobody. And, even if I could persuade her otherwise, nobody in her life could compete with Otto.'

I looked into his eyes, glowing with relief, and a twinkle shone there briefly in the cold blue.

Max ran a finger along the welt that her riding crop had left on my bottom.

'A disobedient slave,' he said. 'What did you do to deserve this?'

'I nearly came without permission, Master,' I replied.

I was sure the flicker of a smile played across the corner of his eye, but he only shook his head.

'That is not allowed,' he said seriously. 'You were lucky that it was only a "nearly". Imagine the stripes that an orgasm would have left across your pretty flesh.'

Max stood before me, so close the leather of his jacket brushed, cool and stiff, against my nipples. He put his arms around me, his hands gripping my buttocks, and pulled me hard against him. I moaned again as he rubbed my hips against his, so the leather of his jeans pushed into my bare sex and slid against my clitoris. He kissed my throat just above the collar, setting needles of pleasure dancing across my whole body.

Then he stood back and undid his jeans, letting them fall to the floor. He stripped off his jacket and T-shirt and stood, gloriously naked, in the red light of the setting sun. It was the first time I had seen his body, and his beauty took my breath away. He was perfectly proportioned, muscled but not muscle-bound, with a down of fair hair across his chest and running down to where his prick stood, a fat smooth column of glowing flesh that pointed straight towards me.

He stepped back to me, put his mouth on mine and pulled me on to his cock. My body went crazy. After so much teasing, I was getting full-body contact at last, at least where my corset and boots were not covering my skin. Max's tongue roamed over my mouth, his chest was warm and rough against my tingling breasts, and his fingers dug into my buttocks as if he thought I might float away from him.

As for my sex, the sensation of Max's hairy body moving against my naked skin was almost unbearably strong. I was being pounded deep inside, feeding the hunger I had felt since the girl's tongue had made its token trip into my folds, and he was banging against my clit with every stroke. I felt my orgasm ready to engulf me, but I didn't want to brazenly disobey Max by coming without being given the order.

I willed him to do whatever it took to attain his own climax, hoping that, as before, he would command mine to accompany his. Usually I could speed up my partner's orgasm by rocking on him, or squeezing down on him, but I couldn't do anything to Max, not so much as run my fingernails down his back. Desperately I fought against my oncoming torrent, tensing every muscle against the onslaught of sensation.

'You want to come, don't you?' Max whispered in my ear.

'Yes, Sir,' I pleaded. 'Yes, please.'

'Come then,' he said. 'Come now.'

And the wave broke, and I shook with pleasure in his embrace. Only the rope that suspended my wrists from the beam prevented me from falling in his arms. And still he pumped himself into me, pulling me on to his driving shaft with strong hands.

My orgasm receded, but I didn't want him to stop. After all the teasing I had endured, to have him give himself to me so fully, to feel the engulfing touch of his skin on mine, was too good to give up. So I let out a sob of disappointment as he suddenly slid out of me, still hard, and stood back. His skin glistened with sweat, and with my own wetness.

'Fear not, little slave girl,' he said softly. 'I am not done with you yet.' He ran his hand over my breast, and I strained against my bonds to arch against his touch. The caress turned without warning to a sharp pinch, and I could not help flinching, though there was nothing I could do to escape him. The cruel half-smile flickered across his mouth and blazed in his blue eyes.

I watched in the mirror as he moved behind me. His face appeared over my shoulder, and his eyes burned into mine as he ran his hands over my corseted body. Even through the stiff leather, their warmth sent flickers of excitement through my skin. Then he slid them down to my hips and dug his fingers into the thin flesh stretched over my hip bones. I winced, but at the same time Max was kissing my neck below the collar, so the stabs of pain from his hands mingled with the ripples of pleasure set off by his lips and tongue.

Then I stiffened in fear. His grip tightened and, at the same time, I felt the head of his prick pushing against the ring of my rear entrance.

'Yes,' he whispered in my ear, 'you will suffer pain for my pleasure.'

If I could have pulled away, I would have, but I was held rigid by the ropes above me, the metal bar holding my legs so wide apart, and by his hands that braced me mercilessly against his once-more invading cock. I tried not to complain when I felt him force the first inch through the resisting muscle.

Nothing so big had ever been pushed into my back passage, and the delicate skin was being stretched and rubbed by Max's enormous cock. I tried to relax, but my panic was only making me tense up more. Relentlessly, he kept pushing himself into me, deeper than I had ever been penetrated this way. I felt the hair on his balls scratch against my shaved pussy, and knew he must be buried in me right to the hilt.

Then he began to thrust into me, as hard as before, ignoring the gasps of discomfort that I could not stifle. Or perhaps they added to his pleasure, for he was more intoxicated with lust than I had ever seen him. His eyes, fixed on mine in the mirror, blazed with a dark cruelty I had never witnessed. As pain pulsed with the pleasure, fear sent a shiver through my body. I had put myself at this man's mercy, and I was suddenly aware that he, not I, set the limits to that mercy. If indeed, he knew limits at all.

But a dark pleasure flowed through my suffering body. Max's strokes into me were finding hidden places that had never been stimulated this way. The sight of myself being used in such a sadistic and degrading way was perversely exciting. I watched myself being jerked against my ropes by every throe of Max's fucking, breasts bouncing like the sex toy I was. Hanging like this, I was wide open and ready for any use that Max could dream up.

I imagined another man at my front, thrusting into my pussy against Max's strokes from behind. Or the female slave, kneeling at my feet, licking at me, running her tongue over my clit, lapping at the root of Max's cock where it pumped in and out of my tender hole. Or a circle of men watching, waiting their turn to use me, or wanking as they watched, till I was splattered with their come, unable to wipe it away from my breasts, my face.

Max's low voice, breathless from exertion, hissed in my ear. 'I knew you would enjoy my cruelty. Does it excite you to be my plaything, my mistreated slave?'

'Yes, Master,' I panted back.

'Then come for me again,' he said, putting one hand against my bare pink sex. 'Come now.'

At the first touch of his thumb on my clit, I felt another climax overtake me, sharp and hot, so I thrashed between his gripping fingers and his pounding cock. I could feel my back passage convulse against his shaft, and the answering shudder that told me he too was coming, emptying himself into my deepest crevices. Pain and ecstasy fought in me, but the ecstasy was stronger, too strong to give way.

I was still dazed as Max released my legs and arms and carried me bodily into the house. He laid me gently on the bed and stroked the red marks around my wrists.

'Thank you, Master,' I said weakly, and the shy tender smile flickered across his face again.

'Good girl,' he said, and kissed me gently.

10

Night was falling as we pulled up in a cobbled alley off a canalside road in Amsterdam. I was exhausted, and I had no idea how Max had ridden for so long, stopping only to buy fierce black coffee and bland sandwiches for the two of us while the bike was refuelled. We had left Alexandra's place at first light, while the air was so cold I huddled gratefully into my new clothes. From the Victorian cut of the long leather skirt, split like a riding habit, and the matching jacket, I guessed they came from Alex's wardrobe, not Max's.

Nor did I get too hot, as we rode northwards into the mountains and down through the hills of France and Belgium. This time we were using motorways, so I crouched behind Max's broad shoulders to shelter from the wind of our speed. Curious eyes looked from the passenger seats of cars at us as we overtook. Though my collar and cuffs were hidden beneath my coat, we must have made quite a sight: the biker and his woman, all in black leather, cruising in the summer sun.

I was glad of the long journey at first, glad of the time to think without having to talk, or even to meet the power in Max's cobalt gaze. I was shaken by the experience in Alexandra's barn. Not only had I realised just how deeply I was under Max's power, but I had been forced to recognise how much I wanted it. Images still ricocheted through my mind, and every time I caught Max looking at me, the picture of his face shining with cruel lust came into my mind.

Then, as the hours stretched on and the miles unrolled, I grew weary of sitting passively on the pillion seat, watching Europe flow past the motorway's verge. I began to think about what else I could have been doing, how I could have been riding my own bike along more interesting roads. My mind kicked against the tedium. The next time we stopped at a service station, Max caught me gazing enviously at a couple arriving on sports bikes.

'You know you can go back any time you want?' he said. I nodded. 'Kit will be missing you,' he went on.

'I know.' I missed Kit too – but he was the one who had sent me on this adventure. I planned to call his bluff.

By the time we rolled down the ramp into Max's underground garage and dismounted, stiff and cold, I had no fight left in me. All I wanted was to be off that bike and in the warm, and to sleep. I followed Max humbly into a lift, glad that we had no luggage to unload and carry in. 'This is your new home,' said Max, and the doors opened on to a blaze of neon light.

We stepped out into a huge room, four walls of glass looking out over Amsterdam's red light district. Garish signs advertising live sex shows, girls, and XXX movies blazed like a perverse parody of Christmas decorations. One side overlooked the canal, where the explicit displays made a surreal contrast with beautiful old buildings, and the lights in the sex shop windows reflected in the dark water.

At the sides of the building, the narrow alleyways scarcely separated Max's apartment from his neighbours. One side looked on to a modern block, sleek venetian blinds concealing the brightly lit rooms behind. The other building was older, and I could clearly see the dining room, lit by an opulent chandelier and painted a deep, lush red.

Apart from the lift in the centre, Max's place was completely open plan. Even the bath stood on a plinth in one corner, a single chrome pipe arching over it to a showerhead the size of a dinner plate. A gleaming modern kitchen and a dining table filled one end of the room, and the other was dominated by the curve of a vast black leather sofa.

It was beautiful. The architect in me was filled with admiration at the daring use of space, and the engineering that allowed the sweep of glass to be a panorama interrupted only by narrow steel pillars. The London flat-dweller in me was flooded with pure envy at the space, the view, the generous proportions.

'You are tired?' Max asked me.

'Yes, Master,' I answered, surprised to find my mouth dry and my voice croaky.

Max opened a giant American refrigerator and poured two glasses of water from a jug. He handed me one and pointed to the sofa.

'Sleep here while I cook,' he said. I sat gratefully on the smooth, soft leather and drank the water. I wanted to watch him work, to see if he lavished the same meticulous attention on food as he bestowed on his motorbike, or on me. But I could not keep my head away from the suede cushion beneath it, and before Max had finished taking things from cupboards and shelves, I was asleep.

The smell of the food woke me before Max's hand touched my face. The fresh smells of garlic and basil rose from a steaming dish, and after a day of bland motorway food, I relished every flavour. It seemed that Max was as discerning a cook as he was a lover. As we dined, Max lifted the veil on his persona a little – enough to give me the basic background story of his sexual proclivities and his lifestyle. His father had died young, leaving him a huge property portfolio and a huge inheritance. In his twenties, living the life of the northern European playboy, he had once attended a ritzy party in Switzerland, and had happened upon the dungeon room – the party behind the party, as it were – and had instantly been fascinated. At first he had been led into the scene by an imperious dominatrix, but had soon found his true tastes were those of what he called 'the caring sadist'.

I watched as he ate and spoke with the perfect manners of the urbane sophisticate. It was amusing to think that I'd thought of him as a bit of rough; yet now he struck me as some kind of Dutch duke; a member of the Euro-fetish aristocracy. He seemed happy with his masquerade; keen to perfect his image and train what he called 'beautiful adventuresses'. I glowed at that, as the sounds from the streets below filtered up to the apartment – the intermittent growl of a car or boat engine, and the buzz of tourists.

When we had finished, Max handed his plate to me and sat back on the sofa. From his expression I sensed we were back into role. I took the dishes over to the kitchen and washed them. Max pointed to a drinks cabinet that stood near the sofa.

'Pour me a brandy,' he ordered me, 'and run me a bath.'

I obeyed, wondering as I handed him the glass whether domestic duties were a fundamental part of my new status. The water splashed into the stone bathtub from a single chrome tap, filling the apartment with its sound.

Max took a sip of the golden liquid and watched me.

'Now I want you to strip,' he said.

I looked at him, glancing first at the red dining room

that seemed so close. A dinner party was getting under way, six respectable-looking people sitting at an oval table only a few yards from Max's panoramic windows.

'Do you think you will be the first naked woman they have seen in this room?' Max inquired, somewhat imperiously. 'Do as you are told.'

Turning my back on the diners, for my own benefit rather than theirs, I slipped off the heavy leather jacket, and unlaced the boots. Max watched, a frown once more passing across his brow.

'I said strip, not get undressed,' he growled. 'Remember your little pole-dance?'

He pointed a remote control at the lift column, and suddenly a sultry blues number reverberated around the apartment. I struggled with the second boot's lacing, trying to at least strike a sexy pose with my leg outstretched, and pulled it off with a flourish. Now I stood in skirt and corset, collar and cuffs. The skirt fell heavy into my hands as soon as the waistband was undone, and I shimmied it down my thighs. Alexandra had not seen fit to provide me with knickers, so I felt horribly naked as I kept my back resolutely turned to Max's neighbours, wishing I had at least my modest covering of hair.

I hesitated. The corset was still tightly laced and, though I had already grown accustomed to the constriction, I doubted that I could remove it unaided. Collar and cuffs were more uniform than clothes, so perhaps Max wanted them to stay in place.

'Come here,' he said with a flick of the head.

I knelt submissively before him while he loosened the lacing down my back, and felt my ribs expand with relief as he undid the buckles and let the corset fall on to the carpet.

He turned the music down, rose and walked over to the bath, which was filling rapidly.

'Turn the water off,' he said, and I walked over to turn off the tap, inches from his hand.

I felt more embarrassed to be seen in the collar than if I had been entirely naked. Hurrying so obviously to perform Max's menial tasks, my status was only too clear to any observer.

However, I was not to be alone in my nakedness.

'Undress me,' he ordered and I removed his T-shirt, laid it aside and knelt to undo his jeans. As I pulled them down and he stepped free, I felt humiliated to see that he was apparently completely unaroused by my naked body. Max stepped into the bath.

'Wash me,' he said.

I picked up the natural sponge that sat beside the bath, and rubbed it over his outstretched legs. Max lay, brandy glass still in hand, eyes shut. As I slid my wet soapy hand under his thighs I felt my own desire growing again. His body was beautiful, not in a flashy, film-star way, but in its simple grace. I slid the sponge over his warm, soft cock, hoping to feel it stir beneath my touch, but it resisted my attentions and I moved on to his belly.

When I had caressed each part of his skin and shampooed his fine blond hair, he opened his eyes and looked at me.

'Good,' he said, and rose out of the water.

I picked up a towel and wrapped it around him as he stood dripping, and he stepped out on to the carpet. I was starting to pick up the habit of anticipating his needs.

I rubbed him dry, and stood awaiting his next command, trying to forget that I was providing a free cabaret for the diners next door. He handed me his glass and I hastened to refill it, then he undid my cuffs and collar.

'Wash yourself,' he told me, indicating his bath with a careless flick of the finger.

I sat in the bath and washed myself with the sponge, trying to angle my body so Max could see everything and the neighbours could see as little as possible. Not that he seemed at all interested. Glancing over a few times to check my progress, he was more focused on his brandy, and on flicking through the different styles of music that the remote control had on offer. Seeing that I had finished washing, he gestured with a nod of the head for me to get out.

'Wash out the bath,' he said as I reached for the towel he had let fall, so I stood dripping and rinsed away the soapy water.

Only then did he point a lazy finger at the towel, permission for me to wipe away the rapidly cooling moisture from my skin.

'Bring me your collar,' he ordered, and stood as I approached to fasten it once more around my neck. There was something comforting about the gentle pressure it exerted, demeaning though it was to stand once more collared like a dog. Obeying another gesture, I replaced the cuffs around my wrists. Max stood and walked over to the lift doors, opened a flap beside them and pressed the button.

I followed him back into the lift, hoping silently that he didn't intend to take me on to the street in my worse-than-naked state. The lift started moving, but I staggered as the floor lurched upwards, not down as I was expecting. Max smiled, a mysterious smile but with a hint of human warmth. 'You are ready to come upstairs,' he said, as the lift stopped and the doors slid open. This time, with a light slap on my behind, he propelled me before him into the room.

I saw nothing at first, but then he must have hit a control because the lights came on. A dull red glow illuminated a windowless room, the square platform of a bed the only recognisable piece of furniture, draped with a black fur cover. All around the walls, brutal industrial shapes and the glint of metal hinted at equipment that stood ready to torment a willing submissive, or to tease her to the extremes of pleasure. Pulleys hung from the ceiling, and a mirror-fronted cabinet concealed who knew what instruments of correction.

I recoiled, but my instinctive step back towards the lift was blocked by Max. I was aware, as I blundered into his warm body, that his interest was finally stirring at last. What my naked body had not been able to rouse, my fear was awakening at last. He put a firm hand on my waist and pushed me ahead of him, straight towards the bed.

'Welcome to your quarters, my sweet,' he said. 'As you see, I have many things prepared for you. Ever since the first moment I saw you, I began thinking of the ways in which I could use you, could enjoy you, could make you suffer for me. I knew, though you did not, that what you sought was strict discipline and merciless training, and finally the deep joy that comes from total obedience.'

Panic filled me. I reached the bed and his strong hand pushed me down on to it, burying my face in the fur. I tried to resist, but Max's superior strength and sheer body weight held me down while he clipped my cuffs together behind my back and ran a narrow strap around my ankles. He continued, as he pulled my feet back towards my wrists and clipped them together, to talk to me in the same even tone.

'I know you will fight me, that your defiance will bring more punishment upon you before you learn to submit entirely to my command. But you will submit, Emma, because you will come at last to realise that you need to be mastered, just as I need to master you and just as your husband, Kit, wants you to be mastered.

Such a privilege is your destiny, and one day very soon you will kneel willingly at my feet and thank me for the great gift I bring you.'

The bed shifted as Max stood up, and I heard his steps crossing the room. I lay, immobilised, hog-tied and naked, my heart pounding with fear and denial. What a fool I had been, to throw myself so eagerly into this man's hands. I tried not to remember how I had lost myself in our last encounter, how I had found, just as he was saying, a perverse and guilty joy in his mistreatment of me.

The silence in the room was profound. I couldn't even hear the sound of the traffic, so it must be soundproofed as well as windowless. My blood thumped in my ears as I strained to hear what Max was doing. I thought I made out a rattle of buckles before he came back to the bed, but the first thing he did was slide a soft band under my face and fasten it over my eyes. Only then did he roll me on to my side, blindfolded as well as bound.

'So begins your training,' he said. 'Open your mouth.'

I dared not disobey, and felt a springy mass pushed between my teeth, and tasted leather. A couple of seconds later, a strap pulled tight over my mouth, forcing the gag on to my tongue. I could swallow, but I could neither speak nor close my mouth.

Max moved away from me again and I heard him prowling around the room. Deprived of my sight, my hearing sharpened and my skin became alive to every stimulus: the warm softness of the fur, the cooler air around me, the tightness of cuffs and ankle strap.

How long did he intend to keep me like this? Now I was here, he could go out and leave me all evening, all night if he wished, knowing that I would be in the same position when he returned. I shivered to think of it, but at the same time a frisson of excitement ran through me to imagine him drinking in a bar with his friends, knowing all the time that his slave lay naked and helpless at home.

Max sat down beside me again, and a current of pleasure sparked from my nipples as he caressed them with rough fingers. I was bent into a bow shape, my breasts thrust forwards by the tension holding my arms back. Seeing nothing, I could only feel each delicious touch of his hand.

It moved down, over the taut plane of my belly that quivered at his touch, and fondled the hairless mound above my sex. This new sensitive area tingled at his unimpeded contact and I was starting to become aroused. Max's hand pushed between my legs, finding the moist crease that betrayed my enjoyment. Holding my body against his, he rubbed his prick against my clit. Now I keened with desire. I couldn't part my legs to admit him, but I wanted to feel him inside me.

Between my thighs the wetness of my arousal made a tight, slippery crevice. Into this Max pushed his cock, and worked it in and out. He was masturbating against me, maliciously ensuring now that he was not rubbing against my clitoris. I moaned in protest.

Max redoubled his thrusts. He was actually pressing my legs together with his, giving himself a tighter crack in which to slake his lust. How could he do this to me? My body was shaken to and fro by the rhythm of his hips, but my most sensitive parts were deprived of any direct friction.

I wished I could at least see his face, to read in his fierce blue eyes some hint of compassion, or merely animal desire for me. Silenced by the gag that filled my mouth like a leather cock, I truly was an object in his arms. At that thought, twisted excitement pulsed through my body, increasing my hunger for stimulation.

But his violent thrusts told me he was reaching his own climax without regard for mine. An explosion of hot liquid between my thighs, a few slow shudders of his hips, and he pulled away from me. I was left – still unable to move or see – with the warm trickle of Max's come a humiliating reminder of the way he had used me. I felt the bed shift as he got up and walked away.

Desire and discomfort battled inside me, but there was nothing I could do to ease either. Until Max chose to return and release me I must lie here and wait. My mind returned to the scene in the clubhouse yard. If he was serious about treating me the way he treated his motorbike, I must expect to be ridden hard and ruthlessly, but I might also hope to be cleaned up and looked after, just as the bike was always oiled, polished and refuelled.

Then again, he was making a point of bending me to his will. If he was deliberately leaving me thus unsatisfied, he might easily leave me here for hours, to teach me that I was merely his plaything. Hoping to show him that I had learned that lesson, I lay still and docile. I heard his footsteps come back towards me.

'Good girl,' he said, then he walked over to the lift. The doors opened and closed, and he was gone.

I shook with frustration and futile rage. I had done everything I was told, had behaved just as I should, and still Max had abandoned me in this state. It was so unfair! I didn't know how long he would be gone, or where he was going. For all I knew, he might be going to another room equipped like this one, where another slave lay bound and waiting for him.

Or he could be going to join his gang of fellow bikers in a bar somewhere. They would sit drinking for hours, laughing about their conquests. Max would tell them about the woman he had acquired in Italy, who lay even now on his bed, sticky with his juices. He might even be planning to bring them back, to pass me around the gang so each of them could use me as mercilessly as he had.

The faces I had seen on the ferry rose into my mind's eye. I remembered them looking up at me as I writhed in Kit's arms. Now I was the property of their leader, would I be shared out like the spoils of war? There was something deliciously degrading about the idea. I imagined myself as they would see me, stepping out of the lift to find me lying here, pulled backwards by the leather straps, the gag and blindfold obliterating my face.

My nipples – erect with excitement – and my shaved sex would be offered up to their eyes, their hands, their mouths and pricks. I groaned in frustration as the heat of excitement at this thought flushed through my skin, and squeezed my thighs together in a pathetic attempt to answer the pulsing call of my clit.

I jumped to hear the lift door open again, and heard Max laugh softly.

'You weren't expecting me back so soon?' he teased as he walked over to me.

I was almost disappointed to hear no footsteps follow him in. He sat beside me and undid the strap that held the gag in my mouth. I felt a thread of spit follow it out, as I closed my stiff jaw at last.

'Thank you, Master,' I said, determined to give him no reason to punish me further.

I felt the clip that held my feet and hands together released, and I stretched gratefully into a more normal position, my joints recovering.

'Thank you, Master,' I said again.

Max stroked my trembling skin and kissed my lips.

'Well done, little Emma,' he whispered. 'You are learning fast, as I knew you would. It is time to reward you with a gift.'

I blinked in the unaccustomed light as he removed the blindfold, and saw him sitting beside me, dressed as before in his leathers.

'Come and wash yourself,' he said. 'We are going out.'

11

I had been to Amsterdam once before, on a school trip to tour the art galleries, but I would not have recognised the city from that visit to this. Though the high, narrow buildings that leaned higgledy-piggledy beside the canals were faintly familiar, my overwhelming impression now was of crowded alleyways and garish, seedy shopfronts.

Nor would the city have recognised me. From a scruffy tomboy in jeans and school sweatshirt, I was transformed into something from a fetish magazine. Laced once more into the corset, I tottered behind Max on the impossibly high boots, a PVC miniskirt barely covering my naked bottom. My collar and cuffs were now on open display in the cool night air, and only a chiffon scarf covered my breasts above the corset. Under Max's orders I had painted my lips again with a gash of scarlet, and darkened my eyes with a smudge of kohl.

I was deeply embarrassed, but I soon realised that in this district I was nothing remarkable. In every lighted window stood a woman wearing less than I, brazenly eyeing up the potential customers strolling past. Some stood casually in underwear, or in shiny bikinis or lacy basques. A few were aiming for a more specialised market, and brandished whips, handcuffs, or other paraphernalia I didn't recognise, as they posed in PVC catsuits or latex uniforms.

Max caught me peeking shyly at the prostitutes in their windows.

'Perhaps I should a rent a window and put you up for

hire,' he said, loud enough for anyone to hear. 'I think you'd like that, wouldn't you?'

I blushed and muttered, 'No, Master,' though I had felt a spasm of sordid excitement as he spoke. Would he really put me on public display like that, and let other men pay to use my services?

A sharp slap on my bare thigh made me stumble on the cobblestones.

'Don't lie to me,' said Max. 'You think I can't see it in your eyes, how you'd like me to show you off to every dirty tourist who comes here for a stag party? You are a slut, down to the core, and before I am done with you, we will see how much you love to be treated as one.'

'Yes, Sir,' I said. I kept my eyes down, partly in respectful obedience, and partly to watch the uneven surface of the road. In these boots it was hard to negotiate the cobbles. I was also avoiding looking at the graphic displays in every second shop. There were sex shops in Soho, but their window displays looked like M&S next to these.

As usual, Max could see what I was up to, and wasn't going to let me get away with it. With a hand in the small of my back, he steered me towards a lighted window. A blow-up doll, painted eyes wide and mouth gaping around a red rubber ball, lay across the display, trussed into a web of leather straps. In her orifices, brightly coloured dildoes quivered, making her plastic body shake inside her harness. Even the ball was held in place by thin straps that criss-crossed her face.

Along the front of the display, gyrating like a twisted chorus line, a row of assorted vibrators demonstrated their range of movements. Friendly coloured plastics, some of them filled with jiggling multicoloured balls, were interspersed with rubber, glass, and even chrome replicas of the male member, ranging in size from the impressive to the alarming. There were even rubber hands, clenched into a fist and actual size, rotating on their stands.

But these were mere toys, hen party jokes, compared to the implements that hung behind them. Riding crops of different sizes, a selection of flat paddles and the sinister coils of a bull whip, promised a multitude of ways to inflict pain. I had no doubt that Max already owned plenty of these, so heaven knew what he intended to buy for me. I was about to find out, though, for he was pushing me firmly through the beaded curtain in front of him.

We were not the only customers. A giggling couple fingered the handcuffs on the shelf, and a tall woman in an expensively cut business suit was holding up a rubber garment against an equally well-dressed man. The young man behind the counter seemed to know Max, as he nodded a greeting to him, bestowing a friendly glance on me.

Max was looking through the clothes on the rail: PVC and latex dresses, suits, and strange garments that I didn't recognise at all. He held up a PVC catsuit in metallic blue and said something in Dutch to the shopkeeper. The man came out from behind the counter and looked me over before replying. I could tell they were talking about me, of course, but not what they were saying. What made it more humiliating was the knowledge that, had they wanted me to understand, they could easily have spoken in English.

The shopkeeper took the catsuit off Max and went into the back of the shop. Max turned his attention to a different rail, beckoning me with an arrogant flick of the head. I found him examining a strange leather item, a little like a chastity belt but with a round opening just where a chastity belt would be impenetrable. He handed it to me, and I saw that it also had a smaller hole at the back.

I felt sure the openings were too small to admit more than a finger, but Max was already taking the thing back from me, and fitting a metal dildo into the round hole. My mind tried to make sense of it – if this was a strap-on dildo, he was assembling it inside out. Then, with appalled delight, I saw the idea. Just as the gag had been held deep in my mouth by a strap around my head, the dildo was intended to be held inside me by this harness.

Max held it up and I saw that he had selected a steel member even thicker and longer than his own real one. Before I could formulate a protest at the size, he said, 'I think you need to try this on,' and gestured for me to follow him to the changing room.

The shopkeeper was already in the small cubicle, apparently waiting for us with a tape measure. Max stood patiently holding the terrifying dildo-belt while I was expertly measured, watching with a detached gaze as the younger man ran his tape around my hips, bust and waist, instructing me when to turn and when to raise my arms so he could hold the tape from shoulder to wrist. When all my dimensions had been noted down, he left me alone with Max.

'Turn around,' said Max.

I thought better of saying anything in protest, and turned my back on him.

'Bend over, and open your legs,' he instructed me, and I obeyed, steadying myself with a hand on the solitary chair.

Out of the corner of my eye I could see myself in the mirror, long straight legs tapering to exaggerated points in the high boots, tiny waist, and breasts pushing out of the top of the corset.

Max grabbed the back of the skirt's waistband to hold me still, and lifted the short panel of PVC out of the way.

Carefully, he placed the cold metal of the dildo against my pussy entrance, which shrank from the hard chilly touch. There was no resisting the invading shaft. It forced its way in, hard and smooth, stretching me open as it came, till it touched the very neck of my womb.

'Beautiful,' said Max, looking down at me. Then he pulled me around, so my back was to the mirror.

'Look,' he said, pushing my head down between my legs to see the reflection.

Above the black of the boots, my pale slender legs rose to the curve of my buttocks. Between them, the shaved pink slit of my sex was stretched tight around the huge shiny rod that stuck out of me. I was impaled on this steel bar, my soft, naked flesh a vivid contrast to the rigid, geometric shaft.

I watched him run a finger lightly over my sex, right at the point where the metal pulled it wide open. The delicate touch set off a strong convulsion deep within me that squeezed against the cold steel. He picked up the leather harness with the socket, and screwed the dildo into place. It turned inside me, dragging at my deepest parts, as if it was drilling into me.

Max did up the two buckles at my hips that held it in place. As he tugged them tight, the dildo was forced into me still further, pushing so deep that I could feel myself being stretched as never before. I groaned; the feeling was weirdly intense. He stood back to admire his handiwork. The effect was like black leather hotpants, a ring of bright metal the only sign that I was being penetrated by a steel member. Just bellow the lifted flap of the skirt, a smaller hole behind revealed a glimpse of my own puckered opening.

He seemed satisfied.

'That will do for now,' he said, and turned to go.

I must have stared, open-mouthed. Making me test

such things in a changing room was no more than I had come to expect from him, but did he intend me to wear it on the street? He looked at me, impatient.

'What are you waiting for?' he asked me. 'We have people to meet.'

So I stood up, carefully, feeling the steel rod inside me shift its position as I did so. The leather felt bulky between my legs, forcing me to stand with feet slightly apart. I took a first delicate step and felt the dildo churn against my most sensitive parts. If I had found walking in these boots a challenge, moving around in this self-penetrating underwear was going to be a hundred times more difficult.

By the time I had reached the front of the shop, Max was dropping a receipt into his carrier bag. He waved a friendly goodbye to the shopkeeper, and held open the door for me to step outside. The few inches drop from shop to pavement rocked the end of the metal prick against a new sensitive patch deep inside me. I could tell that every new movement was going to bring novel sensations.

Max slowed his walk a little to let me keep up, but that was his only concession to my new equipment. I followed close behind him through the dark narrow streets of the red-light district, aware of the curious eyes that followed my collar with its silver insignia, and the cuffs that adorned my bare arms. I wondered if anyone watching could tell how I was hobbled by the rigid bar inside me.

We reached a bar, loud cheerful rock music spilling out of its open door along with heavy-scented smoke. I breathed in the cannabis-laden fug as I followed Max in, squeezing with difficulty past the drinkers who sat on high stools along the bar.

There were low sofas at the back that overlooked the dark waters of a canal, but Max headed straight for a staircase that descended to the lower room. As I picked my way down the stairs, my inner depths were churned by the dildo. I wasn't sure which disturbed me more: my lack of control over the sensations, or the fact that I was enjoying them deeply.

The lower room was dominated by two pool tables, but among a group of men seated in the far corner I recognised a couple of the faces from the ferry. They all stood up at Max's approach and greeted him, some with a handshake and others with a respectful nod. Their eyes turned to me, took in at a glance the collar that bore Max's mark, and looked straight back to him for guidance in how to treat me.

'A seat,' said Max, pointing to one of the higher stools, and it was brought to me at once. I perched gratefully, relieved to take the weight off my toes without having to disturb the position of my metal guest too much. Max ordered two beers, and I sipped the cool, malty liquid and listened to the conversation.

I guessed that not everyone in the group was a local, as the discussion was mostly in English, and it seemed in fact that three of the faces I hadn't recognised were visiting from Denmark and Norway. The talk was innocuous, a sharing of travellers' tales and news of new motorbikes bought, sold or considered. Nobody addressed a remark to me, though I was included in the circle.

I began to tune out and watch the body language instead, noting how everyone deferred to Max, even the visitors. A couple of the men were smoking, but I couldn't tell if they were joints or just hand-rolled cigarettes. Certainly, nobody was working very hard on becoming intoxicated, either through drugs or alcohol.

One of the Norwegians made a comment about Max's shopping, indicating the carrier bag. It bore a striking logo that showed a fifties-style pin-up girl bound with ropes and chained to a lamp-post, so it was obvious what kind of shop Max had been in. With no sign of shame or embarrassment, Max pulled out a small box. I blushed in preparation. Whatever he had chosen in the shop, it was obviously intended for use on me.

I was surprised to see him take out a small remote control, a simple grey plastic device with not a hint of PVC or rubber. He passed it across the table, and the Norwegian examined it with interest. I was transferring my attention to the game of pool beside me, when I felt the dildo stir inside me.

I nearly leapt out of my skin. It was as if the inanimate metal bar had suddenly come to life. It quivered inside me like a motorbike engine, setting off the most intense waves of arousal throughout my body. Thankful that it was, at least, silent, I looked imploringly at Max for mercy. He ignored me, and pointed out another button to the man who had unknowingly (or so I hoped) set off the machine.

There was some confusion over the controls, so Max himself leaned over and fiddled with them. I braced myself for an increase in tempo, but was not prepared to feel vibrations in another quarter. There must have been a plate embedded in the very lining of the leather shorts, because they were shaking at the exact spot that was pressed against my clitoris.

The two movements together were astonishingly effective, working on me inside and out, in a way that threatened to bring me rapidly to orgasm. I tried shifting back a little on my stool, but the devices were attached to me too closely for escape. All I could do was cling to my self-control and hope that Max would soon tire of this new game.

Some hope. Max took the control box back and put it into his pocket, and the conversation moved on to other things, but as he slipped it into his jeans, he very deliberately flicked a third switch. Now the dildo was not only throbbing, but also rotating inside me. I was being churned from within, like thick cream.

I tried to steady my breathing, to fight against the excitement that threatened to overpower me. Not only was I too embarrassed to let Max's group see me lose control – some of them for the second time in our brief acquaintance – but it felt too degrading to be brought to orgasm in this mechanical way, with a remote control, of all things. I fought the ripples of pleasure that spread out from my centre and my tingling clit, overlapping as they met to create waves too strong for me to ignore.

More than anything, though, I knew that to come without Max's direct command would bring down punishment on me that could be painful. As I smiled and sipped my beer, I squirmed inwardly at Max's cruelty. He even glanced over at me as he talked about our ride up through the Alps, as if to include me in the conversation, though I merely nodded affirmation. I did not want to add speaking out of turn to my list of punishable misdemeanours.

Max slipped a hand into his pocket to bring out a box of matches, taking the opportunity to increase the pace of the dildo's rotation. I couldn't believe that a mere device could exercise this power over my responses, but I could feel my breathing quickening and my ribs pushing against the corset's boning as I fought for equilibrium. I actually felt that I might faint and fall off the stool.

What subtle and perverse cruelty to ensure I was deprived of an orgasm when he took his, in private, and then drive me towards one in public! I begged him with my eyes to desist, or at least to give me permission to give in to the effects of this device.

He turned to me at last and asked casually, 'Are you feeling all right?'

'No, Master,' I answered shakily, hoping that he would take me home under the pretext of illness.

The eyes of the group were on me now, and I tried to preserve the illusion of normality while suggesting mild illness.

'What's the matter?' asked Max, 'Do you want to come? Do you want to have an orgasm here, in front of all my friends, like some kind of a slut?'

I couldn't believe he had said it so baldly, but with the flood of shame came relief.

'Yes, Sir, please,' I panted, every muscle tensed against losing control.

Max did not reply, but produced the grey remote control from his pocket. Handing it back to the Norwegian, he said, 'See how long she can hold out.' Then he turned back to me.

'I forbid you to come,' he said. 'If you do, you will be punished. Understand?'

Yes, Sir,' I whispered. Even as I spoke, the Norwegian was playing with the controls, increasing the speed and the tempo of the vibrations against my clit, and varying the pace of the dildo. He seemed delighted to discover that his actions had an immediate effect on me.

I gripped the sides of the stool in an attempt to hang on also to my body's responses, but at a nod from Max, one of his gang came behind me and grabbed my elbows. He pulled my arms back, forcing my chest forwards against the corset and making me struggle to breathe normally. My breasts rose and fell so strongly that the chiffon scarf fell to the floor, exposing me to the watching men.

They were enjoying this game, eagerly watching the Norwegian's hands at the control, as if I were nothing but a human Scalextric set, or a PlayStation. When I did the striptease in the clubhouse, I had been the one in control. Now the tables were turned completely. I had no control: not even over my own orgasm. With humiliation, I noted that one of the men had his watch out, apparently counting the seconds until I gave in to the machine.

A black-haired girl with a pierced lip came down the stairs and over to our table to collect the empty beer glasses. She cast a curious glance at me, but at the sight of the insignia on my collar, her eyes flicked to Max and she took the glasses away without a word. I was alone again with this pack of men who were baiting me like an animal.

Max put a hand into his carrier bag. 'Try this,' he said to one of his men, and passed a small rubber thing across the table. The man behind me pulled me to my feet and walked me over to the pool table, where he pushed me forwards, still holding on to my arms. I pressed my face into the green baize. The change of angle had pushed the dildo deeper into me, and forced the vibrating plate still tighter against my clitoris.

Then I felt something through the hole at the back of the shorts, something cool and smooth. Held down as I was over the table, I couldn't see what was happening, but I could clearly feel that something was being inserted into the hole, and into me. My anus clenched around something the size of a man's finger, but firmer. It slid a couple of inches inside me, then I heard Max say something in Dutch.

I was manhandled on to my back on the table, one man holding my wrists above my head, though I was making no move to resist. With a flourish, the Norwegian hit a button, and the new invader in my rear entrance began to quiver.

Now I was being shipwrecked on the waves of three separate currents, one in each hole and one at the front. If a man could have produced these vibrations unaided, he would have been the most skilful lover ever born. Even two or three people would have done well to set off such intense feelings of pleasure in me. But what was making my back arch and my thighs tremble was a mere gadget, and it was turning me into an arcade game for a group of men to whom I was nothing but Max's latest toy.

They gathered around the pool table for a better view. Only Max still sat and drank his beer, his cool blue eyes on me for any sign of transgression. My hips rocked on the green cloth in time with the dildo's throbbing, and the Norwegian whooped. I had fantasised about being stretched out on a pool table and used by a group of men, but in my scenario they had been fucking me in person. This was a situation in which I alone lost control, and they stood fully dressed around me.

The operator of the control was becoming expert in using all three buttons to combine the effects of the vibrators. I looked up into the eyes of the watching men and saw cruel excitement as well as laddish fun. They were enjoying my helpless arousal as much as I had enjoyed teasing the audience with my strip show. They would not be happy until they had seen me climax in spite of myself.

I looked imploringly into Max's eyes as I came, sobbing with shame and ecstasy, jerking in the leather shorts that kept dildo and plug drilling relentlessly into my softest, most sensitive places. His eyes were cold and pitiless, promising me that I would suffer for this disobedience. I anticipated the pain I would feel from his hand, but it could not extinguish the pleasure that made me writhe on the pool table. After holding out for so long, I lingered in the oblivion of orgasm for what felt like hours. Only after the last shudders of release had subsided did the Norwegian turn off the equipment and let me lie still.

The men turned away, returned to their seats, chatting in light-hearted excitement about the novelty of the remote-control woman. I lay, breathing heavily, my body lax and heavy on the cloth-covered slate of the table. I did not dare look back at Max, afraid to read the displeasure in his eyes. Finally he stood, and I looked at his impassive face.

'Emma, did you come without permission?'

'Yes, Sir,' I said, my heart beating in apprehension.

'Then I must take you home for your punishment,' he said.

The Norwegian and the other visitors exchanged amused smiles at this, but Max's men, the ones who knew him, looked soberly at us. I shivered as I caught one of them look at me; it was the look you give to somebody who doesn't yet know how much trouble they are in. I followed Max up the stairs to the exit, dreading the moment when he got me back into his private world, but also feeling an illicit thrill of anticipation.

As usual, Max was not going to throw away my suspense too quickly. From the garage the lift rose straight to the bedroom and I stepped out into the red glow, bracing myself for whatever cruel games he had in mind. I stood, still and obedient, as he hung his jacket up by the door.

'Turn around,' he ordered, and clipped my cuffs together so my hands were once more fastened behind me.

Then he pointed to the bed.

'Sleep,' he said. I lay awkwardly on the fur cover, dressed as I was and still wearing the crippling boots. Max stripped off his T-shirt and jeans and lay beside me, pulling the edges of the fur over us both. Then, with a hand down to some control beside the bed, he dimmed the lights almost to black.

His breathing told me that he fell asleep fast and deeply. I lay listening to him. With my arms behind me, I could only lie on my side, and even that was far from comfortable, especially with the corset digging into me. I also still had the dildo rammed up me, and now the thick mass of the butt-plug also kept me aware that I was kitted up for instant stimulation at the touch of a finger.

After a while I stopped trying to find a comfortable position and resigned myself to discomfort. As the prospect of immediate pain receded, I began to find my state mildly arousing. Even in his sleep, Max was reminding me that I was his slave, bound and dressed, ready for him to use. His warm, naked skin beside me gave off his unique smell – male sweat, leather and a faint tang of motorcycle oil. I wanted to rub myself against him, to feel his firm muscles with my bare nipples, but I was afraid to wake him and be caught taking my pleasure without permission.

Tiredness seeped into me. Apart from a short nap on the sofa I had not slept since we left Alexandra's villa, and that felt like a lifetime ago. Jane's villa, and the shock of finding Kit prepared to sell me to Max, felt like another life. This weird existence, which had become my only reality, was more like an imagined fantasy. I still couldn't believe Kit had done what he did. I told myself it had been arranged to teach me a lesson; for being so stupidly reckless on the bikes that day and ultimately responsible for causing Kit considerable pain and inconvenience. I thought it over and over and eventually I found that I was lying unresisting in my bonds and sleep overtook me.

Some time later, half-awake, I went to roll over and was confused to find myself unable to free my arm from behind me. I blinked against the light in my face, realising with a start that I was still cuffed and still in the bed. Max stood above me, looking down thoughtfully at my half-naked form. He was already dressed, and had in his hand a glass of orange juice, which he held out to me. I wriggled to a sitting position and drank as he held it to my lips.

It was humiliating to be unable to use my hands, but there was something comforting about being given a drink like a small child or a much-loved pet. As Max took the glass away I saw that in his other hand was a glossy black whip, its coils plaited from leather thongs, and its handle adorned with the familiar insignia of the eagle claw gripping a snake by its throat. He saw my eyes go to it before rising to meet his in a silent question.

'Yes,' he said, 'it's time for your punishment.' He motioned me to lie face down on the bed and I tensed, ready for the first blow. Instead, I felt his hands undoing the buckles on my shorts, and pulling them off. As the plug and dildo slid out of me, I felt suddenly empty, the cool air flowing fresh over my shaved skin. Then he unlaced the corset and finally released my hands.

'First, wash yourself.' Max pointed to a glass cubicle in one corner, where a high-tech shower hung over a stone tray. I took off my remaining clothes and boots, noting the indentations on my skin where my body had yielded to the shape imposed on it. Max was busy with something in the corner of the room, some kind of frame on which he was fitting straps. I felt my insides lurch as I pictured myself stretched upon it, helpless under the lash.

Standing in the shower, aware that Max could see my every move, I surreptitiously examined my body. Apart from the creases left by the corset, and faint pressure marks from the cuffs, I was unmarked. My rear hole felt slightly stretched, but not sore. I wanted to slip a soapy finger in to see if it really was looser after a night pursed around a rubber plug, but I feared Max's disapproval if I touched myself without his command.

I stepped out on to the floor, noticing for the first time that it seemed to be covered in black rubber, studded for a better grip. Without even thinking, I replaced my collar; already I felt naked without it. As I rubbed myself dry, I looked at what Max had been preparing for me, and felt delicious fear dart through me.

It was a ring of metal, toothed around the outside edge, like a giant cog. On the inside, four leather cuffs were bolted, ready for my hands and feet. The thick links of a chain around the wheel allowed it to be turned, so the slave suspended within it could be whichever way up her master chose. The chrome glinted coldly in the daylight. Max held out a hand to me, palm up in perverse gallantry, a twinkle in his blue eyes.

'Come on, slut,' he said. 'Time to receive your punishment.'

I stepped towards him and placed my wrist in his hand. The leather cuff closed around it, holding my hand firmly against the cold steel. My other hand was pulled out and fixed in place, my arms stretched wide and high above my head. Then Max buckled my ankles into their restraints, stretching my legs even wider than the metal bar had done, so I felt the pull along my thighs.

I hung, my sex throbbing already at the thought that I was completely at Max's mercy. I knew that he was about to hurt me, but still I longed for this, to be dominated and possessed by him. Silently he looked at me, a light burning in his icy blue eyes the only sign that he found my state arousing. 'Slave, what do you wish me to punish you for?' he asked.

'For disobeying your command,' I answered.

'What command, slave?' he asked, stroking my defenceless nipple with a rough palm.

'Your command that I was not to come, Sir,' I replied, my clit already pulsing in excitement.

Without another word, Max turned and picked up the whip, and walked around me so I could no longer see him. A crack like a gunshot rang through the room, and

I jerked involuntarily against my bonds. I flinched again as my bare buttock felt a touch, but it was only the gentle stroking of Max's hand. Now I shivered in fear, remembering how the alternation of pain and pleasure had heightened my senses to both; how the intensity of each blow had seared me even through my leathers before turning to a glow of well being.

I willed my skin to ignore the temptation of the caressing hand, to stay resolutely insensitive, but it was too late. I could feel the air moving over my rear when the lash of the whip struck it with a loud snap. A low sound escaped me through gritted teeth, as the path of the whip burned on my skin. Now I prepared for more caresses, but a second blow took me by surprise and I cried aloud.

This was more painful than anything I had felt at Max's hands. As the whip fell again, the strokes criss-crossing my rear in a steady rhythm, I forgot everything except the waves of pain that hit me, turning each time to the heat of arousal. After half a dozen lashes I heard Max step towards me, and then I felt his hand at my pussy. He pushed a finger into me and found me moist, then rubbed a few times at my clit. The pain of my whipped behind had already receded into a stinging soreness that added to the pleasure of his fondling.

He moved his caresses up my bare back, his hand softly straying over my shoulders and around my flanks. I was almost starting to relax when the next whiplash came, a long stroke that snaked from my shoulder down across my skin almost to my waist. Now my whole back was his target, and I writhed in vain as the burning trail of his whip drew a grid of smarting that covered me from neck to waist.

Again, the short offering of pleasure twisted the after-burn of the pain into a dark glow of excitement, and then I was spinning in my wheel. I heard the cog mesh into the chain with metallic clunks, as my feet were turned from under me and my head fell sideways. Already disorientated by the alternating pain and pleasure, I felt weightless as I spun, turning over a few times before I came to rest, head down, hanging from my ankles.

Max recommenced his preparatory stroking, this time over my thighs and calves. I whimpered, knowing how sensitive the skin on my legs was, and how much more the whip would hurt there, yet Max would have paid more attention to me if I had been a squeaking brake pad on his motorbike. The first blow of the whip caught both thighs, and left a momentary trace as sharp as if I had been cut with a knife. My legs blazed with his lashes.

Now Max came around to the front of the wheel and stood in front of me. I looked up at him where he stood in his black leather. Once more I trembled to see the cruel lust in his eyes. My head hung level with his belt, and I could see the bulge below the merciless grip of the silver eagle's claw. It excited me to know that he was so aroused.

'You are looking at my penis?' he asked softly.

'Yes, Sir,' I answered.

With his free hand, Max undid the buttons of his jeans and freed himself. His cock sprang forwards, swollen and already glistening with moisture. 'You want to suck it, don't you?' he teased.

My mouth watered at the words. To hang there and take him between my lips was a thought so thrilling that my sex clenched in anticipation.

Max laughed harshly. Since my hairless mound was at his eye level, I must have betrayed myself immediately to him.

'Yes, Master,' I answered aloud. 'Please let me suck your cock.'

'Not yet,' was his only reply. Instead, he began to run

his hand over my belly and breasts. Surely he didn't intend to use his whip on these sensitive areas?

'No, Master, please,' I begged him, forgetting in my fear the rule of speaking only when I was spoken to.

But Max had not forgotten it, and a spiteful pinch of my nipple reminded me.

'It is not your place to tell me no,' he said. Then he walked over to the mirror-doored cabinet and returned with something I couldn't see. I was rotated again, but only halfway, so I hung horizontally from one arm and one leg. My whole back still glowed, from nape to ankle.

Max pushed a leather bar into my mouth, stretching the corners of my lips back as he tightened the strap behind my head. It was more a bit than a gag, but it still muffled my frightened whimpering as he spun me back to my inverted position and resumed his caressing of my breasts. I closed my eyes as he raised the whip, and felt it sting across my belly.

The lashes ignited my skin, each blow planting a row of fleeting pain that seeded stinging and then a rush of blood that brought strange invigoration. When he had set me afire from collar to navel, Max gently rubbed my wet pussy once again. My nipples throbbed with twisted arousal, and my clit leapt to feel Max's tongue flick against it. Now it was a groan of pleasure that the bit distorted into an incoherent grunt.

He looked down at me, then bent to remove the bit from my mouth.

'Thank you, Sir,' I said, eager to please him.

'Good girl,' he said. 'Will you ever disobey me again?'

'No, Sir,' I promised him, 'I will never disobey you again.'

'Then you may please me as you asked,' he said. He stood close to me, and held his prick to my lips.

'Suck me,' he ordered.

I opened my mouth and sucked him into me, tasting

the clean salty skin. Now the aftermath of the pain had turned to the slow fire of excitement, I felt grateful submission to Max, and the thought of my complete surrender to him thrilled me darkly. Now I was truly his slave, serving him exactly as he commanded. He could keep me hanging here for days, rotating me at will to bring any of my orifices to a convenient height for penetration.

I swung my head against him, moving my lips up and down his shaft, working my tongue over the head. If I was going to be a willing object, I was going to do a good job of it. My body twitched as I felt the wet touch of Max's tongue on my clit. My sex was already tingling from his caresses, and almost unbearably sensitive. Determined not to disobey him again, I fought against my own arousal and tried to concentrate on pleasuring him.

His tongue ran up and down my cleft, plunging into my pussy and returning to lap against my clit. At the same time, he began to thrust against my mouth, his hand on the back of my head to steady it against him. As his tongue delved further into me, I felt his cock sliding deeper into my mouth, touching the back of my throat with every stroke.

Then, tongue still exploring, he pushed a wet finger into my other hole. I knew I couldn't resist this double stimulation, sensitised as I was. His finger flicked gently, setting off delicious contractions that made me groan against his cock.

Max lifted his face, his beard shiny with my juices, and looked at my quivering sex.

'Come now,' he said, and bent to flick his tongue against my hungry clit. My whole body shook with the violence of my climax, and my cries were only muffled by his eager thrusting into my mouth. I was still trembling with my own receding orgasm as he came down my throat.

I was spent, hanging from aching ankles, Max's seed dripping from my face on to the rubber floor. He stood back, his face shiny with sweat, and looked down at me. In his eyes shone gratitude, affection even.

'Thank you, Master,' I said, and he smiled a warm, open smile.

'It is my pleasure, sweet slave,' he replied.

12

It was strange to roll into the port on the back of Max's bike. I turned my head to see the dozen other bikes that followed us, remembering the first time I had seen Max and his group in the hold of that other ferry. Now it was I who bent obediently to tether the sleek black cruiser as the others pulled up alongside it. Max watched critically, less concerned to enjoy the view up my leather skirt than to ensure his precious bike would suffer no damage during the crossing. As I straightened up, I half expected to see my old self watching, standing hand-in-hand with Kit on that first day of our honeymoon.

I shivered, as if I had seen a ghost. I couldn't even say how long I had been in Max's apartment: days, weeks, maybe. I was so moulded to his life that he seldom had to give me a direct order now. I anticipated his needs, sexual or otherwise. And, when he felt like it, Max anticipated mine.

Now, for example, he took me straight to the on-board restaurant, knowing I would be cold and hungry. Over my uniform of corset, collar and cuffs I wore a black leather jacket, Max's eagle and snake insignia stitched on the back. Nobody stared at the accoutrements of my enslavement, though I did see a few eyes following my legs between the short skirt and the long boots.

We weren't the only group of motorcyclists on the ferry. I had not asked, of course, where we were going, but from the conversations I overheard it was clear that all of us were headed for a big biker gathering. I hoped it was somewhere near the port; it was already midafternoon when we disembarked, and my heart sank at the thought of a long night shivering behind Max on a moving bike.

The deference Max commanded was still in evidence. The other groups of bikers on the ferry pulled to one side and let us pass, so ours was the first bike to roll on to the quayside. I turned my head as we swung on to the road, to see the long stream of black leather and shining metal, like a mediaeval army going forth. Though I was nobody here – my only status that of Max's property – I felt a rush of pride and excitement to be part of such a horde.

With the sinking sun in our eyes, we rode across flat countryside along straight roads edged by ditches. The thunder of our engines filled the silence, drowning out the birdsong and the sounds of the tractors working in the fields. We met little traffic, and what there was pulled aside to let us pass with ease.

As the sky began to darken to a dull gold, we pulled off the road at a sign that read 'Serpent Hall'. The long drive ran between two rows of oak trees, straight towards a grand old country house. This certainly didn't look like any biker clubhouse I had ever seen. Then, as Max rode through the wrought-iron gates on to the stone-paved carriage sweep, a slender, imperious figure stepped out of the front door, and I recognised Alexandra.

I stood respectfully by while Max dismounted, eager to show Alexandra how well I had been trained since last we met. She still held that riding crop, I noted. Then, to my surprise, Max pointed to the bike. 'Take it to the stables,' he said, 'the others will show you where.' I stood confused. Ride Max's precious bike? I had never seen him let anybody else do more than clean it.

Alexandra's riding crop stung across my bare leg.

'Quick, girl, your Master has spoken,' she said.

Swiftly, I swung my legs back over the saddle, sitting for the first time in Max's seat. I kicked up the side stand and let the bike roll forwards, following the stream of other machines around the side of the house. It was lower and heavier than I was used to, but nothing unusual to ride. Mindful that the bike probably stood higher than me in Max's affections, though, I took great care as I rode smoothly between Max's followers and into the stall they had reserved for it in the stable block.

I thought again of the mediaeval king and his followers, as we sat down to dine in the banqueting hall. There must have been nearly a hundred bikers along two huge tables, and the uncouth clamour was very like the one that probably echoed through a castle hall in the Middle Ages.

I sat beside Max at the top table, along with Alexandra and a couple of other men. There were a few women among the bikers below, some here as pillions and others riding their own bikes, but the atmosphere was overwhelmingly masculine. Feeling Alexandra's stern gaze on me, I took care to anticipate Max's every need, keeping his cup and plate full all evening.

As the meal ended, Alexandra stood and clapped her hands.

'Enjoy the hospitality of my home,' she said in a loud voice. 'Head riders of each chapter, we will convene in the library for our meeting in fifteen minutes.'

Max rose to follow her out, and I stood too, uncertain of whether I should follow. Alexandra glanced at me, and exchanged a look with Max.

'And you,' she said to me, 'since you are so much improved, are ready to meet Otto.' She turned, and I followed her out, trembling with excitement and alarm. Who was this Otto with who even Max could not compete? And why had he not been with us for dinner?

As we left the house and headed for the stable block,

my alarm turned to panic. Was he some kind of mino-taur, too terrible for the human gaze? Or was Otto an animal? Looking at Alexandra's erect gait and tightly laced waist, I could believe that her irreplaceable partner was a slavering dog, beaten into perfect submission, or a big glossy stallion.

Indeed, Alexandra swung open the door of a stable. My eyes fought to adjust to the gloom, and I strained my ears for the rough breathing of a thoroughbred horse. Silence. Then Alexandra hit the light switch and I saw, glossy and sleek, gorgeously curved and extravagantly adorned with polished metal, a huge, powerful motor-bike. Alexandra's figure-of-eight snake insignia was tooled on to the tank.

'Otto,' said Alexandra, 'I have brought you a new playmate.'

I gaped. My eyes, running over the vision of inspired engineering before me, had caught on an interruption to the classic lines. There, in the middle of the black leather saddle, stood an erect penis, moulded as one with the upholstery.

'Come, Emma,' she said, and I walked behind her towards the bike. I wanted to reach out and stroke that unique feature, at once so realistically crafted and so outrageously proportioned. No wonder even Max felt he could not compete. I wondered if Alexandra allowed any other member to penetrate her, or if Otto truly was the only male allowed to fuck her.

Alexandra lifted up my skirt, nodding with approval when she saw my bare sex, still shaved.

'You may ride Otto,' she said simply. 'Stay here till I return.' Then, with a rustle of leather petticoats, she was gone. I looked at the bike in front of me, wondering whether I could actually get it out of the stable. Then I realised that Otto's rear wheel was mounted on a rolling road, allowing it to spin without moving the bike, and that a large fan was mounted in the wall behind, clearly designed to carry out the exhaust fumes before the rider could be choked by them.

So she really did mean me to ride Otto in the sexual sense. I ran a hand over the leather prick, admiring the silky smoothness of the finish and the detail of each ridge and vein. This time I was glad this was a low-seated cruiser bike, as I slipped a booted leg over the saddle and on to the footrest. Even standing on tiptoe, I could only just lift myself high enough to place the tip of Otto's penis at the lips of my sex.

I slid myself down on to it, feeling the ridges grate against my inner folds, and bobbed up and down a few times. It was wonderful to feel the length of it inside me, and a wonderful change to be completely in control. With Max I was always under his control, and often so immobilised that I could do nothing but submit to his actions.

Wanting more stimulation, I turned the keys and looked for the ignition button. Of course – Otto was clearly an old-school gentleman, with no new-fangled electric start switches. I felt for the start lever and felt my pussy push against Otto's penis as I kicked down hard on the kick-start. At once, he juddered into life, sending delicious vibrations through the whole chassis. The petrol tank shook against my clit, and the leather prick quivered inside me.

This was good, but I was eager to explore what else Otto had to offer me. Pulling in the clutch lever, I kicked the bike into first gear and let the clutch out gently. We didn't glide forwards, of course, but I was quite unready for what did happen. As first gear engaged, the prick began to thrust inside me, a simple in-and-out motion that rubbed excitingly against my sensitive parts.

This was very interesting. I pulled the throttle open a little, and felt the thrusting speed up. By rolling the power on and off, I could get Otto to change his pace to my requirements, the general vibrations through me following the same rhythm. I pushed him to the limit, watching the needle on the rev counter creep past 12,000 revs and into the red as Otto's thrusts went frantic. I laughed. This was, indeed, the ultimate riding machine.

Wondering if I could get more speed out of Otto, I put him into second gear. This time, as the clutch bit, the penis started to thrust at an angle, flicking from side to side to hit every part of my inner surfaces. Now, my pulling at the throttle brought faster rotation as well as quicker thrusts. I suddenly began to worry about the imminence of my climax. If Max was not there to give me permission, would I displease him by giving in fully to Otto's capabilities?

Nevertheless, I could not resist trying third gear. Another surprise, as Otto's apparently rigid tool suddenly revealed a degree of flexibility, twitching and writhing inside me more like a snake than any real penis. Alexandra did seem to have created a lover that no real man could match. Fourth gear brought the saddle to life, as the front section rippled against my clit in little waves that gripped it and released it while the penis continued to gyrate within me. I was on the verge of giving in to my excitement and risking the consequences, when the door opened and Max came in.

'Not thinking of coming without permission, I hope?' he asked good-naturedly.

'No, Master,' I panted.

'Good,' he replied, 'because I was hoping you could take me for a ride.' He swung his leg over the seat behind me and sat down, the leather of his jeans rubbing against my bum in time with Otto's engine.

'Very nice,' declared Max. I could feel him swelling against my back already.

He slipped his hand around my front and into the top

of my corset. My nipples, which were being shaken against the leather of the corset, were already stiff and tender, and he rolled them between finger and thumb. His mouth was nibbling my neck above the collar, so I arched my head back to give him better access.

Then I felt his other hand pushing under me from behind, touching my lips where Otto's penis was pumping in and out, feeling the wetness of my excitement. I wriggled against his fingers as he played with my shaven skin, and sighed with pleasure as he slid a wet finger into the opening of my smaller hole.

'You filthy slut,' he whispered in my ear, 'even Otto's not enough cock for you.'

I could already feel Max undoing his jeans behind me, but he said, 'Go on, ask me.'

'Please, Master,' I gasped, 'please sodomise me.'

His penis rubbed against my buttocks as I bounced, but still he repeated, 'What do you want?'

'Please, Sir,' I begged, 'please fuck me up the arse. I want your cock up my arse.'

'Very well,' he said, and pushed me roughly forwards over the petrol tank.

I heard Max open a small tin and felt him smear something warm and slippery around my anus. The familiar dirty smell of mechanic's grease rose to my nostrils as he massaged it around my opening, pushing a careful finger in to open me to him. Then I felt his penis sliding into my well-oiled ring of muscle. Otto's mechanical cock continued to pump away inside me as Max pushed his hot flesh into my other channel.

This time there was no pain as he slipped in easily, and the pleasure was unbelievable. Max's thrusts kept time with the engine that was bouncing us both on the leather saddle and fucking me with mechanical precision from the front.

Laid forwards over the tank, even my nipples were

pressed against the vibrating metal. It was a motorbike turned into a vast vibrator, and it was working on me everywhere except where Max himself was caressing me, kissing my neck and running his rough hands over my flanks and buttocks.

'Give it more revs,' he whispered, and I pulled obediently on the throttle, feeling the two cocks, human and machine, quicken their thrusts in perfect synchronisation. I was fast approaching my climax, watching the needle creep towards the red line as if it were the dial of my own excitement, inexorably rising to the point of no return.

The needle passed 10,000 revs, 11,000. I knew that when it passed into the red, so would I. As it lined up with the 1 of 12,000 I heard at last Max's voice. 'Come now,' he panted, and my cries were drowned out by the roaring of Otto's engine as it hit its limits. Max had to reach over my shoulder and turn the ignition off, as I lay gasping over the tank. In the silence I heard the hot metal clicking.

'Thank you, Master,' I said.

'Thank you, *Otto*,' Max corrected.

With the rising sun behind us casting long shadows on the road ahead, we cavalcaded out of the iron gates and back on to the road. Beside Max's bike now rode Alexandra on Otto. Her full leather skirt was strapped around her boots, giving an effect like Cossack britches. The folds of the skirt were bunched in her lap, and I couldn't help stealing a curious look, wondering whether she was riding Otto in both senses of the word.

As we left the flat fen country behind, the sun rose higher and warmed my back through the leather jacket. The landscape was softening into gentle hills, and we passed through small towns built in brick or golden stone. The rumble of so many bikes was a hypnotic song, a droning chorus over which the deep roar of Otto and the snarl of Max's bike rose and fell like a baritone duet. As we reached the brow of a long rise, I looked over my shoulder and saw the sunlight turning our dust to golden haze, in which the black shapes of so many riders faded to shadows.

Alexandra looked magnificent, sitting upright in her tight-waisted leather coat, black gauntlets on her slender arms. Beneath the shades, her mouth was a narrow slash of plum red, the merest hint of a smile playing at the corners. There was no sign of the two slaves I had met in Italy, but another woman rode behind her on a smaller bike, also marked with Alexandra's serpent emblem.

As the air grew hotter, I opened my jacket a little, trying not to reveal my collar to public gaze. Without looking around, Max told me to take it off. I hesitated; although I was getting too hot, I was only wearing the corset underneath, and the cuffs would be clearly visible to anyone else on the road. Max repeated his instruction, this time with no ambiguity.

'Take the jacket off.'

I obeyed, enjoying the flow of warm air over my bare shoulders, trying not to notice the stares of drivers we passed.

More bikes joined the cavalcade, all kinds of machines from slick sports designs to muddy off-roaders. Riders waiting at junctions nodded a respectful greeting to Max and Alexandra, then pulled out and tucked into the crowd. We must be getting close, I thought, but still we rode on and on, an unstoppable tide.

Then I saw the first steward, a leather-jacketed man with a shaved head and heavy moustache who stood at a junction, apparently waiting for us. He had a black flag, which he swung to direct us on to the left-hand fork of the road. At every major turning-point or landmark, another man waited to show us the route and, in some cases, to bar the oncoming traffic while the stream of bikes poured across the road. Each of them wore the same black T-shirt, sporting a white dragon spitting flames.

These small country roads were now dominated by the flow of bikes that poured in from all directions. The few cars and vans we encountered had to sit patiently and let us pass. None of the drivers made any protest and, looking back at the army of riders that followed us, eyes hidden behind shades, limbs clothed in a uniform of denim and leather, I didn't blame them.

Then we passed a steward signalling us to slow down, and saw our destination ahead. Across a farm gateway, a massive arch of scaffolding had been erected, topped with a glinting metal dragon that crouched menacingly, snarling down at the queue of bikes waiting to get in. A cloud of bluish smoke hovered above them, as if the dragon was breathing fire for real.

Alexandra's follower pulled ahead and rode straight to the head of the queue, passing the throng of waiting bikes. A few voices were raised in protest, but they quickly fell silent when they saw her insignia and who came behind her. The mass of machines parted before us, and Max and Alexandra rode side by side to the gate. All eyes were on us, and each rider we passed nodded deferentially to Max.

A thrill of pride ran through me; everyone here recognised Max's power, and I was with him, chosen by him. Underneath the pride I felt a shameful frisson to know that everyone here could see my collar and knew what it meant: that I was Max's property, his slave, his plaything. Though they would not dare to show me disrespect now, in their minds they were already picturing me at Max's mercy, used by him, perhaps punished and degraded.

At the gate, the man taking the money waved us through, and we entered the ground. Music was already coming from the big blue tent ahead of us, and fairground rides were moving beyond it. As we got closer, riding between makeshift campsites and rows of bikes parked beside the muddy road, I saw more structures around the music tent: marquees and toilet blocks; seating stands and rows of stalls like a bazaar.

I forgot to be self-conscious about my collar as I looked around me. Though people were still arriving, a steady trickle of bikes laden with camping equipment heading for the grassy areas around the site, there was already a buzz of activity. A small crowd was gathered around the Test Your Strength sideshow, mostly young men out to prove themselves to their mates. Another popular attraction seemed to be simply a bike wash, but as we rode past I saw that the girls wielding the sponges were dressed only in tiny G-strings. One man had chosen to stay on his bike and be washed with it, and grinned as a pair of soapy breasts was rubbed in his face.

As we rode towards a fenced-off area, the gate was opened for us. Max pulled up beside a classic American trailer, a long sheath of corrugated metal. I stood admiring the clean, simple shape as Max dismounted.

'You didn't expect me to sleep in a tent, did you?' he asked teasingly.

'No, Sir,' I answered.

It was true, I had wondered how the fastidious Max, so used to luxury, would cope with the mud and shower blocks. The trailer was small, compared to his spacious Dutch apartment, but it had the basic comforts of home: fridge, shower and central heating. Max lay back on the generous bed, already made up with a duvet and suede bedspread. I opened the fridge, and was pleased to find beer already chilling there. As was now my habit, I opened a bottle and handed it to Max.

'If you need anything while we are here,' he said as he sipped the beer, 'ask one of the stewards. Your collar will be sign enough of whose you are.'

'Yes, Master,' I answered.

He stretched out his legs towards me, ordering me to undress him, then telling me I could have a drink while he showered. I knelt to pull off his boots. Every movement was instinctive now. I could perform each duty just as Max liked it, without him needing to say anything.

I watched him walk naked across the trailer and into the shower, the muscles shifting beneath his skin. His easy gait belied his strength, but the power in his arms and shoulders was hinted at by the sculpted blocks of his flesh. A glow of desire warmed me, but I knew that the merest hint of interest on my part would only guarantee a longer wait. Max derived great pleasure from keeping me in suspense.

Just as I suspected, he was keen to get out of the trailer and look around the site. I followed him as he strolled through the display of customised motorbikes, admiring the artistry in paint and metalwork, and wondering how it was possible to ride some of the more extreme modifications. One cruiser had front forks as long as the bike itself, the front wheel a good five feet away from the handlebars.

Everybody seemed to know Max. Every few yards he stopped for a brief conversation, leaving me free to stare around me. I was intrigued by the stalls, which seemed to be selling not only bike accessories and clothes, but a range of other things from aromatherapy candles to crossbows. Catching sight of a stall offering fetish clothing, vibrators and bondage equipment, I averted my eyes before Max decided to buy me more presents. As usual, he was too quick for me, though.

'Thinking about a little shopping?' he asked me, his blue eyes twinkling.

'No, Sir,' I muttered.

'Pity,' he said as we walked on. 'I hoped you might be planning to surprise me.'

He was more relaxed with me on this trip than he had been in Amsterdam. Perhaps he felt that I had been trained enough, and could be allowed a longer leash. I smiled inwardly at my own choice of analogy. Max had walked me through the streets of his home city on a literal leash one night, punishing me for some minor transgression.

Outside the main tent, from which the raw sounds of a rock band's sound check spilled forth, a board listed the weekend's attractions. We could expect music from noon till eleven, including some major bands I would not have expected to find performing at a biker rally. Then, for the final hour before midnight, the board simply listed a 'live show'. Max pointed to it.

'You know what that is?' he asked me.

'No, Master,' I replied.

'The live sex show,' he told me.

I looked at him in some alarm. Did he intend to add me to the menu, to have me perform some degrading act in front of thousands of bikers? Even as the fear shot through me, a thrill of excitement quivered between my legs. Max laughed.

'You'd like that, wouldn't you?' he said. 'Performing to all those men. Dirty slut. No, I have something else in mind for you.'

I followed him away, relieved and disappointed all at once.

The noise of music diminished, and another sound took over as we approached the stands: bike engines, pushed to their limits, reverberating in the hollow of the racetrack. Max led me into the pit lane, walking close to the wall of the sheds to keep well clear of the bikes coming in from the track. I gazed enviously at the sports bikes tearing around the curves – the riders' knees grazing the tarmac as they leaned over. I missed my Ducati. I was trying not to think how much I missed Kit as well.

Max was talking to a man seated at a table, and seemed to have agreed something.

'First heat, ten o'clock sharp,' the man said.

Max returned to me, and followed my gaze to where the bikes were flicking over in a sharp change of direction between bends.

'Think my bike could get around that?' he asked.

I looked doubtfully at him. Max's bike was not designed for fast cornering, but for the kind of long, straight cruising we had been doing all the way here.

I opted for the tactful reply. 'If anybody could get around it, you could,' I said.

It was true; Max was a consummate rider. Even so, I wouldn't have put money on him to outrun a sports bike on this track.

'That's a shame,' he said, watching a rider hurtle by, 'because you are going to be the one riding it.'

13

I looked ahead at the lights above the starting grid. From the moment I had rolled Max's powerful machine on to the smooth tarmac of the pit lane, my nerves had vanished and I felt only calm anticipation. In fact, I was happy to be here. It was a few years since I had last raced a motorbike, and that had been an informal affair on a track day – a little game to finish off an afternoon of concentrated learning.

This was the full Monty: starting lights, marshals' flags, the works. I was only sorry that instead of a nippy race bike I was riding Max's heavy cruiser. I had already abandoned hope of winning this race, and I felt I'd be doing well if I got it back without dropping it on a corner. Putting a dent or scratch on Max's pride and joy was more than my life was worth.

I checked out my rivals. Everyone else was on something more sporty than my mount, but several were unfaired, streetfighter-style muscle bikes. The most impressive machine was a brand-new Japanese race bike, not a scuff on the sleek white fairing, that purred between the legs of its rider. He was in white race leathers, a perfect match for the bike, distinguished only by a snarling fox's head picked out in white stitching on his back.

He was almost a total contrast to me. I was the most unlikely looking racer on the grid, straddling Max's black lump of a bike, and dressed in an outfit more fit for the late-night 'live show' than for riding. Max had given me a package only that morning containing a black all-in-one suit made to my exact measurements. However, it was made not from tough leather but from skintight PVC.

As I had turned around in the trailer to let Max admire the effect, I was reminded of the suit I wore for the film shoot. This was far better on me, cut to show off my curves exactly. It would offer me little protection if I came off, but I had no intention of doing anything that would leave a mark on the bike, or on me. A scattering of people had turned out to watch the racing, mostly sitting in the stands with coffee and bacon rolls. I stretched, arching my back, and heard a couple of wolf whistles.

The arctic fox turned his head and caught my eye. There was no friendly competition in his gaze, only a sneer of contempt, for me or for my unsuitable mount, I couldn't tell. My blood was fired with a fierce competitive urge. I might look out of place here, all kinky catsuit and old-fashioned biker equipment, but I knew I could ride. You may have the shiniest, most expensive machine, I thought angrily, but let's see what you can do with it.

The lights turned to green, and we were off. Max's bike did not take off as fast as its lighter, sportier competitors, but it was pulling well. My lighter weight compensated slightly for the weight of metal I was carrying, and there was power in the huge engine if you knew where to find it. What was more, I could see that some of the other riders were new to track riding, and were taking the wrong lines into the first bend.

Pulling the throttle wide open, I accelerated smoothly past them on the inside, just as they had to brake suddenly to avoid running wide. I wished I had time to look back at their faces, but I was too busy testing the bike's limits as we flew out of the bend and into the long straight.

My tactics paid off. I was coming up fast on the next biker, who had obviously had to lose speed to negotiate the tightening radius of the corner. I thanked my stars that I had walked the course this morning, noting where such traps might catch me out. That rider was probably in his tent nursing a hangover while I was reconnoitering the race, I thought, as I pulled past him.

On a straight, Max's bike came into its own, the huge engine piling on the horsepower till even a race bike would struggle to overtake us. I was gaining on the next group of riders, but I knew we were closing on a tight hairpin, and I didn't want to risk entering it too fast. I let the throttle roll off a little and followed the group into the turn.

Still too fast for this hefty machine. Feeling the weight pulling me too quickly towards the wall of tyres that edged the curve, I pressed gently on the back brake, and steered a clean line across the hairpin. My head followed the tarmac where it vanished from my view, and I saw the curve begin to open up into the straight.

I took my moment and accelerated hard and smooth, and the bike found its path straight down the middle of the lane. By halfway down the straight, I had overtaken the group of three bikes. They would probably catch me on the next bend, but I had certainly shaken them up. I grinned below my goggles.

Knowing that this curve was gentle and opened out into the longest straight, I kept my speed quite high on the way in, and picked it up again as soon as I could see the stands that lined the straight. One of the bikes I had just overtaken drew level again just before the first stand, but I matched him and, for half a mile, we rode neck and neck. The crowd roared their encouragement, some shouting for one or other of us, most just shouting in excitement.

I knew that Max was watching from the pit lane, but

he was a blur as we flew past. I had forgotten everything except the exhilaration of racing. The bike and I were one, the track our whole world. The massive pistons pounded furiously beneath me, and inch by inch I drew ahead of the other rider.

Now I had only one more bike to beat: the arctic fox. I saw him ahead of me, entering the long sweep that would take us back to the pit, a good twenty seconds in the lead. I chose a bold line that would get me around that curve in one unchanging arc, screwed up my nerve, and held the throttle steady. The low-slung footplate scraped as the bike leaned low, but the fat tyres held their course. Coming back on to the straight I saw the fox closer ahead. I was gaining on him.

Since his was a true race bike with no mirrors, he had no idea I was there as I narrowed the gap with painful slowness along that straight. He knew what he was doing, picking his line for that first bend so well he hardly had to slow down at all. As I came out of it and opened up my own throttle I swore under my breath to see he had made up his lead by a few yards.

I gave the longer straight all the speed I could, redlining the revs and lying low over the tank to try to make myself a little more aerodynamic. I knew that on the hairpin he could flick that white bike to and fro in a way that Max's beast would never manage. Sure enough, he made back most of the lead I had eaten into on the straight, but after this curve was the dragstrip where I could really do justice to my engine.

Letting the footrest spark all the way around, I kept the gap constant through the bend and emerged less than five seconds behind him. Flattening myself behind the token windscreen, I made my machine scream in agony as I jammed the throttle open and went for my chance.

The fox still didn't know who it was on his tail, but

the noise from the crowd told him that he had competition. It was only fifteen seconds from one end of that strip to the other, but I measured each of those seconds by the pounding of my heart. All my plans to take no risks with the bike or with myself were forgotten. I was prepared to risk anything to beat this man, to avenge that sneering look on the starting grid.

His bike was fast, very fast. Even giving it all I had, I was only gaining on him an inch at a time, and he still went into the last curve a couple of seconds ahead of me. Once again I pushed the bike around that bend as fast as I thought it could stand. He was laid over so far himself that boot and knee were sparking from his plastic sliders all the way around.

He widened the gap by a second on the curve, but we had one lap to go. If I could gain on him the way I did in the last lap, he was mine. I was totally focused on him, watching his lines, looking for any weakness that I could exploit. Again we chased around the twists of the track, the gap between us narrowing on every straight and easing out again after each corner.

At the hairpin we were so close that he turned out as I entered it, and his face was looking almost directly at mine. I wanted some sign that he had seen me – that he knew who it was so close behind him – but he seemed to see only the track ahead. The fox on his leathers snarled back at me as I came out of the curve and on to the long straight only a second behind him.

The crowd was wild, shouting obscenities at us in their excitement. This was my only chance to take him, to put such a distance between us that he would not be able to regain the lead on the final curve. He was heading straight down the middle of the track. If I overtook him on the right, I would enter the curve too tight and have to brake sharply to get around at all. If I came past his left-hand side, there was the danger that he would collide with me as he swung over in preparation for the curve.

I had no longer than a heartbeat to make my decision. In a couple of seconds I would be drawing close to his back tyre, and any big changes in my line would cost me time. I kept left, gambling that I would be able to pass him before he moved that way, and my front wheel edged past his rear one and came level with his foot. Our speeds were so closely matched that we seemed to be moving in slow motion, but the blur of the stands and the pressure of the wind on my face told me that we were moving very fast indeed.

I felt sure I could be level with him in another second, and past him in three, but the corner was hurtling towards us. One thing was certain: if I was sitting here by his back wheel when he began to shift left, he would hit me and we would both be sliding across the tarmac, bikes flying after us.

It didn't even cross my mind to drop back into the safe space behind him. I urged Max's bike on, and saw my rival apparently slipping backwards beside me, but so slowly that it seemed impossible I would ever get past him. The corner was nearly on us; if I were him I would be moving across to the left-hand edge of the road about now.

Then I pulled level with his front wheel and felt, rather than saw, his head flick sideways as he was suddenly aware of my presence. The gap he wanted to move into was abruptly filled by another bike, and he shot backwards out of my gaze, forced to brake so he could tuck in behind me or take a tighter line.

I could still hear the crowd, even over the din of our engines. If I could get around this curve as fast as he did, the race was mine. In fact, since I was now holding the best line through the bend, he would have to match me for speed on an even tighter radius, to have any chance of passing me before the finish line.

I put my absolute trust in the bike, letting my eyes trace the path I wanted to follow through the corner, and holding the throttle steady all the way round. Out of the corner of my eye I saw a flash of white on my right; the fox was going for a tight corner, staking the race on his bike's appetite for curves. Too late, for I was already accelerating away, feeling the bike stand upright as it hurled itself towards the line. He passed me at last, but the checkered flag had already come down for me.

I let him roll into the pit lane ahead of me. What did it matter? I had won the race, and on a bike that could scarcely have been less suitable for a twisty racetrack. I took my time, in fact, taking my lap of honour like a pro, acknowledging with a wave the cheers of the crowd. One man seemed to be blowing me kisses from the back row, so I waved back to him, my eye drawn to his windblown brown hair. My hand froze as I recognised him. It was Kit.

Max stood waiting for me as I rolled in, already shaking from the adrenaline. Though his mouth was a straight line, a smile shone through his face, lighting up the blue eyes that looked into mine.

'Good girl,' was all he said, but I could tell I had surpassed his expectations.

The man in the white leathers walked over to us, taking his helmet off as he came. Ignoring me, he spoke directly to Max.

'Since when have birds been allowed to race?' he asked, his voice shaking with anger.

I was shocked, not by his reaction, but by the way he addressed Max. Nobody had ever shown him less than complete respect in my presence. Max looked back at him, his eyes turned to blue lasers. Anybody else would have taken that as their answer, but this man was actually opening his mouth to speak again when Max answered him, 'Since they got to be better riders than you, Damon.'

The man's face clouded with rage. He turned to me, with a look that was pure hatred, and walked off.

I shivered. Just my luck to make an enemy of the one person on the site who seemed unimpressed by Max's standing. And I was shaken by having seen Kit. If he was here, why hadn't he come to find me? Somehow, being with Max in Amsterdam had felt fine, had all been part of the adventure. Now I was back in England I was missing my normal life and, above all, Kit.

I was suddenly a bit of a celebrity in my own right, it seemed, as Max rode back to the trailer with me sitting behind him.

'Well ridden, fetish queen,' shouted one man as we passed the crowd streaming away from the stands. 'You can ride mine anytime,' called another, his gestures suggesting it wasn't his bike he was offering. I waved back graciously.

Max stopped the bike.

'Did I tell you to wave at your fans?' he asked sharply.

'No, Master,' I replied. His eyes on me were cold now, and he seemed genuinely displeased that I was revelling in my success.

'I think I need to remind you, at least, that you are here for one purpose alone. What is the reason for your life?'

'To please you, Sir,' I replied.

'Get off the bike,' he ordered, and I obeyed at once. 'Bend over,' he told me, and I bent to present my PVC-wrapped bottom to him, bracing myself for the spanking I had no doubt provoked. It was a humiliating come-down for the race-winning heroine, and I prayed that Damon was nowhere nearby to see it.

But no slap resounded against my rear. Instead, I felt the tight suit ease as the zip between my legs was released. From the top of the crease that separated my buttocks, round to my navel, was now exposed to the air, and to the eyes of anyone who passed. I blushed deeply, thinking of how my image had just changed in the eyes of those who had just seen me race.

'Take out my cock,' said Max, in a voice so loud and clear that everyone within ten yards turned to watch. Nobody made a comment now; they could see who was talking to me. Burning with shame, I undid the buttons of his jeans and pulled out his prick, which was already swelling in my hand.

'Now suck it,' he told me.

I bent again and took him into my mouth, glad that at least I could not see who was staring at me.

If Damon did come past now, how happy he would be to see me put in my place, I thought, servicing my man the way he no doubt thought a woman should. And yet the idea of being made so publicly to perform this act on Max was exciting too, sleazier somehow than being in an organised sex show or a striptease act. I sucked and licked at him, my own desire rising with his as he stiffened against my tongue.

'Now get on here,' said Max, patting the saddle in front of him. I stared. Surely he didn't intend to fuck me here and now, in the middle of the rally? A blow that resounded across the site struck me across the backside, so I hurried to obey him. Though he slid back a little to make room for me, we were so close that I had to hook my legs over his.

He rubbed his penis against me, my spittle letting it slide across my shaven skin. My clit pulsed at the contact. With his other hand on my PVC-covered breasts he pushed me backwards over the petrol tank. I lay arched over it, nipples pointing skywards through the thin, shiny catsuit. Then with one motion he took hold of my hips and slid me, up and down, on to his cock.

I looked up at his face. He was unsmiling, a glint of animal lust in his blue eyes. He blipped the throttle and the vibrations of the engine went right through me and made my pussy clench around him.

'We're going to take a little tour,' he said to me, 'just to make sure nobody has got the wrong idea about who – or what – you are.'

'Yes, Master,' I replied.

I felt the bike clunk into gear and start rolling, and clutched at the sides of the tank for balance. We were being shaken around as we rolled over the rough ground, so I hooked my legs around Max's waist and pulled myself closer against him. Without even thrusting, he was being bounced about inside me, and the throbbing of the engine was rubbing my sensitive spot against his body.

I looked down at myself, shiny and black like an inflatable doll, with just a slash of bare pink skin exposed at the bottom of my zip. Alexandra had Otto to service her as she rode around, and Max had me. I was no more than an accessory to the bike, a sex toy to be used when he felt like it. The idea was weirdly arousing.

The ground got smoother beneath the tyres; Max must have found a roadway with tarmac. Now he began to thrust into me as he rode, taking his left hand from the grip to squeeze my breast through the PVC. I groaned as the silver buckle on his belt banged against my clit, a contact that was slightly painful but deeply arousing.

'What are you?' he grunted as he thrust, the bike keeping a steady course across the ground.

'Your slave, Sir,' I groaned back, willing him to increase his pace inside me.

'That's right,' he answered, pounding into me so hard I was being slapped against the petrol tank. 'My slave to fuck when I choose, to race when I choose, to do with whatever I wish.'

'Yes, Master,' I cried. So long as he was doing me like this, I wanted nothing else. My whole body was alive with arousal, the vibration of the engine quivering through me and meeting the rhythmic blows of Max's pelvis.

He laid forwards, his weight pinning me to the bike and his leather jacket rubbing my nipples through the PVC. I feared only two things at that moment – that he would forbid me to come, or that he would stop what he was doing.

My prayers were answered as he accelerated along the drive, riding through crowds of people who scattered from his path, his fucking also built to a frantic pace. The engine sound grew with the intense feeling between my legs, till I thought I couldn't control myself a moment longer. Then, at last, he panted, 'Come now,' and I lost myself in orgasm: a sobbing, shaking mess, my hands gripping his shoulders and my legs locked behind his back.

Max sat up again, his breathing slowly returning to normal, and looked down at me.

'Thank you, Master,' I said, automatically.

'You have her well trained in something, then,' said a familiar voice, and I opened my eyes to see Damon leering down at me. 'Not that I'd let her come if she was mine, of course,' he went on. 'She'd be bolted into a frame for me to fuck her till I got bored, and then I'd pass her on to the lads.'

Max looked back at Damon, betraying no emotion.

'You couldn't afford her, Damon,' was all he said.

'How much?' Damon asked, his manhood piqued again.

I lay silent, humiliated to be the object of this discussion as I lay, worse than naked, still impaled on Max's cock. I was afraid of where this was leading. Could Max be planning to provoke Damon into paying some huge amount of money for me? Max named an outrageous sum, and then added, 'That's what I paid for her. But that was completely untrained. Considering the work I've put into her, I'd have to double that now.'

Damon pretended to be considering the figure, but I could tell, with some relief, that he was bluffing. Though the idea of being priced as a trained slave gave me a frisson of excitement, I had no doubt that Damon would be an infinitely crueller master than Max. He seemed to take everything as a test of his dominance, and Max must have known this because he added, 'And of course I'd have to add something on for her racing talent.'

Anger darkened Damon's face again, and I had to resist the urge to laugh.

'That was a fluke,' retorted Damon hotly.

Max shrugged.

'If you say so.'

'Want to bet on it?' he challenged Max.

'If you like,' Max replied. 'How about your bike?'

Damon nodded.

He must be feeling confident, I thought, or too macho to show any doubt about his chances against me.

'My bike against yours, then,' said Damon. Max laughed.

'No,' he replied, 'not my bike. That's worth more to me than money. If she beats you again, I take your bike. If you win, you get her.'

My blood ran cold. I looked up at Max's face, but he didn't even look down at me. His eyes were on Damon.

Damon met his gaze, then ran his eyes over my body. In that outfit, and that position, he could see exactly what he would get as his prize. Though Max could be both ruthless and cruel, I somehow trusted him not to go too far. He had stretched my limits, but never gone beyond them. But Damon was different. He had a vicious streak and would stop at nothing, I could tell, to avenge upon me the humiliating defeat he had suffered. I would give anything not to lie beneath him as I lay now beneath Max, at his mercy and under his control.

Damon looked into my eyes as he answered Max.

'Done,' he said. 'My ride against yours. Make sure you wash her before you send her out.' Then he turned and walked off. Max watched him with quiet contempt. Only when he was out of sight did he look down into my terrified eyes.

'You'd better make sure you beat him then,' he said.

As I clung to Max's back on the ride back to the trailer, my eyes searched the crowd for Kit. If he could buy me back from Max before the race, I would be safe. Or even afterwards, if he could use the greed I'd seen in Damon's eyes against him. But that depended on two things: whether I could get hold of Kit before the race, and whether he could lay his hands on the money.

I had been a complete idiot, getting myself into this position. I knew that at the start I could have opted out, put a stop to the whole thing, and now I was faced with the horrific prospect of real enslavement to a man whose hatred of women, and of me in particular, was plain to see.

14

Max must have suspected that I had plans to find a way out because, before he left the trailer, he handcuffed me firmly to the bar across the foot of the bed, and stuffed the leather gag into my mouth. I lay across the bed, listening to the voices of people passing. Some of them were talking about the drama of this morning's race, but that gave me no pleasure now, even when I heard them laugh about the expression on Damon's face when I had passed him on the last lap.

Max returned after an hour.

'All arranged,' he said briskly. 'You race at six, right after the pro show.'

I lay in despair. The crowds that had gathered to watch the stunt bikes and drag racers would be delighted to stay on and see a rematch of Damon versus the fetish queen, I had no doubt. But I also knew by how tight a margin I had beaten him last time. This time it was a grudge match, and Damon would not be taken by surprise.

I was surprised when Max threw a brand-new one-piece race leather on to the bed – red and black, with his eagle insignia stitched on the back.

'Put that on,' he said, and bent to release me from the handcuffs and gag.

At least he's giving me a chance to escape injury, I thought. He must care about me a little.

I did feel less vulnerable in the armoured suit, and was even more pleased when Max handed me a full-face helmet and serious boots to match the suit. I already felt like a gladiator about to fight for my life, so it was a psychological lift to know I could withstand a slide across the track if I pushed Max's bike beyond its capabilities. Since dropping the bike would mean losing the race, I would be beyond Max's punishment in any case.

Max led me straight past the bike, and we walked towards the stands. I was glad we were going to watch the entertainment, as it would keep my mind off the impending race for a little, and give me the chance to study the track again from a spectator's-eye view. A slight buzz of interest followed us across the ground. Word was already getting about that Damon was getting a second chance against 'that bird on the cruiser'.

I tried to concentrate on the stunts, but all I could think about was how to squeeze even more performance from Max's bike. Perhaps I could let the back wheel slide out to give me more pace on the corners, I thought, but I wasn't at all sure that the low, heavy bike would sustain it. I looked in vain for Kit among the crowd.

I watched the drag racers scream down the straight, covering the distance in half the time we had taken. These were machines that really couldn't tackle corners, built purely to accelerate to ridiculously high speeds in a minimum time along a straight quarter-mile. The riders lay almost flat along the tank, relying on the long bars behind the back wheel to prevent the enormous surge of power from lifting the front wheel off the ground.

Then it was time for the grand finale. In the hush that descended on the crowd, I heard an unfamiliar engine sound, a pulsing beat approaching from some distance. I looked along the track, but the sound seemed to be coming from above. Just as my distracted brain finally placed where I had heard that sound before, I looked up to see the helicopter fly into view above the track.

The crowd whooped with delight, and with good

reason, because below the helicopter, swinging slightly on two wires, was a bright red motorbike, and, sitting on the suspended bike, was a man, his bare torso covered in a web of tattoos. It was Geoff.

My heart rose to see him. He was a true friend, and always knew what to do in a crisis. Suddenly my situation didn't feel quite so hopeless. I relaxed a little, and prepared to enjoy whatever show he had prepared for the cheering crowd.

The helicopter circled the track, making sure that all of us got a good view of Geoff on his two-wheeled trapeze. Then it descended slowly, coming to a perfect hover when the bike's wheels were a few inches above the ground. Beneath the thunder of the rotor, we could hear that the bike's engine was already roaring, and my nostalgic ears told me it was a Ducati.

Geoff let the rear wheel spin in the air, and the engine screamed. It took a minute for the tyre to slow to a stop again, and for the crowd to stop yelling. The helicopter sank gently on the spot, till the tyres touched down and the bike's weight pressed on to its suspension. With another rev of the engine to please the crowd, the bike started moving along the track, the helicopter keeping its position perfectly above. It was as precise as ballet, but far more dangerous.

Smoothly, evenly, bike and chopper accelerated until it seemed impossible they could remain synchronised. Then, with a sharp crack and two puffs of smoke, the wires left the bike and the helicopter was reversing, pulling the swinging lines away behind the speeding Ducati. My heart pounded. Among the thousands watching, I was probably the only one who knew just how hard that stunt must be.

Now began a *pas de deux* of two machines, airborne and earthbound. Everything Geoff was doing with the bike – wheelies, stoppies, and tight circles that left a black ring of rubber on the tarmac, the chopper mirrored above him. It was partly comical and partly beautiful, two pinnacles of engineering dancing together for an appreciative crowd.

It was like a curious mating dance, as the two moved backwards and forwards along the track, bowing and circling to each other. I forgot my own predicament for a few minutes as I watched, and I joined the crowd in delighted applause as Geoff stood on the tank for the finale, letting the bike hold its tight circle below the helicopter rotating on the spot above.

But my happiness was soon deflated by the tannoy announcement that followed, telling the audience to stay in their seats for the race. Sick fear flooded through me. Geoff had come, but too late to help me. I had no time to find him before I would be looked for to warm up Max's bike. I must have been as white as a sheet as I rose and followed Max down the steps towards the pit lane. He must have had his bike brought over already, I thought, then wondered who else he would trust to ride it, since we had both been here.

There was no sign of the black beast, but we did find Geoff wheeling the Ducati towards the sheds. I felt another shock of recognition as I looked properly at the bike for the first time. It was *my* Ducati, the one Kit's mother had given me as a wedding present, the partner of Kit's that was still, presumably, being mended in Italy. Geoff beamed at me as he pushed my bike straight towards me.

'I've warmed the tyres up for you,' he said.

Max laughed at my confusion.

'I'm not risking my bike in a real race,' he said. 'If you're going to send anything crashing through the barriers, you can use your own.'

I couldn't kelp beaming. Geoff had come to the rescue indeed. Damon was a good rider, and his bike was quick, but if I could beat him on Max's lump, I was sure I could beat him on my Italian thoroughbred.

I decided, since Damon had not yet arrived, that I had time for a practice lap. Being back on the hard, narrow saddle, bent over the hunchbacked tank, felt like returning to the arms of a lover. I relished each twist, feeling the bike beneath me find its own line unfailingly, flicking down to trace a tight corner, and then rising with the throttle to power into the straight. Grudge or no, I was in with a good chance now.

I rolled back into the pit lane as Damon started the engine of his white racer. He did a double take that was positively comical as I drew up beside him, then looked across at Max, who was chatting with Geoff.

'What the fuck's this?' he shouted, pointing at my bike. 'That's not what she was riding this morning!'

Max nodded.

'The bet was on the rider,' he said, 'not the bike.'

Damon looked so angry I thought he might take a swing at Max, but neither he nor Geoff was somebody I'd pick a fight with even one at a time, and I'm sure Damon's cowardice would stop him taking them both on together.

Geoff said, 'If you want to back out now, that's fine. I'll get them to make an announcement.'

Damon looked at my bike. It still had a smaller engine than his, so on sheer horsepower he might yet outrun me, though I had the advantage of being a lighter rider. His expression said that he'd been set up, but he was not prepared to back down and risk ridicule for being unwilling to race a woman on a bike in the same league as his.

'Three laps,' was all he said, and he pulled on the white helmet and rode off to the starting grid.

Geoff gave me the thumbs up and said, 'Go for it, danger girl.'

Max just looked at me. My practised eye saw the

warmth in his blue eyes, but all he said was, 'Please me.'

'Yes, Master,' I answered, and I meant it. Max had proved that he did care about me, and I cared for him too.

Damon was already on the starting grid, and the stands were packed with people expecting to see me join him in my black PVC suit on Max's bike. When I rolled into place beside him on the red Ducati, there was a moment of uncomprehending silence, then cheers and laughter. Some of the crowd had seen me snatch victory on the equivalent of a shire horse running at Newmarket. Now I was under starter's orders on an Arab stallion, they wanted to see me win by more than a second.

Damon flashed me a venomous look, then our eyes went up to the starting lights. I was not complacent. I knew that Damon would do anything he could to beat me, by fair means or foul. I would have to ride the race of my life. The light turned to green, and I felt the Ducati fly forwards so fast the front wheel tried to lift from the tarmac. I was determined to get ahead before the first bend, so that Damon would have to take the second-best line, or to ride behind me till we regained the straight.

I heard his engine roar beside me, but my lightness gave me the edge on pure acceleration, and I turned into the first bend exactly where I wanted. It was a joy to feel the bike hug the curve. Having ridden this course once on a bike designed to cross America on long, straight highways, I was staggered by how much faster it felt on a true racing bike.

Out of the corner of my eye I saw Damon gaining on me, but before he could get in my way I was into the hairpin, laying so low that the knee of the red suit scraped on the track. I had never taken a corner so fast in my life, but there was no uncertainty in this bike. As I opened up the throttle it sat upright and flung itself out into the straight at lightning speed.

I knew I was in the clear at least through the next curve, but as I lined up along the strip before the stands I awaited the white flash that would take Damon past me. The tables were turned as far as sheer horsepower went, and if he got enough lead on this longest straight he could block me out of the bends the same way I had outmanoeuvred him.

The crowd was behind me, yelling encouragement, and I was holding the left-hand side of the track. It gave Damon more room to pass me, but it gave me a fighting chance of taking the best entry point into the curve. I was counting the seconds under my breath, trying to work out how much faster I was riding than last time. I was already shifting my weight into the curve when Damon roared past me, cutting right into my line and forcing me to slack the speed a little to avoid a collision.

Now I was caught in his slipstream, using his wake to match his speed, but badly placed to pass him. I was thinking hard. This was a three-lap race, and we were just entering the second lap. If I could keep up for this lap, I might be able to pass him at the last minute, when he would be too late to regain the lead. It was a risky strategy, but I was unlikely to win this race on muscle alone.

So I matched him for an entire lap, following his lines, my front tyre a foot or less behind his rear one. Round the bends I held him effortlessly, my nimble little machine flicking around them smoothly. I could have passed him several times on a corner, but he would only have regained his position on the straight.

The crowd seemed puzzled as I came past them for the second time, locked in behind my opponent and seemingly unwilling to try and pass. They shouted encouragement, and I thought I heard a note of frustration in the noise. I was thinking fast, wishing that the layout of the track was reversed, that the twisty corners came after the long straight. That would have allowed me to overtake him on a bend and hang on to my advantage to the finish line. As it was, I had only one final curve on which I could use my bike's superior cornering, in a risky rerun of the first race.

Damon must have been expecting me to try and pass him on a bend, and when at last I slipped inside him on the big curve he didn't twitch a muscle. Giving it everything I had down the straight, I kept a nose ahead, enough to let me take the inside line again on the first bend of the final lap, gaining another few inches. Through the hairpin and the next bend we kept this up, Damon drawing level with me on the straight but losing a little more ground on every corner.

As we entered the long straight for the last time, hearing the crowd roar even louder than our howling engines, I was just clear of the bigger bike, with enough room to sit well over to the left again. With the little Ducati redlining in top gear, if he was going to pass me he had a few seconds to do it. Time slowed down as I saw him appear on my right, nosing forwards as the stands flew past my elbow, inexorably clawing his way ahead with his bigger engine.

We were both flat out; I had no more speed to give. He could not resist a triumphant glance across as he pulled past me and hurtled leftwards across my path, just as the straight gave way to the final bend. I twisted the throttle and slammed down a gear, feeling the back wheel skip as the engine braking kicked in, trusting the bike to power into the corner tight and slow behind Damon, who was drifting too far to the left, having entered the corner way too fast as I knew he would.

I saw him lay the bike down as he realised how tightly he would have to turn to stay out of the crash wall of tyres, but by the time I heard the scream of metal on tarmac that told me the white bike was sliding off the track, my own line had taken me past him and I was feeling the pull of the turn myself. I needed no more speed now to win this race; all I had to do was keep a steady hand on the throttle to power me round the rest of the curve and across the finish line. The back tyre was gripping with the very edge of the rubber, but it didn't fail me. As I looked up and saw the man waiting with his chequered flag, I felt the bike lift up its head with mine, and we were home and dry.

I took my lap of honour, seeing Damon walk across to his bike from where he had rolled clear, his snow-white leathers scuffed and dirty. The bike lay among the tyres, a few scattered pieces of fairing showing where it had hit the ground. I was shallow enough to pull a little wheelie in front of the stands, for no better reason than because I could. All I lacked was the sight of Kit's face among the exuberant spectators.

Max awaited me in the pit lane, grinning broadly. As I dismounted, he put his arms around me affectionately.

'Well done,' he said. 'Even if you have won me a worthless pile of bent metal.'

I beamed with pride as I took off my helmet.

'I should have added another couple of thousand on to your price,' he went on, 'but a deal's a deal.'

It took a moment for his words to sink in. He had made a deal to sell me, in spite of everything; in spite of the way I had won for him twice, had done everything to please him. Worst of all, in spite of the affection I thought he had for me. Tears sprung into my eyes as I searched his face for some sign that this was a joke.

'Ah, here comes the lucky purchaser now,' said Max, 'fresh from collecting his winnings at the bookie's.'

I turned to see where he was looking, hoping above all not to see the white leather suit with Damon's surly face above it. Walking towards us across the tarmac was Kit.

Now the tears that rolled down my face were tears of happiness. I had missed Kit more and more, and as soon as I had glimpsed his face in the crowd, the pain of our separation had cut me like a knife. Now he waved a wad of notes cheerily at Max, and grinned at me in the old wicked way he always had.

In no time at all, money was handed over and Kit held me tight in his arms, my face crushed against his warm chest. I was smiling and crying, speechless with happiness. I was barely aware that Geoff had reappeared, wheeling Damon's mangled bike into the pit lane.

'Ah,' he said, 'isn't it sweet? If slightly premature.'

'I'm afraid so,' said Kit.

I looked up at him. Now what could there be to keep us apart?

'I officially take possession at midnight,' said Kit. 'Till then, you are still under Max's orders.'

I looked to Max, wondering what he would require of me on my final evening. He looked me up and down, enjoying my suspense as usual.

'Luckily, what I have in mind for you should be finished on the stroke of midnight,' he said. 'Tonight you will make your debut appearance at the live show.'

In the trailer, Max washed me for the last time in the tiny shower, his hands moving over me more gently than ever before. He replaced the collar and the cuffs on me with almost ritual care, and stood looking at me as if he wanted to drink in the sight and burn it in his memory. I felt moved, and wanted to say something, but I knew well that he would use any unauthorised speaking on my part as an excuse to punish me. Perhaps that was always his way – to turn closeness into this game of power and powerlessness.

We arrived in the big tent as the final band was playing their encore, a deafening guitar solo ripping through the night air. I peeped out from backstage at the crowd – drunken, rowdy and vocal. There were thousands of them. I shivered. I had been turned on by the idea of performing to this audience, but now I was confronted with the reality I was not so sure.

But it was too late for nerves, and in any case I was still under Max's command. He gave me a little push, and I went behind the backdrop into the darkness at the back of the stage. Alexandra stood there, her wasp-waisted silhouette unmistakable even in the gloom. A long, mechanical shape gleamed beside her, and at first I thought she had brought Otto, but as my eyes adjusted I saw that this was a huge trike, a stage prop built in sturdy chromed steel, more than double life size.

It was an open frame, the mere suggestion of a shape between the three huge wheels, and all over the framework were steel rings, ready to tie or suspend me. In the centre hung a band of leather, strapped and chained firmly to the frame, laces hanging ready to be tightened around me. The trike was to be my corset – or I was to be its bodywork.

Geoff stood by, waiting with a dirty grin to strap me into place. I stood docile as he pulled the boned panel of leather around my middle and adjusted it beneath the swell of my breasts. This was a corset that would conceal nothing. I felt the now familiar squeeze against my waist and ribs, and breathed in against the tightening laces.

Now I was going nowhere. In fact, the chains that stretched from the rings on my corset were already forcing me to bend forwards with my rear in the air and my breasts thrust out towards the front of the trike. Geoff and Max took a wrist each and lifted my arms towards the handlebars, clipping my cuffs to chains that suspended me between the outsized leather grips.

Then my legs got the same treatment, my ankles pulled apart and back, hanging from the centres of the two rear wheels. I hung, spreadeagled, my middle both constrained and supported by the leather band, and my limbs stretched out and upwards. In this position the arch of my chest was exaggerated still more. I could see the excitement in Max's cool blue eyes, and pictured myself, laced and chained, ready to be used.

I was excited by the thought, but hungry for contact. All my most sensitive parts were exposed, offered up to the eye and to the cool air that blew through the tent, and I longed for the stimulus of touch. Max stood in front of me, looking deep into my eyes. I hoped he might kiss me, but he just said, 'Slave, do you wish to please me by performing tonight?'

'Yes, Master, please,' I answered.

'Then I want you to wear something for me.'

I wondered what on earth he could have for me this time, what kind of PVC garment or leather harness he had dreamed up as his parting gift. Whatever it was, I felt ready to try, secure in the knowledge that at midnight I would return to my normal life.

'Whatever you wish, Master,' I replied.

He smiled then, his cruel smile, and said, 'Good girl.'

I felt his hands caress my breasts, tweaking the nipples, making little darts of pleasure pierce my whole body. Then a gentle pinching pulled one nipple out, and I felt a light pressure from something cold. Whatever it was remained there while Max applied the same treatment to the other nipple, and I felt the same gentle pinching.

Max's hands left me, but the pressure continued. After a few seconds, it was uncomfortable, and soon it was downright painful. I whimpered slightly, but nothing happened. I could think of nothing else as the sensation grew to a burning pain, confined to those two sensitive nubs. I twisted against my bondage in a vain attempt to shake them loose.

'Yes, my nipple clamps are painful,' said Max, 'but you will be amazed how quickly the pain serves only to double your pleasure.'

His hand caressed my breast, brushing against the nipple clamp as he did so, and setting off a ripple of pain that merged with the pleasure of his stroking.

Then I writhed with delight to feel his hand at my clit, stroking and flicking, sending waves of joy to meet the jabs of pain from my breasts and mingle with them. I moaned softly, trying to resist the urge to rock myself against his hand. As if reading my mind, Max whispered in my ear, 'Yes, my sweet little Emma. Your Master wants your pleasure as much as his own.'

Then he kissed me deeply on the mouth, his tongue opening me up to pleasure just as the clamps were awakening me to pain. His fingers stroked my neck, wandering along the edge of the collar, tracing the line of my jaw. My eyes closed again as I tried to focus on the pleasant sensations and ignore the painful ones.

Then the soft mouth was replaced by a hard wedge of rubber, and I felt a harness of thin straps over my face. Max buckled it behind my head, and the leather pulled gently across my cheeks and over my nose. Another strap snicked into place, and I felt my face gently lifted, supported in place by the straps around my head. I was gazing forwards into the darkness at the curtain that would shortly open to let me on to the stage, a curtain suddenly illuminated by a circle of white light as Max clicked a button on my forehead. I was a human head-lamp as well as saddle and bodywork.

Max nodded over my head and I felt Geoff's fingers in my cleft; something cold and slippery was being smeared over me. His finger slid wickedly into my rear opening, and I felt the ring of muscle pulse against it. Max smiled again, a dark, lustful smile.

'All warmed up and lubricated, nearly ready to roll,' he said. 'Only the tail light to go.'

On his nod, I felt a slim bar of rubber pushing its way into my greased hole, around which my ring tightened. Another click told me that I was now holding a red light behind me.

I had read about slaves being used as objects, literally turned into furniture, but I had never imagined how utterly degrading it felt to be used that way. I was being treated as some kind of toy, but there was nothing I could do about it. I could neither move nor speak, and the incomprehensible crackle of the tannoy told me my appearance was being announced already.

Max swung a leg over my tight-laced waist, and the trike began to roll. The curtains parted and I was dazzled by the huge banks of lights that shone into my face as we rolled forwards on to the stage. I couldn't see the audience, but I could hear them baying as they saw me, ridden by Max, gliding along the stage that thrust out to the centre of the tent.

As we slid to a halt, I could smell them, the sweat and smoke of a huge crowd of men having a good time, beer, mud and petrol all mingling into the animal stink. I was suddenly afraid. What if they really were overcome by lust and decided to rush the stage and do what they wanted to me? Would Max's authority be enough to protect me? Then my panic subsided as I began to pick out individual voices in the clamour. They were drunk and they were horny, but they were good-natured and relaxed.

Max reached across to the left handlebar and clicked a switch. I felt the straps around my face pull backwards and my head go up, so the light from my head shone in the audience's eyes. Then he clicked again and I dropped back to my first position. The crowd loved it, and I felt humiliated and perversely excited. He really was treating me like a machine.

The throbbing from my nipples was keeping me in a state of arousal that begged for more enjoyable stimulation. I wanted him to at least reach under my chest and rub his hands over my breasts, or put a hand behind him to where my pussy twitched for contact.

Max swung his leg over my rear and walked around me, stroking the curve of my buttock with a hand. He stroked his way down my cleft to where the little torch jutted out of me, and with the heel of his hand gave it a gentle shove. The rubber grated against my delicate crevice, and a jolt of pleasure went through me.

Then his fingers found my pussy and slipped into the opening, already moist with desire. Two, three fingers pushed their way in, flicking against the most sensitive spots inside me. As my clitoris swelled and twitched in response, I hungered for direct stimulation.

Geoff ran on to the stage, waving to the crowd. He was in mechanic's overalls, arms knotted around his waist to show off his muscled torso and the intricate tattoos that covered him like a second skin. He carried a bucket and a sponge that he put down beside me on the stage. In exaggerated pantomime, Max gestured to me, indicating for Geoff to wash me like a muddy motorbike, then stepped back to watch.

My skin tingled as the sponge left a trail of warm, soapy bubbles on my naked arms. Aroused as I was, the soft, moist touch felt decadently pleasurable. Geoff worked his way over my whole body, unhurried, lingering over my breasts so the white froth slid over my skin without catching the nipple clamps with a rough sponge.

Then he started at my bare feet, teasing the tender soles and even bending to suck at one wet, slippery toe so I gasped with helpless pleasure, to the delight of the watching bikers. My legs awoke to his stroking, and finally the caressing sponge moved over my buttocks and into the crevices of my sex.

Geoff stepped back to enjoy the sight of me suspended, soaped up like one of the bikes in the topless bike wash – only this time it was the bare-breasted woman herself who was being washed. As the foam cooled on my skin, I trembled, longing for some decisive attention that would satisfy my growing lust. I could imagine how sexy I looked to Geoff, and to Max and the audience, a tantalising lacework of bubbles shining on my skin, the white of the soap setting off my tanned body.

Then I felt a delicious trickle of warm water running between my shoulder blades, as Geoff poured water from the bucket and rinsed off the soap. I couldn't help twisting and pulling against my bonds, so delightful was the sensation as my whole body was bathed in clean water, the soft sponge following to mop up any residue of soap. The last slosh of water poured down the open cleft of my sex like a giant wet tongue, and I groaned aloud.

Geoff pulled something from the pocket of his overalls with which to dry me. As it dragged sensuously over my shoulders, I realised it was not a towel but a chamois leather. It was like being rubbed all over with the softest suede, warm and gentle but just rough enough to raise a glow in my already sensitised flesh. Now he did give a little squeeze to my clamped nipples, but the pinching only added to the intensity of the pleasure. I couldn't wait for him to reach my most tender parts, to rub that chamois between my legs.

Through the din I somehow made out the familiar sound of Max's buttons being released, and my sex contracted with anticipation. Soon I would feel his cock slide into me, touching my deepest parts with each merciless thrust. Soon I would hang here in front of thousands of bikers while he fucked me. At last, Geoff's rubbing reached my buttocks and slipped between my legs. I tried to rock against his hand, seeking a stronger stimulus, but he teased me with only a couple of strokes before withdrawing his chamois and leaving me unsatisfied.

Now I felt Max's cock nosing against my lips, his fingers digging into my buttocks as he buried himself in me, inch by glorious inch. I swung in my chains as he rocked his hips against me, relishing the touch deep inside me that made my innermost places sing with ecstasy. If only he would use his hand as well, would touch me with his skilful fingers, I knew my climax would not be long in overtaking me. But, of course, being Max, he was making a point of taking his own pleasure and denying me my final release.

I became aware that Geoff was releasing the straps that held my gag in place. He slid the rubber off my tongue and freed my head from its supports, lowering me towards the floor till my head was at the level of his waist. The crowd knew what was coming next, and so did I. Like the well-trained slave I was, I opened my mouth ready to receive his prick. Now I hung between two men, each thrusting into me from opposite ends. I swung slightly in my chains as the two men fell into the same rhythm, rocking me to and fro between them.

The sensation of being so filled, the rubber plug in my

behind and the two men penetrating me, was so strong I felt quite overwhelmed with arousal. My lips, my pussy, my rear hole, all throbbed with the heat of passion. Even my nipples were constantly teased by the clamps, an occasional flicker of pain interrupting the pulsing of excitement. Only my clit twitched in vain, the odd brush of Max's swinging balls the only touch it could find.

More than mere physical sensation, though, was the excitement of being used like this for the entertainment of so many strangers. Thousands of men were watching, imagining it was their own penises inside me, thrusting into my aroused sex or eager mouth. The same men that had cheered me to victory in the bike race were even now rubbing their erections as they saw me used as the object of Max and Geoff's lust. At the thought, a convulsion of dark, shameful pleasure made me jerk in my chains.

I felt Geoff's hands at my nipples and heard Max's voice.

'Take this, my last gift of pain.'

The first clamp released the nub of flesh, and blood began to flow into it again. After a second, though, the relief was overtaken by a stab of pain, like the ache of pins and needles in a numbed arm, but intensified into one tiny sensitive spot. Just as the peak of the pain passed, the agony of being freed from the second nipple clamp cut through me.

Geoff rubbed at my breasts, helping the burning recede into a glow of pleasurable stimulation. They felt impossibly sensitive now, almost as if I could come from this touch alone. Then, just as my nipples were beginning to sing with arousal rather than pain, I felt Max's free hand move to my clitoris.

Still the two men thrust themselves into me, and now

Max's cunning fingers played over my clit the same way Geoff's hands were caressing my breasts. I had forgotten the audience, the thrill of being used in public as Max's sex slave, as I emerged from the pain into an over-whelming landscape of pleasure.

Hanging weightless, I was limp and defenceless, all my resistance exhausted. Eyes closed, I imagined myself lying on a beach, being pounded by waves like the waves of stimulation that were washing through me from all directions. Feeling my climax approaching, slow but inexorable as a landslide, I was dimly aware that I should, for some reason, try to resist it, but I knew I no longer had the strength. Then, as the big wave curled above me, ready to break with overwhelming force, I heard Max's voice.

'Take this, my final gift of pleasure,' he said. 'Come now.'

I must have arched and cried out in my bonds, as Geoff's climax showered me and Max gave his last orgasmic thrusts behind me, but it was only the sound of a gong that brought me back to myself, ringing through the sound of applause and cheering from the crowd. Max and Geoff were releasing me, lowering me tenderly to the ground, supporting me as the corset withdrew its constraint.

I stood, naked, but for my collar, and looked into Max's blue eyes.

'Midnight,' he said softly, and undid the buckle that held my collar in place. Without it my neck felt light and naked.

'Go forth,' he said softly, with a sadness in his eyes I had never seen before. I lifted my face and kissed him tenderly.

'Thank you, Max.' I said.

Then Kit was on the stage, beautiful as ever in his

leathers, holding his arms out to sweep me up and carry me away. I rested my head against his chest as he walked through the whooping horde, ready to be taken home.

15

Kit woke before me, or perhaps he had not slept, but I opened my eyes to find him looking at me from under that floppy brown fringe. He smiled, his golden-brown eyes crinkling up in their familiar way. I smiled back, but beneath the warm glow of affection, a tension lay between us, and he felt it too. He pulled me into his body and whispered softly into my ear.

'Well, Mrs Wilson, have you had enough adventures yet?'

I lay silent. If this was his way of apologising for his outrageous behaviour, he was going to have to work a bit harder.

'Or was that honeymoon a bit boring and uneventful?' he went on. 'I mean, after all the running around you used to do, married life must seem a bit staid.' I couldn't keep quiet any longer.

'Honeymoon?' I cried. 'Is that what you call it? Selling me to some guy who drags me round Europe dressed like a pervert's breakfast? Watching and laughing while I'm half scared out of my wits, thinking that if I lose a bike race I'll be thrown into the arms of a Neolithic misogynist? Then turning up and expecting me to be grateful?'

Kit looked sheepish. I glared at him, enjoying the way he was squirming.

'Sorry,' he muttered. 'I might have gone a bit far. I thought you'd enjoy it.'

I opened my mouth to make a cutting reply, but the image of myself, helpless with pleasure in Max's hands, rose uninvited in my mind. Kit risked a sly half-smile, seeing me close my mouth again in confusion.

'Perhaps I did enjoy some of it,' I conceded, trying not to let Kit off too lightly. 'But that's not the point. You had no business to frighten me that way.'

Now he held me tightly, and I could tell he felt really bad as he rocked me against him.

'I'm sorry you were frightened,' he said, his voice thick with emotion. 'I was frightened too.'

'What, that Max wouldn't sell me back to you?'

'No!' Kit gave a strange laugh that resonated through my whole body. 'Max would never have kept you if you didn't want to stay. No, I was frightened that you might not want to come back. I wanted to give you a real adventure, but when Max told me how eagerly you took to it, I thought you might like to stay with him till I was over my injuries. Then I got scared that you belonged with him, after all. I thought I might not be enough for you.'

Now it was my turn to hold Kit as close as I could, pressing him to me as I wound my fingers in his hair. 'I thought you might choose to stay with Max,' he whispered, so quietly I could barely hear him.

'You fool,' I told him. 'I would always come back to you. Everything else is just a game. The only one I can't do without is the one I married.'

We clung together, closer than we had ever been before. Tears of happiness wet my face as his familiar body wrapped itself around mine, as my skin sang to his touch. His wise hands ran over my body as only he knew how, waking me gently into sleepy arousal, so familiar, so natural.

I could feel his excitement rising, and pressed myself against him. His soft mouth kissed my neck and his hands stroked my breasts and belly. It felt so easy, as he slipped into me and we made slow, lazy love, delighted to rediscover each other after weeks apart. There was no teasing, no withholding of pleasure, just two people who loved each other and fancied each other's socks off. I felt my climax approaching and began to hold back, then realised with amusement that I didn't need to wait for permission any more.

'Why are you laughing, love?' Kit asked as we lay cuddling in the afterglow.

'I was just thinking how well Max had me trained,' I murmured back.

'Oh good,' Kit mumbled into my shoulder. 'Does that mean you're going to get up and cook me breakfast?'

There was a tussle under the duvet as I prodded and pinched him. Under my merciless onslaught of tickling, he escaped from the bed. As I watched his naked beauty retreat into the kitchen and heard the kettle go on, I smiled with pure, simple happiness. The honeymoon might be over, but we were only just beginning.

Visit the Black Lace website at
www.blacklace-books.co.uk

LOOK OUT FOR THE ALL-NEW BLACK LACE BOOKS – AVAILABLE NOW!

All new books priced £7.99 in the UK. Please note publication dates apply to the UK only. For other territories, please contact your retailer.

Coming in July 05

PAGAN HEAT
Monica Belle
ISBN 0 352 33974 8

For Sophie Page, the job of warden at Elmcote Hall is a dream come true. The beauty of the ruined house and the overgrown grounds speaks to her love of nature. As a venue for weddings, films and exotic parties the Hall draws curious and interesting people, including the handsome Richard Fox and his friends – who are equally alluring and more puzzling still. Her aim is to be with Richard, but it quickly becomes plain that he wants rather more than she had expected to give. She suspects he may have something to do with the sexually charged and strange events taking place by night in the woods around the Hall. Sophie wants to give in to her desires, but the consequences of doing that threaten to take her down a road she hardly dare consider.

NICOLE'S REVENGE
Lisette Allen
ISBN O 352 32984 X

It is September 1792 and France is in the throes of violent revolution. Nicole Chabrier came to Paris four years earlier to seek fame and fortune with the Paris Opera but now her life is in danger from the hordes who are venting their anger on the decadent aristocracy. Rescued by a handsome stranger who has been badly wronged by the nobility, Nicole soon becomes ruled by her passion for this man. Together they seek a reversal of fortune using their charm, good looks and sexual magnetism. Against an explosive background of turmoil and danger, Nicole and her lover enjoy some explosions of their own!

Coming in August 05

THE POWER GAME
Carrera Devonshire
ISBN O 352 33990 X

The only thing Luke and Cassandra have in common is that they both work for the Government – he as a Director of Communications for the New Spectrum Party, she significantly lower down in the ranks. Serious and ambitious, he wants to change the world. She just wants to have fun. Cassandra, whose fondness for sexy shoes is exceeded only by her fondness for sexy men, is a woman who knows where she's going, and she certainly isn't going after Luke. But as Cassandra learns more about his mysterious past, her fascination with her new boss grows. She falls hopelessly in lust and vows that she will have him. Luke, however, is not hers for the taking, but knowing what she does about his private life, something has to give.

LORD WRAXALL'S FANCY
Anna Lieff Saxby
ISBN 0 352 33080 5

The year is 1720 and Lady Celine Fortescue is summoned by her father, Sir James, to join him on St Cecilia, the turbulent tropical island which he governs. But the girl who steps off the boat into the languid and intoxicating heat isn't the same girl who was content to stay at needlework in a dull Surrey mansion. On a moonlit night, perfumed with the scent of night-blooming flowers, Celine liaises with Liam O'Brian, one of the ship's officers to whom she became secretly betrothed on the long sea voyage. When Liam falls victim to a plot that threatens his life, the debauched Lord Wraxall promises to intervene, in return for Celine's hand in marriage. Celine, however, has other ideas. Exotic and opulent, this story of indulgent luxury is stimulation for the senses.

Black Lace Booklist

Information is correct at time of printing. To avoid disappointment check availability before ordering. Go to www.blacklace-books.co.uk. All books are priced £6.99 unless another price is given.

☐ RISKY BUSINESS Lisette Allen ISBN 0 352 33280 8 £7.99
☐ OFFICE PERKS Monica Belle ISBN 0 352 33939 X £7.99
☐ CAMPAIGN HEAT Gabrielle Marcola ISBN 0 352 33941 1 £7.99
☐ MS BEHAVIOUR Mini Lee ISBN 0 352 33962 4 £7.99
☐ FIRE AND ICE Laura Hamilton ISBN 0 352 33486 X
☐ VILLAGE OF SECRETS Mercedes Kelly ISBN 0 352 33344 8

BLACK LACE BOOKS WITH AN HISTORICAL SETTING

☐ PRIMAL SKIN Leona Benkt Rhys ISBN 0 352 33500 9 £5.99
☐ DARKER THAN LOVE Kristina Lloyd ISBN 0 352 33279 4
☐ THE CAPTIVATION Natasha Rostova ISBN 0 352 33234 4
☐ MINX Megan Blythe ISBN 0 352 33638 2
☐ DIVINE TORMENT Janine Ashbless ISBN 0 352 33719 2
☐ SATAN'S ANGEL Melissa MacNeal ISBN 0 352 33726 5
☐ THE INTIMATE EYE Georgia Angelis ISBN 0 352 33004 X
☐ SILKEN CHAINS Jodi Nicol ISBN 0 352 33143 7
☐ THE LION LOVER Mercedes Kelly ISBN 0 352 33162 3
☐ THE AMULET Lisette Allen ISBN 0 352 33019 8
☐ WHITE ROSE ENSNARED Juliet Hastings ISBN 0 352 33052 X
☐ UNHALLOWED RITES Martine Marquand ISBN 0 352 33222 0
☐ LA BASQUAISE Angel Strand ISBN 0 352 32988 2
☐ THE HAND OF AMUN Juliet Hastings ISBN 0 352 33144 5
☐ THE SENSES BEJEWELLED Cleo Cordell ISBN 0 352 32904 1
☐ UNDRESSING THE DEVIL Angel Strand ISBN 0 352 33938 1
☐ THE BARBARIAN GEISHA Charlotte Royal ISBN 0 352 33267 0 £7.99
☐ FRENCH MANNERS Olivia Christie ISBN 0 352 33214 X £7.99

BLACK LACE ANTHOLOGIES

☐ WICKED WORDS Various ISBN 0 352 33363 4
☐ MORE WICKED WORDS Various ISBN 0 352 33487 8
☐ WICKED WORDS 3 Various ISBN 0 352 33522 X
☐ WICKED WORDS 4 Various ISBN 0 352 33603 X
☐ WICKED WORDS 5 Various ISBN 0 352 33642 0
☐ WICKED WORDS 6 Various ISBN 0 352 33690 0
☐ WICKED WORDS 7 Various ISBN 0 352 33743 5
☐ WICKED WORDS 8 Various ISBN 0 352 33787 7

To find out the latest information about Black Lace titles, check out the
website: www.blacklace-books.co.uk or send for a booklist with
complete synopses by writing to:

    Black Lace Booklist, Virgin Books Ltd
    Thames Wharf Studios
    Rainville Road
    London W6 9HA

Please include an SAE of decent size. Please note only British stamps
are valid.

Our privacy policy
We will not disclose information you supply us to any other parties.
We will not disclose any information which identifies you personally to
any person without your express consent.

From time to time we may send out information about Black Lace
books and special offers. Please tick here if you do not wish to
receive Black Lace information.   ☐

Please send me the books I have ticked above.

Name ....

Address ....

....

....

....

Post Code ....

Send to: Virgin Books Cash Sales, Thames Wharf Studios, Rainville Road, London W6 9HA.

US customers: for prices and details of how to order books for delivery by mail, call 1-800-343-4499.

Please enclose a cheque or postal order, made payable to Virgin Books Ltd, to the value of the books you have ordered plus postage and packing costs as follows:

UK and BFPO – £1.00 for the first book, 50p for each subsequent book.

Overseas (including Republic of Ireland) – £2.00 for the first book, £1.00 for each subsequent book.

If you would prefer to pay by VISA, ACCESS/MASTERCARD, DINERS CLUB, AMEX or SWITCH, please write your card number and expiry date here:

....

Signature ....

Please allow up to 28 days for delivery.